The BATTLE FOR LIFE

AWAKENING THE WARRIORS

The BATTLE FOR LIFE

AWAKENING THE WARRIORS

LUCAS RYAN

OTTO
Publishing

OTTO Publishing

Edited by Jenieve Fisher
Cover and back cover illustration by Gabriel Tora
Cover production artist by David Moratto
Interior design by David Moratto

First edition,
Printed in Canada.

LCCN: 20169322578
ISBN: 978-0-692-81429-1

DEDICATIONS

I fought cancer and won; enduring a battle fraught with pain, and what in some moments felt like physical and emotional torture; but I fought, and I won.v

This book is dedicated to my father, Mihai, who often donated his blood for me, slept next to me many nights in the hospital for two and a half years. Without you, I never would have been able to complete this book. Your insight and unique perception helped me throughout, but most of all you taught me how to be a warrior, to trust myself, and to honor everyone I meet.

To my mother, you are everything I am, and all I am yet to become in this world. You are my angel.

To my sister, Nicole, thank you for showing me the beauty of unconditional love.

To my grandparents, who have filled my world with joy and meaning, and were right by my side during my battle with cancer.

To Sharon Moses-Solano, you are magical, thank you for making my dreams come true. I'm forever grateful for everything you've done for me.

To Dr. Iftikhar Hanif, Dr. Brian Cauff, Dr. Carmen Ballestas, Dr. Deborah Kramer, and Dr. Anne Schaefer, you made it possible for me to write this book. I am forever grateful to you for saving my life.

To Michael Jordan, meeting you was one of the greatest experiences of my life, you will always be my king.

To Don Yaeger, you inspired me in every way.
Thank you.

To Gabriel Tora, you are an artist with talent beyond measure. Thank you for showing the world in my imagination.

To Jenieve Fisher, thank you for editing my book and doing such a fantastic job on it.

CONTENTS

INTRODUCTION

The day that changed the course of my entire life and nothing would ever be the same.

February 4th, 2013; my mother picked me up from school. It was a typical day for my friends and I; we were playing basketball as we always did after lunch, pretending we were big shot NBA players. It was about 1:00. I heard the office calling my name over the intercom, so I got up, packed my bag to leave, as my mom walked into my classroom. I was astonished to see her there; I didn't know why I was going home early, but I intuitively knew something was seriously wrong. I overheard her asking my teacher if she thought I had been acting weird in any way. My teacher asked what was wrong, and said I had been acting normal as always. My mom was panicking. As I walked out of my classroom, I started to get really worried and panicked, myself. I asked several times if everything was okay. Once we were inside the car she looked at me and asked if I was feeling fine. I tried to calm her down. I kept on telling her I had a fantastic day, and I got my math grade back and had another "A"! She took a deep breath and said, "I want you to get checked out by a doctor. "My mom had never done this before; she was never one of those paranoid moms. I agreed to go with her to the ER. As we walked in, she said, "Don't listen to anything I say. It's not okay to tell a lie, but if I tell them we are here because I "think" something is really wrong, they will never see you. All I said was, "I'll be here reading my book; say whatever you want."

I've always been a reader. I love reading more than anything in the world. I was lost in my book, so it didn't seem long before my name was called. I went back to a room where they took my vitals, then transferred me into one of the patient rooms. I was seriously hoping I wouldn't get a needle! IV's are horrible, and besides that, I was feeling fine! Everyone moved along pretty fast. I had a heart ultrasound, chest x-ray, and finally I had a CT scan. Of course, I ended up getting a needle too, but by that time I was just ready to go home. It was late in the evening when the doctor walked in, and said to my mom, "Okay, so, what your son has, we can treat with chemo." I was thinking, "CHEMO? What is CHEMO? ...And, can I get some food now?" I was starving, and I wanted pretty badly to go home.

It all happened quickly. I didn't go home that day; instead, I went directly to the ICU, and before I knew it, I was going into surgery. My mom was crying in a corner hysterically, assuming I couldn't see her. My dad was trying to console her. My grandparents were with us, too. Everyone was making a pretty big deal out of whatever this was. When I got out of surgery, I felt as if a bus had hit me or how I imagine being hit by a bus would feel like. I had tubes coming out of every possible part of me, and everything hurt. Everything! Even with tons of medications on board.

I was finally transferred into the Oncology Wing of the hospital. I was about done with hospitals, doctors, and all the pain at that point. At eight years old, this was by far the worst experience I ever had, but it was about to get much worse. One of my doctors came in to explain how my life would be "a new normal". All I kept thinking was, "I don't want a new normal; I'm fine with my current normal. After all, I had just turned eight, and my current normal was great! I had a beautiful life, full of innocence and everything childhood should be. Until this point, my biggest problems were getting up for school! I had been struggling with being a bit more tired than normal, which is what triggered my mother's concern, and her reason for thinking something was wrong.

The way I found out I had cancer was by mistake. One of my nurses walked in and said, "I'm so sorry you have cancer." I thought my mother was going to strangle her! My mom had a plan that she would slowly break things down for me, so I could understand what was happening, and not be afraid. At first, I wasn't too worried, because I had no clue what cancer was. I thought cancer was something old people get. My mother's eyes were HUGE with anger. She asked the nurse to leave the room. Figuring out she had just done something wrong; she left straight away. My mother quickly took a seat next to me and said, "Lucas, it's true; you do have cancer, but you don't have to worry. We got this! We are going to kick cancer's butt! Cancer just messed with the wrong kid!" She then grabbed a pillow and again cried hysterically. I then knew I was in trouble.

As chemo treatments progressed, I was responding amazingly, and was able to quickly go home. Although I still had to go to the hospital for chemo every other day, I was able to sleep at home. That made all the difference in the world! There were times when I was so sick, I had to stay in the hospital overnight, but I tried my hardest not to look sick; I did not want to sleep there.

The first year out of the three years of chemotherapy was the worst; I had chemo every other day. I lost all my hair, eyebrows, and eyelashes included. I think that was the worst part. I didn't want to go anywhere. I didn't want anyone to see me. I felt as if people looked at me strangely, and often with pity. Chemo is like sitting in front of a bus that just keeps on running you over, over and over again. I was determined though, and I knew I was going to be okay. I wasn't alone; there were so many other kids there, in a similar situation. When I started working on this book. I was thinking I wanted to make the whole world aware that pediatric cancer isn't rare, that it is just horrible, and no child should ever experience cancer. Cancer stole my childhood, my innocence; now I'm a 25 year old trapped in the body of a 10 year old. I wish I never had to endure all the physical and emotional pains, watching myself deteriorate, and to know everyone I love suffered alongside of me. Cancer affects the whole family; not just the patient. Although I was extremely lucky I caught it in time, it still terrifies me that I was so sick, yet had no symptoms. I had a huge tumor pressing on my heart, lungs, and liver. I had fluid in one lung, and had to have a tube drain it out. I had just finished playing basketball!

I wrote this book to inspire. To inspire not just children but anyone going through any diagnosis. Cancer doesn't care about age, ethnicity, if you're rich or poor, if you're ready or not; cancer just happens at random, and happens way too often, to good people. We need to find a way to cure cancer. I watched as some of my friends lost their battle. I will live with those memories for the rest of my life. The fear cancer leaves in its wake never goes away. Together we can change this together we can kill cancer. No parent should have to watch, as their child fights the battle of their life, and no child should have to lose the battle.

Directory of
Characters & Locations

Alburn — *The star*

Argam — *Fortress village*

Armizeg — *The warrior, king of Getaes people, cousin of Kothar, great-grandson of Dorbald*

Barkon — *The dragon, the ex-wizard of the South, now known as Karken*

Borysth — *The captain of the guards*

Cythun — *Falconer and warrior*

Derron — *The Master Wizard*

Dolong — *The wizard*

Donnar — *River in the Getaes land*

Dorbald — *Ancestor of Armizeg, a king from Getaes*

Dytes — *Bowman escort*

Elidoc — *The boy*

Folmart — *The falconer*

Getaes — *Land across the sea*

Hydal — *King*

Karken — *The dragon, formerly known as Barkon*

Kolnet — *The cook*

Kothar — *The regent, cousin of Armizeg*

Larsa — *Housekeeper for Derron, the Master Wizard*

Loend — *Village in Maedyv's land*

Ludorn — *Stone statue of the warrior*

Maedyv — *The wizard of the East*

Metaur — *Metal alloy of gold and meteorite*

Maryia — *Mother's name*

Nather — *Mother's male name*

Nysgar — *A spy from Loend, reports to Maedyv*
Obert — *The old man's dog*
Partogos — *King of the western lands across
from the Bended River*
Sargem — *Elidoc's village*
Strebo — *A village neighboring the Argam village*
Taiss — *Landlord near the lands of Zurob*
Troko — *Karken's lieutenant of spies*
Tykas — *A spy from Loend, reports to Maedyv*
Wi rgos — *The wizard of the West*
Wolbah — *The wizard of the Getaes people*
Zurob — *Master of stronghold*

The BATTLE FOR LIFE

AWAKENING THE WARRIORS

A Long Forgotten Evil

Alone...at a table made of uncarved wood, resting his head on his left hand, sat the old Wizard, contemplating scrolls written in a long forgotten language, the light from his only candle was playing on the wooden walls like it wanted to fight the unforgivable winter storm raging outside. In his mind he was passing from one world to another, as he has done for centuries. Here, in the Land of Man, he keeps watch over the Dark Evil that has been trying for such a long time to bring all living beings under his heavy spells of grief and desolation. In their minds, he is nothing but an old myth. The truth has been long forgotten by the Man's kin, as his life is short in the eyes of the immortals. The fear of the unknown made them begrudge the Wizard's knowledge and his unexplained long life.

Knock! Knock! Knock! The Wizard startled. Was he dreaming, or was his mind playing tricks? The chilly winter winds were howling, blocking all the outside noises. He got up from the chair and lit another candle. Knock! Knock! Knock! He heard it again. He wasn't imagining it. Someone was outside. He got up slowly and opened the door. What living thing could possibly be outside in this kind of weather? A woman with tears frozen on her cheeks was holding a young boy with a livid face and eyes lost in the darkness.

"Help me! Help me! My child is ailing. I'm afraid that he is passing into the World of Shadows. I don't know how this could happen. He was sleeping peacefully, when suddenly I heard this strange noise coming from his room and from out-side; when I found him he was laying on his bed and could not move, his skin was paling in front of my eyes, then the light from his eyes started fading. Oh, Wizard! Please tell me! What is happening to my son?"

The Wizard touched the little boy's head, whispering words the mother could not understand, and then quickly retreated his trem-bling hand, murmuring,

"Bring him quickly! Inside! What day is it?"

Instantly he remembered; it is the last day of the century. It is the day when the Dark Evil takes his tribute from our lands. Today is the day when his servant, Karken, the Shadow Dragon, takes chil-dren into his realm.

"It's Karken's witchcraft."

The dragon had chosen this child to serve him in his realm of shadow. He was poisoned from within his body. If you had delayed any longer, your entire struggle in this unleashed winter storm would have been in vain; no one would be able to help your son.

The mother laid the child down on a bed of woven twigs while the wizard searched through the dusty shelves cluttered with old books, and bottles with colored potions. He took the child's hand made a small slit with his knife, the child's blood quickly changed from crimson to black. The Wizard began reading to the child out of a book with tattered leather covers, written in a strange and un-known language; words only a Wizard understood. Periodically, the Wizard poured small drops of potion onto the child's lips. The mother sat in a corner, holding her knees to her chest, watching the fire in the grand stone fireplace, distraught by the unknown.

Countless hours passed. Fraught with despair, the mother dared to ask, "Who is this Karken of which you speak; the dragon sorcerer? I remember when I was a child, my grandmother told me stories about a dragon, who would come during the night to steal children's souls."

"Karken is an evil from the bygone age. In the last day of each century the dragon rides through villages and chooses children so they can serve him in his realm of shadows and desolation. Now that he lost one child and cannot take another, he will be searching for your child as long as the poison is in his body, and his spells are upon him."

Many more hours passed, and the Wizard was still whispering those unknown words from the old book. Suddenly the wizard turns to the mother,

"I was able to stop the poison from spreading throughout the child's body, but his heart and lungs were already touched. This is beyond my powers. The evil that was seed inside him is hidden from my sight, and won't show itself easily. We must head to the Master Wizard of the North, he will know what to do, but we need to hurry, because for every hour that passes the evil grows in strength. Find food to prepare for a seven-day journey. Don't be afraid of the roaches; they are my guardians. I will get the horses saddled. We have a long and harsh road ahead of us, and the wind isn't going to do anything but slow us down."

"Who is the one you call Master Wizard? Is he a wizard like you?"

"The Master Wizard is nothing like me. He's the leader of our Order. There are three more wizards like him but he is the most powerful among us. To become a Great Wizard you have to be chosen by the light of the Alburn Star; the star that keeps watch over our world since the beginning of time; fighting to keep the Dark Evil in his cage."

After saying these words, the Wizard pulled on his old cloak, and went outside, closing the door behind him. All that was heard was the long, gnarling creek of the door. The mother, still trembling, laid close to the child, taking his weak hand into hers, and began to cry. She asked herself, "Why has Karken the dragon chosen her beautiful son? Could she have saved him from this curse if she had stayed with him?"

The child slowly opens his eyes, and mumbles, "Where am I?

His wings all over me... It's so cold... red eyes glows in smoke... a shadow is coming through my window. It feels like I'm falling into a deep dark hole...there is no end...I feel dizzy...It is the mist? Where am I..." Then with a long sigh he falls back into a deep sleep.

The crying mother tightens his hand, hoping the Wizard is right, and once they get to the Master Wizard, his great wisdom and power will undo this dreadful spell.

Slowly, with a staggering gait, she enters into the Wizard's kitchen and starts looking through the pots that are as old as the books on the shelves. She wondered if he ever ate. Finding a bag, she begins filling it with old sausages and molded bread. She is moving slowly, as all of her strength has abandoned her.

Finally, the Wizard arrives through the creaking door with a beard laden with ice and snow. He shakes the snow off his legs, and states adamantly,

"It's time to go now! Climb up on the fetched horse; he's a gentle one, but very strong. He will take you without worry. I will take the boy; he is safer, close to me. Do not worry if you cannot see the road; your horse is tethered to mine and will follow my lead. This winter storm is looking to steal those who lose their way.

The Wizard takes the boy outside, wrapped in a shabby old cloak. The woman takes the bag with food for their journey.

The winter is showing all its madness, unleashing its fury from the cold and cruel northern wind, shattering the snow like a spell meant to impeach them from leaving the Man's land. Even the light of the sunrise seemed to be held into darkness' claws. The wind was so strong, it took their breath away. They crossed frozen rivers, winding through ancient forests. The landscape was beautifully Frightening. They were riding through dark forests where no man dares to enter, where even light seems to fear piercing the trees.

"We should be on our guard," says the Wizard. I feel that something or someone is moving unseen behind us, hiding in the shadows of the trees. "What it is; I do not know. It could be that Karken has sent his spies to find your child, and take him to their master. As long as the spell is upon him, and the poison is in his body, they can trace him like a pack of wolves tracing their prey."

Days and nights had passed. They only stopped to eat, and water the horses. Soon they begin to tire, and decided to rest for the night.

"A few hours from here, Northward, there's a ruined fortress," said the Wizard. "We will stop and rest there."

He clutched the boy closer to his chest and kept on riding through the mad storm. They were moving slowly, covering their mouths to avoid breathing the frozen air. The ruined fortress was perched on a steep mountain cliff, with narrow stairs, unfit for a horse. After sheltering their horses beneath a cliff, from the wild winter wind, they began their climb up the narrow stone steps. The Wizard pushed forward on the old, broken doors, and entered what once was the guard's room.

"Let's make a fire and eat something. We need to feed and water the horses in order to regain strength for tomorrow," said the Wizard, bringing the boy close to the mother. He made a fire. The winter didn't feel so harsh from inside. The wizard brought an old, broken cauldron filled with snow, to melt for water.

The boy, eyes closed, started mumbling again. "Where am I? I want to go home. I am scared. I don't want to be alone. Mother? Where is my mother?"

"Do not be afraid, child, you are not alone. Your mother is here; she's holding you in her arms. We have left home and now the three of us have a task to accomplish. A long and perilous way lies before us. Now sleep in peace, child, I will take the night watch."

The mother and the boy fell asleep in each other's arms, close to the fire. Only the Wizard started gazing at the stars and mountains beneath the moon. He is desperate to save this child, for he could be the first one to survive the dragon's witchcraft.

What he didn't realize is the fact that he just woke up dark forces that are way beyond his powers and knowledge. Outside, the howling wind is moving the snow in a circular motion around ruins of the towers and walls of the once grand fortress.

"We must awake!" exclaimed the Wizard; getting up and preparing for the treacherous journey ahead. The white skin of the boy is covered in a cold sweat. His mother lovingly wiped his face with her sleeve. They start riding, as the growing cold of winter is again showing its cruelness. Their home is now far behind them as they have crossed the mountains, the ridged hills and valleys where there is no sign of beast nor man. No one from their village has ever adventured so far into the wild.

An unknown world lies in front of the mother's eyes, a world she's afraid of; beyond her knowledge or understanding, but she has no choice but go forward. The child's life depends on it, and the mother's love is stronger than her fear of the unknown.

"How far are we from home?" asks the mother

"I am not sure, but I think a few hundred leagues are behind us," answers the Wizard.

"How far is the realm of the Master Wizard?" she asks.

"How far it is, no one knows; no one can measure distance in these bewildering forests where even time seems to stop. For us wizards, the distances and time are meaningless."

Hearing all these words causes the mother to tighten her grip on the horse bridle.

"Soon we will pass on a hidden path, leading us deep through the heart of the mountain. Once we enter, do not look back. You will see things, and hear sounds that will terrify your soul, and isolate you from your mind. They are too powerful for a human soul to sense. Better close your eyes and trust your horse, think of all the good moments in your life. We have to tether our horses together, so you will not lose your way."

As they ride, the trees upon them bind their crowns together into an underpass, slowly engulfing the sunlight. It feels like the trees may fall onto them, and take them as hostages. With a limited view, it seems as if they have nowhere to go but forward; deep into the darkness of the forest. The entrance into the mountain suddenly appeared before them. A deep cavern opens like the wide-open mouth of a dark, hungry beast, ready to swallow anything that dare cross its path.

The mother closed her eyes, laying her head on the horse's arched crest, tightening even harder onto the bridles in her weary hands. They entered into the mountain, guided only by the wizard's magic. The mother wondered how he could possibly see the path in such deep darkness. She assumed his senses were guiding them. Strange noises surrounding them seemed as if they had entered into another world. The air became heavy, and the dense smell of wet dirt and decomposing leaves was inescapable. The wet air moved around the mother's face like gigantic wings, pushing forcefully into the dark cave, where screeching bats flew chaotically, feeding on insects. Their frightening scratches made by gigantic claws echo from the stonewalls. The mother breathes slowly, for fear her breath will be sensed, and increase the chaos.

"We are almost out of here, just be still," says the Wizard.

The woman felt how the air was changing; becoming fresh enough to inhale easily. A strange heat traveled over her cheeks; she slowly opened her eyes. Suddenly, and surreally, the landscape changed. It seemed that even the grass was a deeper green; a green that enlivens the senses to the point the color can not only be seen but inhaled. The mother no longer senses the cold, and doesn't even realize winter is gone for another year. In this land on the other side of the mountain there's no winter. "Is this real? Maybe I'm dreaming." As they ride through the meadows, and over the hills, they cross the bold mountains recently covered with snow. Seasons are changing in a strange and rapid manner; the mother wonders why.

"Where are we now? We are not home?" asks the child. "I want to go home, Mother! Please, can we go home?" "I'm sorry, my child, unfortunately, you're very ill and we must take you to the Master Wizard. Your life is in danger. Don't worry; all will be fine once we reach him." "Why is my life in danger? Why are you sad, Mother?" The Wizard interrupted, "You and other children of your age were chosen by Karken, the dragon sorcerer to serve him in his realm.

Your mother brought you to me as you started to become a shadow. I tried to stop the poison from spreading all over your body, but all I could do is to slow it down. The dragon's witchcraft is too powerful for a wizard like me. To save you, we need the power and wisdom of the Great Wizard." "But...but, I thought it was just a bad dream," says the boy. "I'm sorry my child, it wasn't just a bad dream, I wish it was. We have entered into the realm of the Master Wizard, and here the weather is obeying his will, like all living things that move around us," he says, looking into the child's mesmerized eyes. The Master Wizard knows already that we are coming. See those falcons above us in the sky? They are the watchers of these lands, and the eyes of the Master Wizard."

Unending plains stretching as far as the eye can see, with rivers winding throughout, green fields with people harvesting crops, working their land, meadows where the horses run free with their foals, orchards aplenty, a village full of joy; children running and playing in blissful peace.

"The Argam Village," says the wizard, looking toward the mother. "Many people call it the Fortress Village, because it's so close to the White Fortress."

The path leads them onto a wooded hill where village houses can be seen in the distance. They were built with heavy logs and rounded river stones, with have brown shingled roofs and smoking chimneys. The houses were grand, and well maintained; no domestic beasts were on the streets; nothing like the place these three travelers came from. Clean streets paved with square, gray stones; big trees, well trimmed, shading houses, and perfect, green grass surrounding every house and tree. As they pass through on the street, townsfolk begin appearing from nowhere, watching them with eyes of wonder. Some of them smiling at the newcomers; others speaking discreetly.

They passed on a bridge where a strong river flows beneath. Swirling water and seething foam flows between gigantic boulders; seemingly struggling to cut a path straight through. From the top of the hill, outside of the village, they better see all the landscape, draped like a painted cloth over the sloping hills before them. On top of a mountain in the far distance, the white towers of a fortress surrounded by high vertical walls can be seen. Waterfalls flow underneath the four corners of its strong foundation. The buildings inside follow the contour of the mountain on which they were built. On top of what was once the peak of the mountain they could see a gigantic building, which seemed to sparkle in vibrant white. They started descending into a sleepy valley, bathing in the light of the morning sun. These lands seemed to be enchanted. Even the birds sing a tune of peace and joy.

In the horizon they saw riders coming their way; banners waving proudly in the wind.

"The Master Wizard sends heralds for us," says the Wizard. "Do not be afraid, for now we are in good hands."

The soldiers stopped ahead of them, turning their horses in place to take them way. They were robed in silver armor, laden with golden symbols. A falcon with wings wide open, ready to catch its prey, embroidered on their long capes. It's the blazon of the Master Wizard. In their left hands, they hold long spears with banners. One of the soldiers approached, raising his right arm, covered with a silver glove.

"The Master Wizard welcomes you into his realm," says the Herald. "You must be in great trouble to have come such a long and perilous way. I will not waste your precious time with useless words. Follow me."

The Herald turned his horse and rode fast, closely followed by the wizard, the boy, and his mother. Behind them, the other riders were closing the column. The fortress on the mountain looked like it was reaching out and touching the clouds above. The group crossed a narrow packhorse bridge, and took a steep, winding path up and around the mountain, under the waterfalls, ending at the fortress gate. On the embattled walls, colorful banners with embroidered falcons and mystical symbols battered into the mild wind.

"Open the gates!" shouts the Herald. "The Master Wizard's guests are here!"

The massive gate moved slowly, with a loud clang of metal. Atop the embattled walls, the soldiers armed with bows were watching with wandering eyes, as the newcomers entered.

"The Master Wizard is awaiting you in the Great Hall; follow me. You can easily get lost here.", says the Herald. "The fortress streets are built like a maze to make it easier to defend against the outside enemies. The streets are narrow with tall buildings on each side, in order to ambush invaders, and defend the fortress."

"Enemies? How can you have enemies in such a peaceful land?" asks the mother. "Well, there is always someone or something that does not like peace, who wants to rule over all lands, realms, and living things, one who desires to be the only Master. We have to be ready to fight, to prevent evil thriving in our lands."

They rode on the paved streets of the fortress, higher and higher to reach the fantastical structure they had seen from the distance. As they climbed higher along the streets they could clearly see the land they had passed. From the fortress heights the trail looked so thin; the fields appeared now as green and brown patches. The townsfolk on the fields so small, they seemed unreal. Far in the distance, mountain peaks could be seen with snow sparkled like beacons in the sunlight.

"Here it is! The Great Hall of the White Fortress, with its tall and twisted marble columns and arched doors, fit for a giant." The doors were made of wood and polished metal. From the top of the tall stairs one can see all that encompasses the great realm of the Master Wizard; the splendor of the meadows and forests surrounded by tall mountain peaks, where the snow never melts, and only eagles dare pass over.

"What trouble brings you here, Dolong, Wizard of the Man's land?" asks the Master Wizard, with a voice sounding like summer thunder.

He was dressed in white clothes embossed with golden embroidery, his long white hair flowing like rivers atop his shoulders. In his right hand, a staff on which ancient symbols and runes are carved. The top crested with a large, clear stone, seeming to grow from within the grand staff.

"My Lord, I bring you a child from the village of Sargem, chosen by an old enemy of ours, Karken, the dragon sorcerer. His mother brought him to me just in time to stop the poison from spreading, but the witchcraft which lies upon him is too strong for my powers. I come here to seek your wisdom, and your power to undo this heavy spell."

The great Wizard looked at the boy with discerning eyes. He never saw nor heard of any child escaping the dark powers of Karken. He takes the child's hand and whispers in his ear. His face fraught with concern.

"Take him to the Healing Room!" he orders the guards. "...and do it quickly! We have already lost precious time."

They entered the Great Hall, which looked even mightier from within. The tall, stained windows made the majestic walls look like they were made of glass. They represent old battles scenes, battles long forgotten by Man's kin. The light passing through the tall, colorful glass windows made the battles seem like they were written with light. The majestic marble columns of the Great Hall were sustaining the immense, vaulted ceilings of stones that seemed to reach celestial heights. On the sides of the long hall were great statues of kings and warriors who fought and protected the land and its inhabitants for thousands of years. Their faces mysteriously powerful eyes, that seemed to pierce the soul. Each of them was holding their chosen weapon: long double-edged swords of many sizes and shapes, with blades covered in symbols; swords with unusually long grips and curved blades, which were straight for much of its length, but curved at the end, sharp only at the concave underside; axes made not for cutting wood but to fight battles; battle maces of strange shapes, some of them with spikes; double ball spiked flails; bows; double ended spears; enormous shields with strange shapes, carrying the blazons of their kingdoms and their kings. On the pedestal beneath each statue, carved in white marble; the name of these brave warriors.

The silence was so deep, only the echo from their feet was disturbing the mystical air of the Great Hall. At the back of the hall, a gigantic falcon stood erect, carved in stone, sitting on top of a mountain peak. It looked as if it was alive. With its beak agape, feathers that looked like it wore a cuirass breastplate and back plate fastened together as one, meant to protect and make him invincible. His clenched, powerful talons, ready to catch the helpless prey, and great wings, outstretched over the entire width of the Great Hall, seemed to envelop those passing through. As they walked through the Great Hall, the Master Wizard approached the child's mother and in a low voice spoke to her, "Now, you must be strong in your soul. What was done to your child can be undone. You saw things and places no human from your land had yet seen, but now I am asking you to gather all your strength, because what will follow next is not for the faint of heart. Do not worry about Karken any longer; he cannot pass the borders of these lands, his power stops as he enters the lands of the South. It was made to be this way, and cannot be unmade by any magic or dark spells. There are many things you cannot understand, but in time you will."

"I will try to be strong and follow your advice, Master Wizard. Can you tell me if my child would be spared from this nightmare? Can he have a normal life as he did before? I have so many questions."

"Yes, I understand; many questions, yet no answers for this troubled time. Your heart is yearning to know what will happen. Only time will tell, and there's not much time left."

The mother closes her eyes, struggling not to cry. Deep in her soul she feels so alone and hopeless; as if she was falling into a dark void.

They cross the Great Hall, then turned right, under a big, pointed arch made of black stone covered in unknown runes. In the center was a shrine. The light was coming from the top of the ceiling. It appeared like a beam, stopped in the center of a table made of sapphire, surrounded by transparent colored crystals, and covered with a canvas, embroidered with golden runes and strange symbols.

"Lay the child in the middle of the table!" shouts the Master Wizard to the guards carrying the child. "Now, leave me alone with the child, I am commanding you to leave this room. No matter what you hear, do not enter; your strength will wither and your mind will see things beyond your understanding." They leave the Healing Room and walk away from the door.

"Let's go outside," says the wizard, "we both need some sun and fresh air. Do not worry; your child is in good hands. Karken the dragon does not have power here. Great spells are guarding these borders so only those allowed by the Master Wizard can enter his realm. Let's free our minds from dark thoughts, and hope the power and the knowledge of the Master Wizard will heal your child and undo the witchcraft of the old and evil fueled dragon."

"This land is so peaceful, and there's no winter here. The people are so happy. Why is not like this in the Man's land?" asks the mother.

As the Wizard draws a breath, he looks toward her, and then turning his sight to the green plains below the fortress walls, and answers, "The Land of Man was not always as you know it. A dark, cold place, filled with sorrow, where evil and fear ruled over its people. It was the same land as this one."

"But, what happened? Why is it like this now?"

"A few thousands years ago the world was protected by four wizards. They had once been kings, ruling over their own land. They were chosen among many other kings, by the light of a star that we called Alburn. That light gave them the chance to protect this world from the dark evil to come. But it came with a price. They had to give up their thrones, their wealth, and their kingdoms; even their names, in order to become the protectors of this world. That light gave them knowledge, magical powers, and undying life, so no living thing, beast, or man could kill them. Centuries passed in peace, and no trouble disturbed the world until one day a nameless evil came; a dark evil beyond time, far from the darkest corners of the unseen sky, and none of them were aware of its presence. He started growing slowly, hidden deep in the Snowy Mountains so no spell could reach him. He grew in power and strength, waiting for the right moment to unleash his wrath upon the world of the living, but he could not do this alone; he needed an ally; one powerful enough to defy the spells protecting this world. He needed a wizard among the four. He started seeking, contemplating which one of them had a soul easily deceived. He discovered the Wizard from the South, which also had the task to keep watch over the man's land."

"But, why? You told me they where chosen by the star Alburn, and the light of the star gave them wisdom and power so they were not to be weak."

"It seems that deep inside their souls, the weakness of the humans they once were still lies dormant. Some things just cannot be erased. That is what the evil sought, because the human soul is weak, and easily deceived."

"Why can't they feel or see the evil coming? How could the evil get to them? Are not all the borders of this World protected?"

"No matter how powerful they are, there are places in this world no spell can reach or protect. Could be deep underground, under the mountains or forests, or deep into the soul of the living; the evil will always be seeking a place to thrive. No living beast nor man, could not see the evil alike. He has no shape or smell and he's not a shadow either. He's unseen to the eyes of the living. Only the three wizards can feel him. Only the Three can force him to show himself in the light. But for that, they must be all together; his power is way beyond each one of them alone."

As they enter the Fortress City garden, they see trees that have grown in such a fashion to form benches and garden tables, pools plentiful with water lilies, geese playing with their goslings, columns of all shapes and sizes made of rosebuds and yellow flowers bound together to form arches and canopies, bees, rainbows, and butterflies playing among intricate and alluring flowers. Green marble water fountains with water springing up, forming a refreshing rain of rainbow crystal droplets. Small streams were slowly flowing into the garden with bridges made of woven twigs, covered in stone. The streams were flowing around trees with trunks that seemed to be made out of bronze and copper with colorful leaves where birds played, and nightingales sang effortlessly.

"Let us have a seat; we had a long and arduous journey. We are not yet done for today," says the Wizard.

"I am terrified, and have so many questions. I cannot even feel the exhaustion overtaking my body," the mother tells him.

"I understand. Too many things have happened in these past few days; events beyond your understanding."

"Yes, I have begun to feel this is all just a bad dream; we are still within the safety of our home, sleeping in peace. All of this seems unreal to me. Perhaps my mind has made up things that are not real, because I had always feared something bad would happen to my child," said the mother, as guilt enveloped her.

"I wish all these were only the fruit of your imagination, but they are not. This world is much bigger than you can imagine, with plenty of dark places, kingdoms and creatures you have never heard of nor seen. None you ever even imagined. Do not let your hope die; we will walk through this together. I will never leave your side," as he comforts her by placing the mother's hands gently inside his.

NOTHING IS
FOREVER LOST

The Master Wizard uncovers the pale child's chest, letting the light beam from the ceiling warm his weakening body. He walks to a wall lined with bookshelves carved into ancient, cold stone, and looks through countless century- old books.

After a long while, in the far corner of the shelves, he finds what he is looking for; an ancient book written in the times when the light of the Alburn star came to instill its magic, teaching how to fight the Dark Evil that may one day come. With a satisfied smile, he carefully takes the book into his strong hands, and turns over the pages, reading each word written in glowing blue letters. He approaches the child, closes his eyes, and utters the book's magical words.

The child murmurs; his lips a pale blue, eyes gentle closed and starting to move back and forth, as if he was dreaming. His body moves as the Master Wizard places his hand on the child's chest.

"This spell is more powerful than first thought. I may need more than spells to undo this evil. This poor child."

He opened a wooden box lying underneath the table, taking a big blue crystal with precisely chiseled shapes and angles. He approached the light beam, placing the crystal between the light and the child's body. A rainbow light, stronger than the beam itself, appears from the crystal, forming an elongated shape on the child chest.

The Master Wizard whispered spells from the old book of the Alburn star, waving the colorful light over the child's chest. Black spots appear and disappear as the light moves away from them. He removes the crystal from the light beam and covers the child body with the black canvas from the table. He closes his eyes. His fears are validated. The power of Karken has grown in strength and he was not aware of it until this very moment.

All those children he had taken to his world of shadows centuries ago, have become soldiers ready to fight in his dark army, equipped with powerful spells. It Would be just a matter of time before the Dark Evil would unleash his wrath upon all kingdoms and lands. He must warn the others warn them fast. They must all assemble, in order to stop this work of evil, and save the child. If they could make this happen, all the people from all corners of the world would know how to protect their children from Karken, and his dark spells. All the havoc Karken brought to this world over centuries could end at once. He needs the other three wizards to help him win this battle. And he needed them fast! He ran to the writing table and rapidly wrote on small pieces of paper, messages with coded words.

"Guards!" A soldier came from a hidden door, moving quickly toward the writing table. "Yes, my Lord," says the soldier, slowly bowing his head. "Take these letters to the Falconer and tell him to send it with the strongest falcons he possesses! Do it fast, as our lives depend on it!" "Yes, my Lord," says the soldier, as he sprints toward the same door he entered through. "Hang on, my child. You are our last hope to save all living beings from this world. The last chance to stop the evil from stealing our children's souls and taking them into the darkness," says the Master Wizard, lovingly placing his hand on the child's forehead.

In the realm, the sun was setting quietly over the mountains, making the snow on the highest peak sparkle like diamonds. Little by little, silence was taking its place among the people, and the beasts of the land. Candles and rush lights were spreading their vibrant orange light over the villages, looking like beacons burrowing into the vast land. Torches were lit on the fortress' high walls, and the soldiers on guard prepared for whatever the night may bring.

The Master Wizard put a small potion on the child's lips, allowing him to sleep in peace. Slowly he walked away from the shrine to the door leading into the Great Hall. He took a deep breath and asked a guard where the wizard and the child's mother were taken. He found them sitting on a bench in the garden, and slowly walked toward them. The Wizard first saw him. With a discrete gesture, he the mother, letting her know the Master was approaching. She stands up quickly, asking, "Where is my son?"

"He's resting for now. We have much to discuss. Follow me to my quarters where the both of you may eat. Later, I will show you to your rooms where you may rest for the night."

"Will my child survive? When may I see him?"

"All in due time, but you have not to worry, he is fine, he needs rest because all those days that you spend coming here, all that winter cold and sleepless nights have weakened his body which was already weakened by the spells and poison of the Karken, the shadow dragon. I know that you have lost your willingness to endure, but in these moments patience is vital. Often, we have to let time do its work. You will need all your strength, and for that you should rest your body and mind. You need to eat some dinner, too." "I will try, Master Wizard, but I do not think I could rest or sleep until I know my son will be saved," says the mother.

"Do not worry; he will be saved," the Master Wizard tells her, leading their way to his quarters. At the door there is a woman awaiting them.

"Dinner is ready, my Lord," she says with a smile on her face.

"Thank you, Larsa," says the Master Wizard, "but it must wait. Please, lead our guests to their rooms that have been prepared for them. I think they may want to change their clothes and bathe; these past days have been harsh on them. After such a long journey they must be quite tired." As he turns to walk away, he pauses, "Oh! I almost forgot; you have clothing in your rooms, I hope they fit you well. If you need anything, just ask Larsa. She's my housekeeper and a person you can trust. Everything you need is available to you. Do not hesitate to ask. Larsa, would you please care for our guests?" "Yes, my Lord. Follow me, my Lady; do not bother to take off your shoes, I will handle that later," Larsa says softly, walking toward the stairs.

"Thank you, Master Wizard, for your kindness and hospitality," offers the Mother, climbing the stairs, followed closely by the child's mother. "You are more than welcome. In times such as these, we all should help one another. We gather our strength together, as we cannot fight such an evil alone."

Slowly, the mother descends the winding staircase, to the first floor of the Master Wizard's quarters. His house was not ornately decorated like the others; it was a simple, with a polished, white stone floor, covered with hand woven carpets. Supported by three rusty chains, was an old, wooden chandelier. It hung from the ceiling with white consumed candles. The chandelier's arms were engulfed in candle wax. They seemed to be frozen in ice. The walls looked like they were carved in stone, and from place to place paintings were hanging in erratic patterns. It looked more like soldier's quarters; not the house of the Master of the Fortress.

She started walking down the long hall, turning her eyes to the paintings on the walls. On them were depicted long gone kings and lords, landscapes that reminisced of other lands or realms, magnificent beasts in their forests, giant elk with antlers like chandeliers calling their herds, and mysterious, leafless trees with broken branches.

"strange paintings cover the walls of this house," the mother thinks to herself. "I was looking for you, my Lady," says Larsa. "They are waiting in the dining room. Please, my Lady, follow me."

She follows Larsa through the long and narrow hall as they entered into the dining room. The dining room was simple like the other rooms of the house. In the middle was an unusually long table with hand carved, dark wood chairs. Atop the table were three massive, five-arm pedestal candleholders made of brass. Sitting at the far end of the table, the Master Wizard, and Dolong, the wizard from the Man's Land, whisper to one other. They stop as the mother stepped into the room.

"Please, take a seat," says the Master Wizard, rising from his chair. "I hope you found everything you needed."

"Yes, I found all I needed, but when may I see my son?" asks the mother.

"Do not worry; if it makes you feel better, I assure you he is well protected; my guards are watching over him. In order for my medicine to work, he needs to rest and let time heal him. You may see him in the morning, but he will still be sleeping, and we cannot wake him."

"Will he survive? Do you think the witchcraft is still upon him?"

"That is why I have called you here. The fact you brought him here, to my realm, has saved his life and his soul. If you had not done so, the spies of Karken would have searched endlessly for the child. As long as the spell is upon him and the poison is still into his body, they can sense it, and track him. It will be only a matter of time until they find the boy and take him into the Realm of Shadows, where Karken will make him a servant. The borders of this realm are guarded by heavy spells, and my falcons are watching them relentlessly so no one enters unseen. Karken cannot cross them; the spells are meant to keep the evil away."

"Now you have undone the spell, and have taken the poison out of his body, haven't you, Master Wizard?"

"Unfortunately no," answers the Master Wizard.

"But why aren't you? Why can't you?"

"The witchcraft that lies upon your child is something I have never seen before. He is the only child, as far as I know to be stolen, from the Karkens' hand. He will not allow it. If we have this child, we can undo his witchcraft, and in the future we can protect other children from his spells and poison. By doing this, he cannot build his army anymore, he cannot fight against us anymore, and his days in this world may be numbered."

"What army? I thought he was just a shadow, and if my son cannot survive this he will be a shadow too. He will leave the world of living before his time, like the other children taken by Karken."

"You see, in the world of living, when the soul leaves the body, they think it's the end of it all, but they do not know it's only the beginning. The whole world is not made the same, and not all beings see it the way you do; the people from the Man's Land. Karken stole their children souls, and until they get older he trains them to become soldiers of the Dark Evil. He teaches them how to fight against us; they learn how to build their own weapons and how to survive our spells, in case they are caught out of their shadow realm, the realm where the magic of the Dark Evil protects them."

"Dolong, the wizard, told me about Karken, and about how you and the others were chosen to be the wizards who protect this world. But how did the evil succeeded and made Karken his servant? He is not meant to have a strong and trustworthy soul like the others."

"With kindness and wisdom you can change almost anything in this world, but you cannot change the human nature, and that was precisely what the Dark Evil was searching for; the weakness of the human's soul, and the greediness that lies within."

"Indeed, there are many things in this world not many people understand; even when they do, they cannot accept them," said the mother. "Before this happened, I could not have imagined realms like this could exist. I feel as if all my life I have lived in the blindness of a deceiving mist."

"It's unfortunate you have to discover all this at the sacrifice of your son. There are realms and lands that are way beyond your imagination, some of them are like paradise and some are like a nightmare, but you should be assured, knowing this entire world is an eternal battlefield against the evil forces who want to take over this world, man and creature alike, bringing them into the darkness and

sorrow. All those statues in the Great Hall, and many of the paintings hanging on these walls stand witness for those who gave their
lives to protect us from the Eternal Darkness."

"I never imagined Karken existed until now. The truth is even
worst than the stories our elders have told us. Well every story, legend, or myth, has some truth behind it, but with the passing of time,
the truth has been forgotten."

"Lets stop talking and enjoy our dinner; I am sure you will need
it because tomorrow is another long day, and we are far from
through," says the Master Wizard, sending a discrete sign to Larsa, as
she quickly ran into the kitchen.

"Yes my Lord, we have to take care of ourselves in order to continue our battle," says Dolong.

"Let's forget for a moment, all the evil, pain, and sorrow, and enjoy these moments together," encouraged the Master Wizard. "I forgot to mention, in these lands we don't eat the meat of beasts very
often, so I hope you will enjoy our green foods and fresh fish. Green
foods is a medicine to the body, mind, and soul," says the Master
Wizard, smiling.

Larsa made her appearance, followed by two servants who
brought overflowing platters with fresh, ripe fruits and vegetables; a
feast for the eyes and mouth.

"The fish is from the river you crossed in the morning," she says,
placing the heavy tray on the table.

"Thank you, Larsa, I think this will do," says the master Wizard. "Lets us enjoy our feast."

Barkon's Treason

The child was lying on a black, embroidered canvas, draped over the cold table inside the Healing Room, surrounded by glowing crystals. The crystals began glowing stronger and stronger as the light beam faded with the setting of the sun. The guards were changing every few hours at the entrance of the Healing Room. They began to light the lamps around the walls of the hall, as night took the place of day. Stars began making their grand appearance, one by one, on the ceiling where once the beam of light came through, as if they were assembling after a long time apart. They seemed to dance in the darkness, lighting the sky with twinkles of joyful splendor, at the opportunity to meet once again.

The child's body was bathed in a rainbow of colors, from the crystals surrounding the sapphire table. Around the shrine where the table sat, five more soldiers gathered with their long spears and shields; posting them in defense position, ready for a battle against the evil that may come at anytime.

The orders of the Master Wizard were clear; no one except him should approach the child. In the heavy silence of the room the child moaned, writhing in pain, as he lies restless on the table. Strange noises began to emerge from his dry mouth. The soldiers searched each other's eyes for answers; their empathy for the boy growing stronger.

The light of the full moon permeated through the window of his room.

"It will be a quiet night," says his mother. "You will sleep by yourself in this room tonight, Elidoc. You are safe here. I will be downstairs, so do not be afraid."

"What if you just stay with me until I fall asleep," he softly says, "and tell me a story like grandma told to you, when you were a young girl."

"It's too late for that Elidoc, maybe tomorrow, if you aren't be a wayward boy like you were today."

"But I didn't do anything," says the child.

"Indeed, but you fed the dog under the table, the food you were supposed to eat." "I do not like the green leaves; I desire fowl or chicken."

"Well, you cannot thrive on birds alone, regardless of how strong your desire is. The green leaves give you a long life. Your grandmother has lived a long life because she eats the green leaves..."

Interrupting his mother, the boy states, "But I do not want to get old like grandma, old people are rigid, and cannot run with the wind. She cannot even catch the dog."

"Well, you will understand when you get older. It is good to get old like grandma; age is a privilege not to be discounted. Now go to sleep and do not look out of the window, my child."

Softly, he hesitantly asks, "Mother, what if the dragon will come in the middle of the night and steal me away? What if..."

She swiftly interrupts, "Oh, my precious Elidoc, I know you want me to stay with you, but the dragon is only a myth to scare bad children who don't listen to their parents. Now close your eyes, and think of how will you be well tomorrow."

"I will try, Mother," as he pulls the blanket over his head.

She closes the door slowly behind her and descends the spiral stairs into the kitchen.

The Battle for Life

"Tomorrow I will try to behave, and try to eat those stinky green leaves. She said this would be a quiet night. It's quiet for certain, quiet enough to hear my own heart beat!"

As he began to fall asleep under his warm blanket, he dreamt of long, summer days, when he ran effortlessly from morning to night; soaking up the warm sun, and the scent of childhood with the other children in his village. He suddenly felt a cold breeze under his blanket, as if the window was open, allowing winter's cold breath inside. He immediately awoke, searching the window for solace from the light of the moon.

"What just happened?"

The room was dark. There was no longer a fire burning in the stove. "Was it the wind that put the fire out?"

Slowly, he got off the table and tried to open the door, but it was locked. "How can it be locked? It has no locks."

Panic set in, and the trembling of fear quickly became an audible scream. Even then, no one heard him. He hesitantly approached the window, only to see eyes, burning like fire in the foreground of thick, black smoke. A dark silhouette slowly took an eerie shape, appearing as if it hovered over the trees and homes of the land; wings of shadow sprawled outright, but without a distinct origin. Smoke began to billow from under the windows and doors of the little houses. It seemed as if everything in the land was on fire. He started to yell, forcing every ounce of breath he could summon from his damaged lungs, hands over his ears to muzzle the screams, eyes shut tight.

The eyes of fire were rapidly approaching him. From out of the thin layer of smoke arose a black, perfectly formed hand with long, sharp claws, touching his skin, and deep from within the darkness a disembodied, penetrating voice spoke, and "Welcome to my kingdom, child Soon you will serve your only master." The boy's body went limp.

The smoky hand lifted the listless child off the floor and slowly placed him on his makeshift bed, disappearing into the darkness.

"It is so warm now. Who is this old man with silver hair and long beard? What was he telling me? I couldn't understand his words. This is not my room. Where is mother?"

The child slowly opens his eyes.

Back at the Master Wizard's house, a soldier approached, whispering something into the Master's ear.

"Let him be; he's just having bad dreams. Leave him to his memories, and do not disturb him; he is still fighting from inside his body. Just keep watch, and do not let anyone enter the room. It is in these dark hours we cannot be sure who is friend and who is foe. Trust no one."

"I will take care of him. Do not worry, my Lord; he is in good hands, and I have doubled the guard," assures the stout soldier.

"What happened?" asks the mother, frantically. "It's about my child? Is he hurt?"

"He is fine; just dreams, and the guards were concerned for him," assures the wizard.

"It will be a long night. Are you sure he will be saved, Master Wizard?"

"I am sure. How long will it take, that I cannot know. Now sleep,"

"You said the power of Karken is very strong. What should we do? Is there still hope for my son, for others?"

"Karken has grown in power, and is now much stronger than we knew him to be. We've made a grave mistake, letting time pass; hoping it will consume him. I was wrong; we were all wrong. I've send word for Wirgos and Maedyv to come. My falcons should arrive to them by nighttime tomorrow. They will be here in two days if they don't encounter any losses to delay them."

"Who are Wirgos and Maedyv? Are they coming to save my son?"

"They are the other two wizards. Wirgos is of the West, and Maedyv keeps watch over the East. We are the last strongholds against the Dark Evil."

"Do you think the boy will hold strong until they arrive?" inquires Dolong.

"Yes, he is far from evil, and my medicine is at work, but for the poison to be removed completely, the spell has to be undone."

"Do you think my child will be the same again?"

"That I am unsure. He is just a child, but has already passed through trials in which a man of physical and mental strength would struggle. He has seen and heard of things that will change his child's mind to a man's, and there is much still to come."

"I understand," replies the mother.

"This depends only on our will," says the Master Wizard. "We have to help him comprehend things a child cannot. I will instill all I can, but it will take time and patience."

The mother was wringing her hands, gazing down at the table, unable to hear anything more than the sound of her racing heart.

"I want to know how Karken was deceived by the Dark Evil, and why, and how such horrible things were allowed. What did evil find as his weakness?"

"Karken was once one of the great wizards; he was like me, Wirgos, and Maedyv, but before then he was a king of the Southern lands. His name was Barkon. When we gave up our thrones and our wealth, we also gave up our names, and our human condition. The Alburn Light gave us undying life and wisdom, the science of medicine, and the power over all living things within our realms."

When the dark evil came into this world, none of us were aware of its position. It takes time for the evil to thrive, but time was not what it lacked. He needed one of us. The Southern lands were rich in every resource; the mountains overflowed with gold and gems, there were endless fields of nourishing food for the entire kingdom; no man would ever go hungry. Barkon was a powerful king; his army was no match for any army of this world, but his desire was not for more power or land. He ruled his kingdom in peace and harmony. When he gave up all his wealth, his family and his friends, he became one of us; a chosen wizard. He was happy, and content with the tasks of a Master Wizard. The one desire he never divulged was his undying need for glory and fame. It was this weakness the evil longed for. The evil used this weakness to make him dream about the days when he was a king, ruling over the Southern Lands. Each morning, Barkon became increasingly saddened, with dark thoughts were passing through his mind. He started asking himself if his choice to give up all he possessed in the past life was worth what little he had gained. He was thinking the light from the Alburn Star deceived him, covering him not with blessings, with sorrow and regrets.

His mother pleads, "How could he not see and feel that evil toyed with him in his dreams? Was he not protected by the spells?"

Unbeknownst to her, his present form was protected, but not the spirit side of him.

His dreams continued to seem more and more like reality. He dreamed about being the only ruler over the whole world, being the one and only king. The greatest power of all the lands. One day when he was walking through his forest, the Dark Evil met him beneath a veil of flower-laden trees. He promised to make him the king of kings, the only ruler of this world. He promised unthinkable riches and immeasurable power over all living things but on this day, his human nature betrayed him. It betrayed all.

The magic of the Alburn Star was still upon him. He was unaware he couldn't shelter the good and the Dark Evil under the same roof. After the Dark Evil touched him with its spells, the two, powerful, magical forces started to fight inside of him. He started passing from light to darkness; his body fighting against itself. When the Light of Alburn abandoned him, he turned into a shadow; unable to take any shape except that of a shadow dragon, which is how he became a sorcerer, and the slave of the Dark Evil. He now can serve but one master, the Dark Evil, who derives from the depths of the unseen sky.

The Dark Evil gave him power in order to build an army strong enough to fight us. Since then, many centuries have passed; too many for a man's life to add a drop to the bucket. This is how history becomes myth.

"And why can you not fight him and kill him once and for all;

stop all this pain and sorrow he brought into this world?" begs the mother.

"We fought him for centuries, and many brave warriors have died in these battles. We did not kill him because we didn't find a way to end his life. His master, the Dark Evil, protects him and we cannot cross into his realm. The borders are protected against us like our borders protect us against him. We were unaware he has been growing in strength; until I felt the spells he put over your child. We cannot stop him from building his army. Much time has passed and he may be strong enough to defeat all of our spells and pass over our borders."

"Will this become war again? This is why your soldiers are always ready?"

"Indeed, they are ready to fight the army of Karken. Once, all kingdoms were united, but the greed of the kings seeking more wealth and more power divided them. Now our alliances are few, and the few great kings who remain are old."

"We have had enough for today," says Dolong the wizard. "It is time for us to slumber so we may be well rested for tomorrow."

"Indeed; we need plentiful rest by night, because we do not know what the day of tomorrow has prepared for us," says the Master Wizard. "It will be hard for you to sleep. I understand, but you especially, have to rest," he tells the mother, as he leaves the table.

The mother and the wizard climb the winding stairwell that leads them to their rooms.

Into the peaceful realm, the silence of the cloudless night set little by little upon the beasts and people of the land. Only the soldiers on the fortress city walls are keeping watch. At last, the tireless nightingales of the fortress garden have paused their merciful songs.

The Magic of the Three Wizards

The light of the morning sun shines over the mountains, bringing life for the people and beasts of the land. The fields are alive again, after their short slumber, for those who work them relentlessly. The guards of the night watch now change positions for those who found rest in the stillness of night.

The Master Wizard is already in the Healing Room, watching over the boy. He is sleeping deeply, on the sapphire table, surrounded by guards, which have been keeping watch over the night.

"Send word to the Falconer; I need to know when the falcons return," says the Master Wizard to his lead guard. "And tell Larsa to bring the mother when she's awake."

He takes an old book from the carved stone shelf and slowly turns the thick pages, contemplating the drawings alongside the writings. The light beam from the ceiling appears again and showers the child's body with healing light.

"Open all the windows," the Master Wizard commands the guard, "let the fresh morning air replace the old."

The tall, stained windows open one by one, and the cold morning air fills the room with the intoxicating perfume of the awakening garden flowers. The nightingales, perched on the thinnest branches of the tallest trees, sing their morning melody, blessing all creation within ears' reach, with their song of the new day's splendor. The elegant geese with their downy goslings glide like ice dancers around the water lilies of the garden's pools.

In her room, the mother sat on the corner of the bed, impatiently awaiting Larsa. Another sleepless night, as so many before had passed in the last days of struggle. The night seemed endless, like the daylight doesn't want to peer from beneath the mountains. The separation from her child makes her feel minutes pass like hours; waiting lonely in her room for the morning to come.

"My Lady, it is time for you to see your child," says Larsa. "If you are ready, just come down. The guard will take you to him."

She's been ready since they left the Healing Room, the night prior. She descends the stairs, to the entrance hall where the guard was waiting for her.

"It is time to go, my Lady," says the guard. "My Lord has sent for you; please, follow me."

The soldier turned to the right of the building on a narrow, paved street. "We will take the shorter path to the Great Hall. You will be there quickly."

"I can't remember if this is the same path we walked yesterday. Are we passing through the garden?"

"No my Lady, this path will lead us straight to the eastern entrance of the Great Hall."

The mother follows the soldier on the narrow street. After a short time, the Great Hall appears in front of them. Viewed from the side, rising spectacularly from the ground, an intricate spider web of pillars and massive stone arches, sprawled out like a human ribcage, support the majestic walls. Carved on top of each pillar, hideous monsters crouch in sorted, macabre positions, eyes pointed to the horizon.

"What are those stone monsters on the top of the pillars?" asks the mother, inquisitively.

"They protect the Hall from the outside evil," replies the stoic guard.

They climb the stairs that leads them to a stone portal. A small wooden door opens, and another soldier appears.

"This way, my Lady, the Master Wizard is waiting for you."

Sitting on a chair near the shrine, the Master Wizard is reading from a book that is lying on his knees. Slowly, he closes the book, and stands up as he sees the mother coming.

"As you can see, your child is still sleeping; you can stay here as long as you please. I do not know if he can hear you because he is sleeping so deeply, he has yet to open his eyes."

"How long will he be like this?"

"I think he'll be awake by tomorrow afternoon. He will be hungry, and full of questions. If you need anything, I will be right here."

The mother takes the child hand and begins to cry. The beam of light coming from the ceiling makes his body appear ghostly white.

"Why is he so pale?" Asks the mother.

"It is because of the light that covers him. This is not normal sunlight. The light from the sun is passing through a crystal with such a shape, only the purest of light can pass through to the other side. This beam of light will keep his body warm, and renew the energy of the other crystals around him. When night returns they will give him their powers, and help my medicine fight the poison inside his frail body."

"But the spell is still upon him?" she longs to know.

"The dark spell is still there. I am waiting for the others to come, so our combined power draws it out completely, and without harming him. As I told you before, we need to let time do its work. We cannot rush anything, because in the end, we may not like the result of our impatience."

"Where is Dolong, the wizard?"

"He's in the fortress dungeons, searching old scrolls. Which scrolls; I do not know. He said he remembered something about dark spells of the ancient times, but cannot find them in any of these books."

"You have prisoners in those dungeons?" The wizard starts laughing.

"Oh, no; once there was a prison, but now there is just a library where old archives and scrolls are, as well as several writings that had to be hidden and are under guard."

"What kind of writings?"

"That, I cannot tell you," says the wizard. "I'm afraid that is far beyond your understanding."

More than three weeks had passed since they left the village of Sargem from the Man's Land. Word began to spread about the child and his mother. Along with these stories, truth starts to emerge on the streets and taverns; stories telling how the mother and her child have been taken by an unseen evil to the Land of Undying, and how strange folk are searching for them. Some are saying the Wizard has taken them deep into the mountains, to keep them prisoners inside a hidden cave, so he can place spells on the humans, and because of him, the children of the village have disappeared into the night.

This is how the legends and scary stories are born. Ignorance breeds misunderstanding, and it is this way that myths are born. Myth coming from misunderstanding brings fear and doubt into the man's soul. Fear is the oldest and strongest emotion of a man's soul and the greatest fear is the fear of the unknown.

The fireside tales, old legends and myths, are making this fear even greater than it should be. So they prefer to stay on the secure land of their homes and villages, not daring to explore the world surrounding them. They have been fad with myth and scary words, and they do not want to see beyond them. The will explore the unknown that is taken from them without their knowledge, and Karken's spies are taking care of seeding deep into their minds, that primeval fear, to better control them.

In the Man's Land, books are forbidden, and those chosen few who understand the meaning of the written words, hide their secret.

Since the time when the boy was taken to the wizard, Karken searched for him. He recruited spies among the people of the village to inquire about the three of them, but the townsfolk know not to trust strangers. They searched the Wizard's house, knowing they fled, because the horses were missing, and the fire was still burning in the stove; they obviously left in a hurry.

Karken sensed the Wizard stopped the work of his spells and poison over the child's body, and no longer able to steal his soul. But this was not what the servant of the Dark Evil feared most. He feared the Wizard will find a way to undo his spells, and common people will find out the truth; knowing in the future, how to protect their children. The fear and sorrow could be over for the people living on his land's and the possibility they may unite with the Armies of the Orders to take revenge over their children has brought him immeasurable duress. His master will not be pleased.

He searched relentlessly in each house of the each village, but found no sign of them.

Back in his dark fortress, he sends powerful spells into every corner of his realm. Every bird and beast was enchanted, in order to search after the runaway; every tree, every crevasse, every hole and cavern, every fissure of this land. No place went unsearched. All this was fruitless, so Karken, by himself, moving from shadow to shadow, searched for them. He lost their trace at the entrance of the cavern-leading deep into the mountain. "If they are not lost inside the mountain's trap then they are beyond my reach, and they are already into the realm guarded by the master Wizard." The spells guarding the borders of that land are too powerful for him, at least for now.

Consumed with anger and hate, he turns back into his dark realm, hoping his spells are too strong for the Master Wizard alone to undo them. If so, he will never find a way to stop him from building his all powerful, dark army.

He was unaware the other two wizards were en route to the White Fortress City of the Master Wizard, and together they are much stronger than any spells and witchcraft to come from this world or any other; and they are rapidly approaching.

In the Healing Room, the mother gently caresses the face of her ailing child; whispering into his ear, knowing he is unable to her soft voice.

"Do not worry, Elidoc, your body will heal; just be strong, my son; the nightmare will soon be over. Once you awake, you will see a realm like never before, a realm where the winter never comes, where all living things reside in peace and harmony."

A soldier on guard barrels toward the Master Wizard. "The falcons are back, my Lord!"

"This will summon Wirgos and Maedyv. They should arrive by the rise of next light. Send word for the gate's watch to let them pass, and bring them to the Great Hall."

A new hope now enlightens the mother's eyes. Just as the Master Wizard said, she has to be patient, but how is this possible, when her child's life is at stake? It seems so long until morning.

The night approaches at slow pace, covering the Northern Lands in a blanket of deafening silence.

"It is time to retreat to our rooms," says Dolong. "Staying here will not benefit our task."

Startled, the mother replies, "I didn't know you where here. Where have you been all day?"

"I have been searching for old, forgotten writings. I know somewhere, lost in the dungeon archives, are scrolls with old spells that could help your child to regain strength to better fight Karken's witchcraft. Much time has passed, and I no longer remember where to search. My search today was in vain, but I will try again by tomorrow."

"Tomorrow the two wizards arrive."

"Yes, I have heard. I know you are impatient for tomorrow's light."

"I am. I think tomorrow will be much like our first day here, where I could not see my child, as the Master Wizard will stay with him sun up to sun down."

"Yes, I believe so, too. They will want to be alone with your child. But it is better this way."

"I understand. May I help you search for those writings?"

"I apologize; unfortunately you are forbidden. They are only accessible to the wizards...and the writings are in a very old language only wizards comprehend; it is now unspoken."

"I will spend my time with Larsa. Perhaps I can assist her."

"At least you will take your mind off what's happening in the Healing Room. Let's leave for now and allow him rest under the crystals lights. All will be better tomorrow, you will see."

The mother and the wizard leave the room, passing through the same small door on the side of the building she came through this morning. In the Healing Room, only the guards and the Master Wizard keep watch over the child.

"The orders are the unchanged, Borysth," says the Master Wizard to the Captain of the Guards. "I hope by tomorrow's light, the child will no longer require your protection, or at least as long as he will stay inside the borders of the realm."

"Do not worry, my Lord, our borders are well protected, and our falcons keep watch over the places we cannot see or reach," says the Captain.

"Well, after the spell I saw upon this child, I fear we should be more cautious than we have ever required. Karken has grown in strength. His spies are still looking for this child, and I fear he may know he is here. For now, my spells are holding him back, but for how long I cannot know."

"Then we should alert all guards, and double the night watch," urges the Captain.

"I sense we are safe for now. We will seek resolution on this matter tomorrow. I have to consult with Wirgos and Maedyv to gain their input," says the Master Wizard.

"As you wish, my Lord. I will wait for your command."

The Master Wizard slowly approaches the child, placing his hand on the boy's forehead.

"One more night, my child. Soon you will awake from this nightmare."

He organizes his old books on the stone shelves and leaves the room by the Great Hall. As he walks through the narrow corridor, he peers longingly; sadness in his eyes at each glorious statuary of long gone warriors and kings.

"Dark times are coming again," he says aloud. "I pray your sacrifice and struggle was not in vain."

From the top of the high stairs, he watches over the villages in the valley, finding respite in the silence of the night. He takes a deep breath, closes his eyes, and contemplates how long it may be until the Army of Darkness will attack these lands. The people of the valleys have forgotten the battles of bygone ages. Their lives are so short; some things should not be forgotten. How could they enjoy life if the Dark Evil comes upon us? How could they live without worry? Their lives could all end.

"I will find a way to keep the evil away. This is why I am there. This is why I was chosen among the others. This child could give me the tools to stop the evil from building his army."

The moon starts its ascending path behind the mountains, covering with its light all lands of the north. He descends the Great Hall stairs, passing through the garden of the Fortress City.

Everything is so quiet, is seems to be under a spell. The nightingales are crowded one into another, preparing for a good night's sleep.

"Hey! You! The one from the tower," shouts Borysth, to the soldier on watch. "Yes, sir?"

"Tell me; what do you see there in the distance, near the edge of the forest? If my sight does not deceive me, it looks like riders are coming this way. What do you see? Tell me quickly!"

"I see them!" says the soldier. "They are coming this way. They are riding fast. I count five, but there may be more."

"Alert the gate's watch! This should be the wizard our Lord is waiting for. We have to stay on guard until we are certain."

"Tell the archers to prepare, and to stay hidden in the towers. Wait for my orders!", commanded Borysth.

The archers climb the stairs in the watching towers, for a wider field of vision, and greatest range for their arrows, as the riders are close now. In the dark of the night no one can tell who they are.

Through the open window, two falcons enter the Master Wizard room.

"So, they are here at last," he thought to himself. He prepares to leave his room. "Let's see what this new morning will bring us."

The guards lined against the walls are unaware of who approaches. Only the Master Wizard can communicate with his falcons. They all wait, tensed for the rider's approach, which is timely, as they are climbing the sneaking road under the waterfalls to the Fortress City gate.

"Open the gates! We are waited by your Lord," the Master Wizard says to the lead rider.

"And who are you, may I ask?" inquires Borysth sternly. "I am Wirgos. This is Maedyv. The others are our guides." "Why do you claim our Lord is waiting for you?"

The rider answers, "His falcons brought us his messages, and we have sent them back. We know he is already waiting for us in the Great Hall."

"Indeed!" says the Captain, relieved.

"Open the gate!" he shouts to the guards. "Let them pass!"

The cumbersome gate moves slowly; the riders enter the Fortress City, riding on the streets to the Great Hall. From atop the long, winding stairs, the Master Wizard waits patiently for them.

"You have come sooner than I expected."

"We took the shortest route, and we have met in the mountain." replies Wirgos. "Your messages implied a sense of dire urgency."

"Where is the child?" asks Maedyv. "What has Karken done to this boy?" "Follow me, please," says the Master Wizard. "He's in the Healing Room."

The three enters the Healing Room. Elidoc is lying on the table inside the shrine, surrounded by crystals.

"So, how do the stones look? Did they lose any of their light?"

asks Wirgos. "Some. The red stones have faded," answers the Master Wizard.

"That's a good sign, but still, why have you not undone this witchcraft?"

"I was deceived. Karken deceived us all. The evil has strengthened his powers, and I cannot fight against him alone, as I have done in the past," says the Master Wizard.

"This is what I was afraid of," says Maedyv, "the enemy has been preparing for war, and he hid it within deception. How blind are we to allow this to happen."

"Blind... or fools? He took advantage of our good faith, in order to prepare," says Wirgos.

"We should prepare for bad things to come; strengthen our armies, and send word to our allies or what's left of them."

"I do not think this is wise," says Wirgos. "We cannot let him know we are aware of his plan. Let's pretend that we are weak and unprepared. We will gather our armies, but we have to do it wisely; his spies are watching us."

"Yes, that will work. Now let's try to save this child, and undo his witchcraft," says the Master Wizard. "Wirgos, did you bring the medicine I asked for?"

"I have it here," says Wirgos; showing them an emerald green vial. "Let's put it to use."

The three wizards gather around the table where Elidoc is lying.

"Let's do this while he's sleeping, so he will not remember it when he wakes up."

The Master wizard pierces the vial's cork top with a brass needle, then slowly, and painlessly pierces the other end into Elidoc's arm. The potion flows into his veins; slowly, they start glowing blue into the crystal light.

"The medicine is working!" exclaims the Great Wizard. "The poison cannot fight it. Soon his body will be clean."

"How soon, we cannot know," says Maedyv. "If only the poison was utilized to enslave him, then it will soon be gone, but I feel powerful spells upon this child. This may take time. We do not yet know how this will affect him.

"We have to undo the spell; this is our only way so stop Karken from building his army," says the Master Wizard.

"Yes, we have to," agrees Wirgos.

"Then, don't delay," urges Maedyv.

The two wizards took the child's hands, while the Master Wizard placed his hands on Elidoc's temple. They were murmuring unknown words in unison. The crystals around the table were glowing brighter than ever seen, and the child's body is bathed in their colorful lights. Dark spots begin to appear again on Elidoc's body. Maedyv sees this, and takes a golden box from his cloak; withdrawing a handful of translucent crystals. He gently places one on each spot forming on the child's body. The crystal absorbs the dark spots upon contact. Trapped into the crystal, the spots now look like black smoke. Maedyv waves the largest of the crystals over the child's body. Soon the translucent crystal is black, and Maedyv puts it back inside the golden box.

Elidoc's body trembles as cold sweat beads over his entire body. His lips become black.

With a sense of urgency, Wirgos shouts, "Hold on child!!" as he changes the empty vial still attached to the boy's arm by the copper needle.

Dark shadows appear on the room's walls. They look like they want to approach the child's body. They struggle to approach him, as the three wizards are too powerful, and the light from the shrine is too strong for them to succeed. The dark shadows circle like buzzards over a fresh carcass, but are unable to breach the wall of light.

"Maedyv, someone must open the windows," says the Master Wizard. "This evil has to get out of this room. Do it, quickly! Now, Maedyv!"

Maedyv runs to the stained windows, hurriedly throwing them open, one by one. The dark shadows circle the room's walls, only to exit as they reach the open windows.

No shadow remains, and slowly the wizards take their hands from Elidoc's weakened body.

"The spell is undone," says Wirgos, "but now the Evil One will know. He is certain to arrive here soon."

"Yes, he will now know we have taken the poison out of the child," says the Master Wizard. "And he will count on it to work. Let the child rest. He will wake up in a few hours."

"Bring the mother to me, please," asks Wirgos. "I need to speak with her now." "She's in her room," replies the Master Wizard.

"That is good. Then let us go; we have come a long way and are longing for sustenance."

As the three wizards left the Healing Room, headed to the Master Wizard's house, the sun shined upon them. They noticed the guards preparing to change for the second part of day.

"Master Wizard, please tell me, how many allies do we have?"

Wirgos, I am afraid, not as many as we once held. As you already know, the old kings can no longer fight, and the new kings are not the brave warriors their fathers before them were."

"Then we should search for more warriors," replies Wirgos. "Time is not in our favor."

"Maedyv, where are your spies? Did you find a way to pass them into Karken's realm?" asks Wirgos.

"I have three of them who are ready for such a task. I will leave as the morning comes. I will meet them, and tell them what is required of them."

"Now is the time to use them wisely. We need to know what the enemy is prepared for. Not to forget, Karken has his own spies. Warn yours to be aware of this," said the Master Wizard. "My falcons spotted them on the borders, but the spies are unable to cross."

"Not for now," says Wirgos. "Those spells that were upon the child were something I've never seen before. No wonder you cannot do this alone. They were seeded deep into his soul and they were made to work together with the poison from inside his body."

"Indeed, those spells are powerful, you're right. We let the Evil One grow in strength, under our watch," says Maedyv.

"We have to make our plans to be as dark as the night," said Wirgos. "We have to deceive him better than he deceived us."

"We will prepare ourselves. If our plan works, we will attack the unprepared enemy."

"A great victory is one that requires no battle, but I am afraid we have no choice," says the Master Wizard.

"Indeed, we have tried to avoid battles in order to save lives, but he took advantage."

"Let us rest and clear our minds," said the Master Wizard. "The evil will still be there, waiting for us. That is the only thing we don't have to worry about."

"Sadly, not," said Maedyv. "It was always there, somewhere, fighting with Alburn's light."

"Here we are; my home," says the Master Wizard.

"Finally," says Wirgos. "For a moment, I thought we were lost in this maze of streets."

One of the guards opens the door for the three wizards, and then regained his place against the stonewall.

"Larsa, are you home? We have guests."

"Yes, my Lord; I am always here," says Larsa, smiling upon hearing his voice.

Please prepare food; our guests are famished, and I do not believe they will be content with veggies alone."

"And no fish, please," says Wirgos. "I always feel hungry after I eat fish." The three wizards laugh simultaneously. It has been a long time since they were together.

"I understand, my Lord; I will tell Kolnet to prepare meat. Sausage is already prepared. I will bring that immediately."

"Perfect, and wine, please."

"You have not changed at all, Wirgos," chuckles the Master Wizard. "Where is the child's mother?" asks Maedyv.

"Larsa, would you please look for the Elidoc's mother?"

"She's not in her room," answers Larsa. "She told me she would be in the garden, waiting for Wirgos and Maedyv to arrive."

"They've came sooner than we thought," says the Master Wizard, "and we already finished our work in the Healing Room."

"As soon as you can, please find her. Tell her the child is safe now, and she should join us."

"Yes, my Lord; as soon I prepare the lunch."

Larsa headed back into the house's kitchen searching for Kolnet.

"We have guests, and they do not want our green veggies; they want meat. They desire wine too," she says.

"They are not from these lands?" asks Kolnet.

"No, they are not. They are wizards of the Eastern and Western lands; Wirgos and Maedyv."

"Great troubles our Lord has, for them to come all the way here." "It is about the child," says Larsa.

"Poor child; I hope he will survive. Where is his mother? I didn't see her all morning."

"She is in the garden," says Larsa. "She is waiting for our two guests to come; unaware they have arrived early. She didn't know that they have arrived. I will find her when the food is prepared."

"We should hurry," says Kolnet, as he began preparing the feast.

"Bring them some wine while they wait for the food to be done. Take this bread and oil as well."

Elidoc's New Life

In the Fortress Garden, the child's mother sits on the same wooden bench she sat with Dolong, the day of their arrival. She watches the geese play with their goslings and tirelessly singing nightingales filling the air with their sweet song. "They have no worry," she thought to herself. "Perhaps it is better to be a bird, than a human? You are blissfully unaware of the sadness and sorrow of this world. Their offspring have not to worry about being taken by evil shadows."

Suddenly, she hears someone approach, with small but hurried steps.

It's Larsa!"

"My Lady, I was looking for you, my Lord has sent me to tell you the two wizards have arrived."

"How can they be here? I did not see them pass."

"They entered the city early, and have already done their work in the Healing Room."

"That means my child is safe?"

"I cannot tell you that, because he didn't give me any news on your child. They are waiting for you in the house; we should go now."

Larsa left the garden with the child's mother, stepping quickly through the fortress' narrow streets.

"Come, we are waiting for you," said the Master Wizard. "Please take a seat."

"These are our guests; he is the Wizard of the Western lands; Wirgos, and The wizard of the Eastern lands; Maedyv. We have undone the spell laid upon your child, and we have taken out the poison from his body."

"So, is he saved?"

"He is saved from Karken's witchcraft, but now we have to wait and see what damage the poison has made inside his body," says Wirgos.

"Do not worry," says Maedyv, "he will be fine in the end, and that's what truly matters. It will take some time, it's true, but the end result is what's important. Patience it's all we need," said Maedyv.

When may I see him? Is he awake?"

"We will all see him in the afternoon, the guards will inform us when he wakes," says the Master Wizard.

"For now, we need rest and sustenance; we rode without delay for several days," replies Wirgos.

"Please, eat with us," urges Maedyv. "What is the child's name?", asks Wirgos. "His name is Elidoc, and mine is Maryia. "He's very young. How old is he?"

"He was born eight winters and a day, before he become ill." "What about his father? Where is he?"

"His father was gone when Elidoc was only three. He entered into the untamed forest and we never saw nor heard about him again. I was told he lost his path in the mist, on his way back to our village, but no one has ever found him. Since then, we have only each other."

"I am sorry," says Maedyv, drinking from his cup. "Sad, indeed," says Wirgos.

"Do not worry," said the Master Wizard, "you are welcome here, and may remain as long as you please. The child has to stay with us until the enemy spies will lose his trace. Dolong cannot go back there anymore; they know what he did, and will not forgive him."

"Dolong is here?" asks Wirgos.

"Yes, he is here. He was the first one to stop the poison. He brought the boy and his mother to me."

"Where is he now?" Asks Maedyv.

He's searching for old scrolls in the dungeons," interrupts the mother.

"What scrolls? This old wizard always has grand ideas."

"The scary thing is that most of them work," says the Master Wizard.

'He didn't say. He told me that it's pointless to explain such things to me that anyway I cannot understand."

"Sometimes that is best; it could taint your mind," says Maedyv.

"You are right; I feel like my mind is in a dense mist. There are so many things I cannot understand; most of them I cannot believe could exist. It's far beyond my understanding."

"I wonder what he's up to?" asks Maedyv.

'Well you may ask him yourself when he comes up into the sunlight," says Wirgos. "Now, let's eat!"

Larsa, followed closely by Kolnet, enters the dining room, arms loaded with gigantic platters of steak and sausage, potatoes surrounding them, and vegetables in every color.

"Well, it seems we will partake of the vegetables after all," says Wirgos, with a smile.

"All for your nourishment, my Lord. It will not hurt you to eat some."

"...And your horse will be thankful," interrupts Maedyv, laughing hysterically.

They ate slowly, and for a brief moment, it seemed all was well in the world, but deep in their hearts, fear began to grow. They each reflected on time long ago, when countless lives had been lost in perilous wars against evil. The difference then was their many allies. Now, times have changed, and they are forced to move in secrecy.

They also know they will have to forge new weaponry, as the evil cannot be subdued with what they have.

A soldier on guard enters the Master Wizard's house and approaches. The mother looks at him with hope-filled eyes.

"The boy is awake, my Lord; he asked for his mother," says the guard.

"Very well then, it's time to see how the child is feeling," says Maedyv.

"And to see if our work was in vain," says Wirgos.

They left the house in a hurry, taking the short path to the Great Hall. As they entered the Healing Room, the child was still lying on the table. Borysth, the Captain of the Guards was speaking with him. Elidoc was wrapped in the black cloth with golden symbols, shivering from head to toe. His scared eyes searched the soldiers surrounding him, not understanding what was going on, or where he was. This room filled with books and colored windows was not familiar to him, and he was desperately trying to remember how he ended up in this place.

"Where am I?" asks Elidoc.

"Do not be afraid. We are here to protect you. Your mother is on her way as we speak," said the Captain. "You are in the Healing Room of the White Fortress, and you have been here for days. The Master Wizard will answer all your questions as soon as he arrives."

"Where are my clothes? And why I'm laying on this table? I am so cold." As soon as the Captain sees them, he points towards them.

"Here they are! I told you not to worry. You will get your answers soon." The mother ran to Elidoc, as he tries in vain to get up. He was still too weak.

"Oh, my son, you have opened your eyes after all these days!" through tears in her eyes. "I thought I would lose you."

"I thought I was still home, in my room. Was I dreaming then?" says Elidoc, confused. "I can barely remember my dream; it was a place so dark that I could barely see. I saw a forest where all trees were dead. No man was walking on those lands, and I could hear nothing; it was like I was deaf. No noise of wind nor beast."

Wirgos carefully asked. "Do you see the stars, or anything built by men?"

Elidoc closes his eyes and answers. "I saw something ahead... ruins... I saw someone there... No, there are more of them. They are moving toward me, but Icouldn't hear their footsteps...they didn't make any noise." "Did you see their faces?" asks Wirgos.

"No, seemed like they were hidden in black smoke. They barely had faces; I could hardly see their eyes, but I did see they were glowing like red hot coals," says Elidoc opening his eyes.

"How many are they?"

"I can't count them," answers the child. "I have never seen so many people before."

"It is all right child. It was just a bad dream; nothing to worry about," says the Master Wizard looking at Wirgos.

"I do not know how much you remember from the last days, but your mother can help you to remember. Now the guards will help you to get dress and they will bring you to my house. You are not staying here anymore. I am sure you want something to eat," says the Master Wizard, signaling the Captain of the Guards.

"Maryia, you can stay with him and come later; there is no rush now."

"Yes I will help him get dressed," offers the mother. "He is much more calm when I am with him."

"Wirgos and Maedyv, we have to leave the boy. Let's take a walk through the Great Hall," says the Master Wizard.

As they let the guards in charge inside of the Healing Room, the three wizards left. "So, tell me, what do you think about his dream?" asks the Master Wizard.

"Well, after what the child is saying, he saw the realm of Karken, and I think his fortress and guards. Perhaps it's just his imagination."

"But, how? He has never been there before?" asks Maedyv.

"Karken had the control of his consciousness through his spells," said Wirgos. "And yes, it's the thing you were afraid of," he says looking to the Master Wizard.

"What thing?" asks Maedyv.

"What Karken possesses to make his spells able to cross our borders without being stopped," answers the Master Wizard.

"Indeed, he has grown in strength, and we let him," says Wirgos, raising the tone of his voice.

"Did you see his veins?" asks Wirgos. "I do not think it's out of him yet."

"Yes, I saw them. The poison was in his body far too long, and even if we saved him, his blood was poisoned. We must start working on medicine to clean it."

"You have to tell this to his mother," says Maedyv. "She has to know."

"After all these days, we must be patient; I do not think she will understand it yet." As they walk through the Great Hall, Maedyv looks to the statues for answers.

"I hope we can still find warriors such as these; skilled warriors of old."

"I agree; we cannot win this only with our wits and our spells; we will need the armies of old," says Wirgos.

"First, we have to stop Karken; once and for all, from building his own borders, and we must stop being exposed to the evil," says the Master Wizard.

"We will count on your spies, Maedyv; the success of our plans will be depend on them."

"I will leave tomorrow and organize them. We will need more "Dead Spies", and the three will be our inside spies."

"Dead Spies? If they are dead, how they can they spy for us?" asks Wirgos, confused.

The Master Wizard and Maedyv laugh.

"Let me explain," says Maedyv still laughing.

"We called them "Dead Spies" because their role is to give false information to enemy spies. We also have spies that we named them "Living Spies". Those spies come back and report to me. Got it?"

"You and your wicked spy games. I will let you enjoy your spy game; I have to go over the mountains and start gathering the armies, or at least see who is with us," says Wirgos.

"Do not be upset, Wirgos, we all have to do what we know best, in order to save the lives of our people," says the Master Wizard.

"Now let's go to my home; Larsa has prepared your rooms."

The Guards had transported the child on a wooden stretcher, carried over their shoulders to the Master Wizard's dining room., and put him in a chair. All of them were posted in front of the house by Captain's orders. As the mother sat next to Elidoc, holding his cold hand, the child tells her he is hungry, and needs nourishment.

"Larsa is coming from the kitchen, bringing salad and some bread, my child." Elidoc sees the food and asks her, "Do you have any chicken?"

Larsa is looking at him and with a smile answers, "You should be friend with Wirgos; he too doesn't like the green stuff. I will ask Kolnet for some chicken for you."

The mother smiles.

"Elidoc, after all this, you still don't understand you should eat green leaves too?" "But I don't like salad; it takes like nothing."

"Your mother is right," says the Master Wizard entering the dining room. "Green food will help clean your blood. All our medicine and the poison that was inside you have weakened your body."

Elidoc is looking at him with sad eyes. "But... my chicken..."

Larsa comes from the kitchen, carrying a plate in her hands. Elidoc's eyes gaze longingly.

"I am so sorry, child, we do not have chicken, but Kolnet has fish for you. You should try it."

"Fish? I don't like fish."

"See, Maedyv; no child likes these things. How about some sausages and steak?" says Wirgos.

"You two should be friends," Maedyv laughs.

"That's what I told him, too," says Larsa, laughing.

"Finally! There's he is!" exclaims Wirgos with joy, when he sees Dolong coming through the door.

"We've been asking for you, Dolong."

"I've been in the dungeon's archives," answers the wizard.

"How are you child?" he asks Elidoc. "How do you feel?"

"I am hungry, and they are giving me fish and green leaves to eat."

"Well, you should get used to it, because here they do not like meat much," says Dolong. "Do you remember me?"

"I cannot be sure."

"I was the one who brought you and your mother here. I was carrying you all the way here on my horse."

"So, tell us, what are you up too? I heard you are searching for some old scrolls, or books?" asks Wirgos.

"Yes, I barely can remember. A long time ago, when Barkon the Wizard was not yet Karken the dragon sorcerer, he was spending much time in the dungeons, writing what he told me to be his realm's history. Back then I didn't give them much interest, but now they are starting to make sense."

"What scrolls are you talking about," asks the Master Wizard.

"I do not know if you are aware of them," answers Dolong. "Karken himself, Barkon back, wrote them, they were a diary of his own memories."

"Well now, that's interesting!" says Wirgos.

"How could this help us?" asks Maedyv.

"I am not sure, because I didn't find them, but I think we will find something we can use."

"Find how the evil deceived him. Go back to the origin of his fall," says the Master Wizard.

"Exactly," says Dolong. "Maybe we will find out how the dark evil protects himself, and were it is hiding."

"I see it now," says Wirgos. "I didn't even think about it until now."

"Maybe Barkon wrote how the evil passed over the spells that protected his realm. I think we all need to know that in order to better protect ourselves."

"Are you sure the writings are still there?" asks Maedyv.

"There's only way to find out; I have to search and look over all writings." "And if they're not here? What then?" asks Wirgos.

"Then we have only one option; we should trust our spies."

"Your spies?" said Wirgos. "I do not want to deal with them. I cannot trust those who work in the shadow, no matter who they are."

"You don't have to worry, Wirgos, you are safe with us. Just stay close to me, and do not look back."

"I prefer my own soldiers."

"I have to say, sadly, it is like in the good old days with these two," says the Master Wizard laughing. "They will never stop teasing each other."

Dolong slowly approaches the Master Wizard and with a low voice asking, "May we please go outside? I have some questions for you, if I may."

The Master Wizard nods. They leave the dining room and close the door behind them.

"What is bothering you?" he asks.

"I watch the child, why is his skin is so white and it looks like dark blood running through his veins," says Dolong. "The poison is still inside him?"

"Maedyv removed all the poison from his body but his kidneys and his lungs were already affected by it. I thing that by the time his mother brought Elidoc to you, the poison was already working inside."

"And what can we do now? Will he be fine, or is he still in danger?"

"He will be fine; we have nothing to worry about for now. Our medicine will continue to work and we should give it to him every day. For how long, I do not know for sure, could be a few years," says the Master Wizard.

"And why has his blood changed? It was affected too?"

"Yes it was. When our medicine was fighting against Karken's poison. The child may need his blood replaced, but not soon. Now we have to work on the vegetables and the herbs from this realm. They could help him clean what's left from the poison's damage."

"I see he's not used to eating our food; it will be difficult to make him understand; he's just a child."

"Yes, it will be very difficult, I know; but we have to be patient and watch over him, because he's a child.

"And you warned the mother about all this?"

"No, we have to let some time pass, she has heard and seen enough already. We have to let things settle for a while."

"I understand, now let's go inside before they become suspicious about our absence."

"I agree and we don't have to talk about his in front of her. I will find a way to explain it so she can handle it."

"I will respect your wish," says Dolong. "You know better than I, what lies within her soul."

The two rejoined the others in the Dining Room. Wirgos was enjoying his cup of wine, and Elidoc with his mother, and Maedyv at his side, trying to convince him how strong, brave, and wise he will be if he eats all the fish and vegetables. The night is setting over the realm with fast pace, and the moon appears between the mountains like a sentinel keeping watch over the borders. One by one the Master Wizard's guests are retreating to their rooms. Dolong and the mother helped Elidoc climb the stairs to his chamber. Silence takes over the folks and beasts; only the soldiers on guard seem to never sleep; keeping watch over the fortress city.

The sun rose purple the next morning, like in the days of great battles of the old. Dense clouds gather over the realm, and the rains begin.

Maedyv was already on his horse when he felt the first drop. "Can you please stop the rain?" he begs the Master Wizard. "The crops and beasts need it."

Maedyv's horse gallops along the narrow streets to the fortress gate. "Where are the child and his mother? Have you seen them?" asks Wirgos.

"They are still sleeping," says the Master Wizard. "Let them rest, there's no hurry." "I will be in the Healing Room, preparing his medicine."

"I think I will join Dolong in the dungeons to help him find the writings he spoke of. Maybe he is right," says Wirgos.

"He's already there," says the Master Wizard.

Wirgos pulls the hood of his cloak over his head and starts heading into the dungeon entrance, beneath the Great Hall. On the northern side of the Great Hall, hidden from view by trees and bushes, is a narrow, stone stair that descends beneath the building foundations. Wirgos descends the narrow steps slowly, and soon enters through a heavy gate made of thick and rusty metal. In front were two guards, slowing his pace even more. He fires up a torch and advances into the dark and narrow underground tunnels. As he fires up torches along the walls, he asks himself why Dolong did not light them. He descends another narrow stair, and in a niche sees a burning torch; a sure sign Dolong is somewhere near. He finds Dolong in what once was a prison cell, sitting on a table with a pile of old books and scrolls. He was reading at a lantern light, and seemed not to notice Wirgos' presence.

Clearing his throat, "Did you find something?"

Dolong startles.

"I thought I was alone here, I didn't here you coming. I found some writings from those ages but not what I am looking for. I still have many to look at. What brings you here, Wirgos?"

"I thought I would help you find those writings. I also wish to know what Barkon was dreaming about."

"Then you may start in the next room."

He fires up this lantern, and quenches his torch.

"You don't want to start a fire with that," says Dolong, giving him a lantern. "Why would anyone keep such a library in dark underground?"

"Because some things are better if they're hidden underground."

The sunrays are entering through a curtain into the room where Elidoc and his mother are sleeping. She slowly opens her eyes checking on Elidoc and moves close to him. The boy wakes up, watching how the sunrays are fighting to pierce the window curtain. Their room seems larger, with higher ceilings compared to one from their house from the village of Sargem. A big chimney made from rover stone is on the other side of the room and a massive table is sitting in the middle. In a corner near the chimney is a wooden bathtub. The bed on which they sleep is made out of carved wood, with high bedstead and curtains around and above it sustained by thick square pillars at its corners. It was soft and comfortable. They were not sleeping on a pad made of straws but on one made of soft feathers. The floor was paved with dark red polished stone and covered in some places with simple squared rugs.

"Mother, are you waking up?" asks Elidoc. "I am already awake."

"I am hungry. May we have some breakfast?"

"Let me see if Larsa is home, so we don't have to bother our hosts. You wait here; I will go to see if someone is home."

"But I don't want to be alone, Mother."

"You have no reasons to be afraid; there are soldiers at the house entrance, and all over the Fortress City. I will be back right away."

The mother leaves the room closing the door and Elidoc pulls the blanket over his head.

"Good morning, my lady," says Kolnet. "How is Elidoc feeling this morning?" "Good morning, Kolnet, he is awake and he's hungry."

"Oh, that's a good sign. I will prepare something for him. What do you think he may like? I have milk, eggs, goat cheese, some tea; maybe some bread with butter?"

"Knowing my son, I think he would like milk with some bread." "Very well then, I will prepare what he desires."

"Kolnet, have you seen Larsa?"

"She left this morning to the village to bring food for our house. You should have gone with her, it would have done you good. The guards are with her to help so you should not worry about anything."

"I will ask her to take me with her next time. When we came here we passed through the village, but the folks were looking at us suspiciously."

"That's because they do not like strangers, and especially those who came from the forest. They are afraid that the Karken's spies can cross our borders."

"They know about Karken?"

"Yes they do; the master Wizard is not allowing for the history to be forgotten. They know about the old wars and about the kings and warriors that you have seen in the Great Hall. They know that they sacrificed their lives so the people of this world can leave in peace. No, my lady, they cannot forgot that, they should newer forget that."

"You are right. We, from the Man's land we don't know the history. We only heard about Karken in our myths and night stories."

"Karken wants it to be like this. The less you know about him the better he can do his work."

"Ohh, we almost forget about Elidoc's breakfast. Give me a few moments, please." Meanwhile the Master Wizard enters into the dining room.

"Good morning, how's the child doing? Did he sleep well?"

"Yes, he did not have any bad dreams," says the mother. "Now he's hungry, and I asked Kolnet if he could prepare something for breakfast."

"That's good news, he will need to eat in order to regain his strength. I came in time to let you give him this medicine."

"What is that?" asks the mother.

"This potion he has to take every morning and before he sleeps. This will help his body to recover faster, and to repair what the poison has damaged inside him."

"I will take care of it, because I have to fool him like I do with everything he doesn't like."

"Very well then, we have to do whatever it takes for him to be well." "His breakfast is ready," says Kolnet. "I should prepare one for you too."

"Do not bother for me; I will find something in the kitchen, I don't want to slow you down from what you're doing."

"You don't bother me at all; you are our Lord's guests; we are at your service my lady."

"Thank you, Kolnet."

She climbs the stairs to their chamber. As soon as she opens the door, Elidoc takes his head out from under the blanket he was covering with.

"I almost fell asleep."

"I have your breakfast; milk and bread, just as you like it."

"Thank you. For one moment I thought that I had to eat fish and vegetables for breakfast too."

"No, Elidoc not for breakfast, and the Master Wizard has given me a gift for you." "What gift?" asks Elidoc, with eyes sparking with curiosity.

"Well, he told me to give it to you only if you are a good boy. He says that it will make you stronger and taller if you take it."

The mother shows him the small bottle with the green potion in it.

"This is a magical potion, Elidoc, and if you take it all mornings before breakfast and before you go to sleep, you will grow three times faster than any child of your age."

"Give it to me, please, I was a good boy; I ate all the fish yesterday!" "Very well then, open your lips, I have to give it to you."

The mother starts pouring small drops of the green potion into his mouth. Elidoc starts crooking his lips, disgusted.

"Arghhh it tastes so bad! What is it? I fell like I want to throw up, and it smells so bad!

"It's the magic potion Elidoc!" "I don't want it anymore!"

"Then I will tell the Master Wizard that you don't like his gift and you want to rest a tiny weak little boy for the rest of your life."

Elidoc is looking at her, not knowing what to do.

"Fine! I will take it! Do not tell the Master Wizard I do not like his gift." Elidoc takes the potion with tears in his eyes, almost crying.

"I would rather eat fish all day long!"

"Eat your breakfast now, I will go downstairs and if I see the Master Wizard I will tell you how much you liked his gift."

The mother left the plate on the table and left the room closing the door behind her. "Do not close the door!" shouts Elidoc.

"We are safe here; there are soldiers over the streets of this city and guards are watching this house."

"I am not afraid, I want you to leave the door open because it's too hot in here," says Elidoc.

"Did you find something?" Wirgos asks Dolong.

"No, not even a trace of it. I have a feeling it is not here."

"I was thinking about that too, and if it's here for sure it should be hidden somewhere. Maybe we're just wasting our time searching for it."

"Maybe, but what choices do we have?"

"We have none, but to enjoy our dinner," says Wirgos, smiling. "I didn't even realize how quickly time has passed."

"Well, my belly did. Let's go outside; I've had enough of staying underground." "I agree," says Dolong, "we should continue another time."

Soon they entered the Master Wizard's dining room. At the table Maryia and Larsa are talking about women's chores.

"Good evening ladies," says Dolong, smiling. "Where's Elidoc?"

"He is in our chamber," the mother answers. "He was asleep all day and only ate his breakfast."

"Well I don't blame him. He doesn't want to be thinner than he already is," he says, looking to Larsa.

Dolong starts laughing, and takes a seat near Larsa.

"Wirgos was complaining about your food, he told me that you want him to starve and he's having dreams about eating beef and sheep meat, and drinking wine till I fell under the table."

"Well, I have good news for you, my Lord, we have lamb for dinner with potatoes and green beans; Kolnet just put it in the oven."

"See Wirgos, nothing is as bad as it seems," says Dolong.

"Indeed, at least we have some real food in here," says Wirgos appeased. "Mother, are you there?" Shouted Elidoc. "Can you come here please?" "He woke up at last," says Larsa.

As the mother enters, Elidoc cries, "You told me that you'll come back but you never did."

"I was downstairs, Elidoc. Why are you scared?"

"I am not scared but I am not used to sleeping in any other room except mine. I feel like a stranger here."

"Well, my son, you have to get used to it because I think we will have to spend some good time in this house."

"But why? I want to go home, I miss my room even if this one is bigger and nicer."

"We are not ready to go back, you are still weak and you have to drink the magic potion, remember?"

"I don't want to eat fish. I am not hungry."

"No fish this time, they have chicken, but not the one like you know; here they have big chickens that taste better than the one you know."

"Really, they have chicken? I though they ate only fish and grass."

The mother took his arm help him to stand up. Step by step they descend the stairs to the dining room. Everyone starts smiling and acclaimed him as they saw him walking into the dining room. Elidoc's cheeks reddened and his self-confidence starts growing in him.

"I told him about how big the chickens are growing on these land," says the mother to Larsa, "it was the only think that convinced him to descend for dinner."

"The chicken is ready," says Kolnet, bringing a huge food tray with the lamb and potatoes.

"Tell me, Elidoc," asks the Master Wizard, "do you know how to read?"

"No, my mother knows a little but in our village nobody knows, it is forbidden."

"Well, here it is not forbidden and I propose to your mother that myself and Dolong will teach you. A child like him has to know more about this world, now that he escaped Karken's wrath he will have to be smart and clever. The enemy will not rest until he finds who this child is."

"I agreed, my Lord," says the mother, "it will not do him any harm to lean how to read."

"You will have to stay here quite some time, we are already talked about it, so why not take advantage of this and make your time here useful."

"I agree," says Dolong. "We can teach him and when he will get his strength back Wirgos can teach him how to fight and use weapons."

Elidoc's eyes twinkled with happiness. He looked at Wirgos, who eats his lamb thigh like he was fighting with it.

"It is true? You can teach me how to fight?" he asks Wirgos.

"I can, but for that you need to regain your strength, so you should start to eat that chicken."

Elidoc starting eating the lamb like he never ate before. With his mouth full he asks Wirgos again, "and how to fight with a sword? And... and you know how to shoot a bow?"

"Elidoc, he knows everything about weapons and how to use them," says the Master Wizard. "Wirgos was not always a wizard, once he was a warrior king."

Elidoc gazes at Wirgos but this one he acts like he didn't heard what the Master Wizard just said, continuing eating and drinking his wine.

"He knew all those warriors from the Great Hall?" inquires the mother.

"Yes, he knew them all, and most of them were his friends," says Dolong with a low voice.

"He doesn't like to talk about them; he suffered too much, when one by one they all died in battles or by wounds that cannot be healed by any of our medicine. Sometimes he wished not to be immortal, and that's why he and Maedyv made such a good team. Even if they never stop teasing each other, one is renowned for his sneaky methods, and the other for his brute force. When their minds working together nobody can stop them, they are unstoppable.

"But making them work together is much harder than you think."

"Indeed, they are both stubborn like an ox, but once they start to like you, there's nobody like these two. They will do anything to protect you no matter the cost, and when they have same goal."

"And I can feel that he likes your son, Elidoc. If he agreed to teach him how to fight it means that he had seen something in this child."

"What he saw in Elidoc?" asks the mother.

"We do not know, but let's trust his warrior instinct. Who knows what future is made of?"

"Better stop talking and enjoy this wonderful food," says Wirgos. "Or what's left of it," he said smiling; pouring more wine is his huge cup.

"We all know you prefer to eat than talk."

"Fish for tomorrow, Wirgos?" as they join in simultaneous laughter.

ASSASSINS

At last the rain subsided. Maedyv was relieved, as he rode his grey horse, followed closely by his guards, who, too, were content to be past the rains.

"What did Dolong remembers about Barkon's good old days? I am curious to know," Maedyv contemplates, "but who knows, life is full of surprises; like this child, Elidoc."

They were almost out of the realm of the Master Wizard, cautiously taking secret roads and paths, where one can quickly reach the borders of the realm, but only a wizard can cross them. They arrive in front of a gigantic waterfall billowing out of the cloud covered mountain peaks; chaotic waters pouring down along the vertical mountain wall, falling into a churning cauldron. They took a slippery trail on the side of the water cauldron; a trail that cannot be seen by untrained eyes. The trail led them under the water curtain, sheltering them from the outside world. Over the millennia, the water carved frightening shapes in its struggle with the mountain rock, forming caverns beneath its restless waters.

"It is time to dismount from our horses," orders Maedyv. "We will march through the mountain, aware of every single step."

As they enter the dark cavern, the overwhelming noise armor

the waterfall subsides. All they hear, from time to time, is water trickling from the cavern's walls. The air was cold and wet, and gradually grew frigid as they transcended deeper into the unknown.

"May we light our torches?" asks one of the guards. "We can't see anything ahead of us."

"That is the last thing you want to do in a place like this. Into this cave are beasts we do not want to awake. We can pass through it only by day; they wake up to feed as the night comes."

"What beasts are you talking about, my Lord?"

"Blood sucking bats; giant bats strong enough to take your horse and fly into unknown places in this cave; just as an eagle lifts its prey."

Silence falls over the group.

"They are here to protect this secret pass from our enemies; no common folk may take this path. You need spells to cover the smells and noises of those who are with you, or they will hear and smell everything that has no place in their cave."

Their presence becomes known, and they begin to hear the rustling of beating wings, wild squealing, and claws dragging along the stonewalls of the cavern.

"Do not be afraid; we will be out soon."

Far in front of them they began to see a glimmer of light; a beacon of hope they each sense palpably.

"Well here we are, all together and whole," says Maedyv. "We have to water our horses and take a rest on higher ground. Do not make a fire; I have a feeling someone or something is watching us."

The guards mount their horses and ride through the forest, far from the cave. "Follow me," says Maedyv, "I know a place here where we can rest."

They leave the path and turn straight into the forest, riding through the trees without a path or trail, following Maedyv. A grassy glade opens before them, hidden under the canopy of the trees.

"Someone has to check our surroundings and listen to the noises of the forest," suggests Maedyv. "Go on foot, and not alone; we don't know what may lie in the shadows even by daylight."

Two guards dismount their horses and disappeared into the thick bushes.

"Let's make our camp; we stay here for tonight. We have to avoid moving by night, the enemy spies could hide anywhere in the darkness."

The guards prepare for the night, and unsaddle the horses.

"Leave the saddle on them, we may be forced to get out of here fast! And keep your swords close at all times," he said, as he lay down near the trunk of an old oak tree.

Dark clouds gather, hiding the moon's light. In the old forest, Maedyv and his guards are resting under the trees. All forest's beasts are under the spell of the night darkness, and a deep silence surrounds the woods. Suddenly strange and frightening noises are disturbing the silence of night.

"What are these noises?" asks a soldier.

"Those are the blood sucking bats that came out of the cave we've been in. They are feeding now, but do not worry; as long as we stay under the trees we are safe from them," assures Maedyv, pulling his cape over his head.

The Eastern wind slowly drives the clouds, opening up their view. Now they can see in the foreground of the moonlight, how those bats are fighting each other for their prey.

"We have to check our horse, in moments like these they should be quiet and not make any noises."

With that said, the guards get up, go towards their horses, protected by tree's canopy. The horses were tied to a Leafy Oak trunk, neighing softly ups their master's approach. Maedyv pats his horse's cheek to comfort him. The noise of rustling leaves and broken branches begin to be heard from deep within the forest. Someone or something is surrounding the glade.

"Mount your horses slowly, and draw our swords. We have to make a cycle around this tree."

They are slowly encroached by the mysterious sounds, and without delay, body shaped silhouettes walking on foot start to profile among the trees.

"From this side I can count only five of them," whispers a soldier. "Three on this side," whispers another.

"Four on this one, but I cannot be sure; there may be more. They're coming in my direction and they are all on foot, no horses," says Maedyv.

Simultaneously, a few of them pause, unsteadily standing in the grass, looking around the glade; dagger blades shine in the moonlight. From their awkward gait and unkempt clothes, they look to be thieves or mercenaries.

"Let them get closer," whispers Maedyv. "We will wait until all of them come into the glade so we can count them. They think we're sleeping somewhere in the glade; they do not know that we are right here. We did well to leave our resting place and hide under the trees."

"Who are they?" Asks a soldier.

"By the way they're moving, it looks like they're thieves or mercenaries, but this does not matter because now they are just assassins and they are after us. They have no swords and no horses so we have the advantage here. Hide your sword blades from the moonlight; I do not want our location to be disclosed. We have to hide until we know with whom we're dealing."

More continue to arrive, and gathering in the middle of the glades, stepping slowly on the grass, unaware of the blood sucking bats that swarm above them. Maedyv counted twelve total. They decide to wait for some time before going to attack them. The assassins are lying on the grass like they are waiting for someone to come. Another one is showing from behind the bushes, crawling to the group. He seemed to be their leader. It appeared he gave the others orders, which Maedyv realized was their opportunity to attack them, as they were all together.

"Prepare for attack!" he orders his soldiers. "Remember, whatever happens we have to stay together; we will break the line and start encircling them. We have to move fast. Our enemies are on land and in the sky."

In complete silence, the five riders break formation and ride at a swift pace to the center of the glade where the assassins are laying in the grass. They break the line, encircling them and closing the circle around their assailants. Taken by surprise, the assassins panic. With a cry of despair, they attack the riders, but their daggers were no match against the long swords of the guards. They fall to the iron of the long blades. The gigantic bats seized their opportunity to feast on those who were wounded; scooping up their mangled bodies, and soaring high into the moonlit sky. Few of them succeed to escape from the encircling, seeking refuge within the forest. Two remain alive, throwing their daggers to the ground, and in despair they beg for mercy.

"Take the prisoners," orders Maedyv, "we have to keep them alive if we want to know who they are, for who they work, and how they found us, because no one knew we are here. Tie them! We have to leave this damned forest. It will be morning soon."

The Maedyv guards tie the prisoners, and pull them behind their horses. In no time they are on the same trail they were on the day before.

"We have to watch for more assassins," says Maedyv, "we don't know if we're out of danger. We will move in silence. Bind their mouths so they cannot scream."

The morning sun is ascending lazily behind the wooded mountains, bringing light for a new day and raising the fog from the belly of the valley below. The riders, along with their prisoners, are moving quietly thought the forest. They reach a stone bridge that crosses a deep valley.

"After this bridge we are safe," says Maedyv, "the master of these lands is an old friend of mine, and his borders are well guarded. We will rest in his stronghold and question our prisoners."

One after another, the riders pass the stone bridge and enter into a new forest. This time they can see the trail well, and from a long distance, they can distinguish the sound made by galloping horses.

"Do not be alarmed, these are the watchmen's of Zurob, the master of these lands."

A dozen riders, all with stern faces come their way. They are dressed simply, with long iron shields and pointed helmets.

Their Captain asks upon approach, "Who are you, and what are you doing on these lands?"

"I am Maedyv, the wizard of the Eastern lands and I'm an old friend of Zurob, your master. Assassins attacked us in the forest and these are my guards. We have taken two prisoners with us. I want to speak with your master. I would be pleased if you could send him word of our arrival."

The Captain makes a sign with his head to a soldier, who rides without hesitation to Zurob's stronghold.

"Very well then," says the Captain, "allow me to escort you to my master's house because strange folk have been seen into these forest these last days. We have orders to check on all travelers."

"I well understand," says Maedyv, "the forest roads are unsafe, especially by night, and you cannot know who is crossing the borders."

As they walk, the road becomes larger and the woods become thinners. Soon they are on a field from which they can see Master Zurob's stronghold. A very old stronghold with thick stonewalls, beaten by wind and rain; moss growing among the stones. A heavy gate opens in front of them, and they all enter a court where Zurob was waiting for them. As he sees Maedyv, Zurob's face is enlightened with joy.

"Maedyv, my old friend, I didn't expect you. What winds have brought you here?"

"Unfortunately, not good winds. I'm afraid that dark times are coming our way."

"That's what I know to be true as well," says Zurob, "until they arrive, you are welcome in my humble house. I heard you were attacked on your way here. Leave the horses, come inside; you must be tired and hungry."

"We have two prisoners with us. We need to use your prison for some time, so I may question them."

"I see. Will you allow me to listen in on what they have to say?"

"Of course. You need to know what to expect at you borders."

Zurob gives the Captain orders. The Captain nods and is followed by four soldiers; taking the prisoners to the stronghold prisons. Maedyv and his guards follow Zurob, and enter the dining room. On the table await simple dishes of fresh food.

"So tell me, my old friend, why are you in such a hurry, and why are you attacked in the night?"

"It seems an old enemy of ours, Karken, the Dragon Sorcerer, wants to start a war against us."

"I only know about Karken from the books of my ancestors. My grandfather and my father have kept those books; they tried teaching me about Karken, but I didn't believe them. I believed he was defeated a long time ago."

"He was defeated, and never to be able to fight against us. We banished him to come on our land, but we cannot impeach him to take his tribute at the end of each century. He has taken children. He brings them to his realm so they will serve him until the next century. But he made them soldiers; he built an army of our children."

"I heard a child was saved from evil. Was this child saved from Karken?"

"Word is spreading fast! Indeed, we saved this child and found that Karken's powers had grown in strength all this time. The Master Wizard alone cannot stop his spells, so he needed Wirgos and I to help him, in order to save the child."

"That's frightening."

"Another concern is how the assassins knew about our position. No one knew we had left the realm, nor that we would pass through the secret shortcut. How did they know, and who sent them?"

"We shall soon know. Rest now, you will need to recover some strength after these trials. I'll go outside and tell my guards to look after your horses and prepare them for the road."

After some time, Zurob enters the dining room. Smiling, he says to Maedyv, "I packed food for your men; it is with the prepped horses."

"Thank you, my friend. We don't have time to waste. We will leave as soon as I have my answers from the prisoners."

"Very well then, follow me to the prisoners."

They exit the dining room with Zurob followed closely by Maedyv and his guards. As they enter the prison, the assassins look frightened.

-"Now you have to choose." says Maedyv. "The easy way, or my way. You will not like the last one. So what do you choose?"

They sit in utter silence.

"Who hired you, and how did you know where we were?" The prisoners only stare at the cold, bare ground.

"Now we will try my way. Guards! Take the one from my right and throw him from the high tower."

The guards approach. The prisoners beg for mercy.

"We were paid to watch over that cave; we do not know who you are." "Then why did you surround us?"

"He told us whoever comes from that cave should be killed." "Why that caves? Who is this HE?"

"We don't know. He came by night and his head was covered with the hood of his black cloak. He spoke in a wretched voice, that penetrated our souls."

"Do you remember the way he walked?"

"No."

"Did you see his hands? How they looked?"

"Yes! I saw one of his hands! He removed his glove, and I saw that his hand was black as night."

Maedyv and Zurob went outside. The guards closed the iron door of the prison. "Karken's spies," says Maedyv, "I wonder if all the secret passages are watched."

"This evil is advancing faster than I expected. I will double the men on watch, as well as those on the borders, but I cannot send my soldiers to the forest to protect the cave."

"And I cannot ask you to do this," says Maedyv, "there are not many who know the passage, and those who know don't get out alive. May I ask you for a service?"

"Anything, my friend."

"You have to send a message to Master Wizard. Tell him that all paths have been compromised, and the enemy expects us. Sign it with my name. Send it as fast as you can, please."

"I will send it with my falcon."

"Thank you, Zurob, for all your help and hospitality. The time is against us; we must leave."

"I well understand your hurry; your horses are read. My soldiers will escort you to the borders, so you will not be delayed. What shall I do with the prisoners?"

"Keep them in their cells for a few days, until I reach my fortress. After that, do whatever you like with them."

"Very well. Anyway, I will need others to fortify my walls, and these two look strong enough to do it."

They exchange friendly handshake, say their goodbyes, and exit the stronghold, headed East.

Wirgos's Promise

Three days passed since Maedyv left the White Fortress. It was now time for Wirgos to leave in search of their old allies, and restore alliances.

"Wirgos," says the Master Wizard, as he enters the dining room, "I just received a message from Maedyv,; he send it from Zurob's stronghold, it says all the secret passages are compromised. If you leave, you will have to take the longer path. Do not take an escort with you. Ride alone and ride fast. Avoid crowded places and hide your weapons."

"Aggghhhh! This is starting to upset me. Maybe I'll have to disguise myself as a woman then?"

"It may sound crazy but it's not a bad idea."

"All right then, I will have to change my clothes and find a way to hide my sword." "I suggest you take a dagger, but you know these things better then me."

"I will not take any of my own then; if Karken has sent his spies after us it is time to unearth the old ones. I wonder how many of these weapons are left among our allies?"

"Indeed, those are made with metaur, the only metal that can kill Karken's shadow soldiers. It is an atrocity we have to bring into light the old relics of dark times."

"It's sad, but necessary. If Maedyv is right, his spies are watching every road leading in or out of this land. The threat is even bigger if he hired assassins among common folk. We cannot know who is friend or foe," says Wirgos, with sadness in his voice.

"You have to avoid contact with anyone, and choose wisely where you will pass the night."

"Like in the old time. What fools we have been to think those days will never come again."

"We cannot change the past."

"Then let's prepare the future better," says Wirgos. "Indeed. Ride careful and always watch your back."

"I will. I hope our old allies from across the sea, the Getaes people, still have sword makers that know how to melt and craft weapons from metaur. We will need them now, more than ever before, because no one knows the science to make and forge that kind of alloy."

"I hope this time we will not be deceived," says the Master Wizard leaving the room.

All this time Elidoc listened from atop the stairs. As soon as Wirgos left the house, Elidoc ran to the window looking outside after him. Feeling better day-by-day, the Master Wizard's medicine fights what's left form Karken's poison. The mother's soul lightens up every day as she sees her son slowly returning to normal. He's still fighting with the food imposed by the Master Wizard, dreaming of his grandmother's roasted chicken.

Elidoc looks with sadness in his eyes from his room's window, remembering how he played with children his age until the sun would set. He felt not hunger, nor slumber when they all played outside. He remembers the summer days when they all went to the lake near the forest to run after wild ducks and geese, splashing in the lake water until they started to see the mist in front of their eyes. He remembers the times when their parents would come at dusk to send them home, and how his mother washed him hard to clean the mud from his ears. Those were better days.

"Time is passing so slowly here," he thinks.

"I wonder if in that village are children of my age? What are they doing now? I am sure that they are playing like I used to play in those summer days, but it is summer here all the time, so they play all day long without stopping. How lucky they are. I wonder if they know how to play with snow. I don't believe they know how snow looks like. Here the snow is only on the mountain peaks and they are too high to reach. I will ask mother if one day we can go in that village so I can play with those kids. I wonder if Master Wizard will let me?" he asked himself.

He looks down and sees Wirgos preparing his horse. He knew he must leave but doesn't want him to know he heard everything he talked with the Master Wizard.

"Where are you leaving to so early?" Elidoc shouts. Wirgos looks up and sees the boy's head at the window. "I have things to do, child."

"And when will you be back?"

"When I finish them."

"You told me you would teach me how to fight with a sword, and how to shoot a bow. If you leave, who will teach me?"

"Do not worry, I will be back. Until then, you get better and stronger. You need strength to lift the sword and to stretch the bow-string. Don't forget that first you have to learn how to read and write. Those things are more important than knowing to fight with swords and shooting bows and arrows. They are important, of course, but not yet child."

"But I want you to teach me how to fight and be a warrior. I want to help the Master Wizard kill that Dragon!"

"All things in their time, and as for killing Karken, I am afraid that is not a task for a child. Learning, Elidoc is like building a house, or a castle; just look at this fortress. It is so grand, and well built, but it all started with the first stone of its foundation. After they build the foundation, they started working on walls, followed by towers, and on and on. Your learning must be the same child."

Elidoc stares at Wirgos, contemplating. "Let me make a deal will you, child." "What deal?"

"Until I get back, you have to eat all the veggies and fish that I eat, and you will not complain."

"But I don't like them. They all taste the same, and then I have to take the Master Wizard's medicine."

"That one is the more important," admits Wirgos.

"But it stinks and taste horrible, and makes me vomit," complains Elidoc.

"Look, child, when I was your age, my mother forced me to eat the same; like your mother forces you. So when the time for supper was near, I hid in my father's castle, but as time passed, hunger hit me. I snuck into the kitchen, stole something to eat, and guess what? No matter how hard I tried to pass unnoticed, my mother always caught me and gave me the same food as you are eating now, but the food was already cold and the taste was gone but she stayed next to me until I finished everything."

"I bet you changed your plan after that, didn't you?"

"I did indeed change my plan, all the time, but my mother would always outsmart me. Year after year she fought with my stubbornness, and me until I realized I was much taller and stronger than all the other children my age. That's how I started to figure out in order to be strong like my father, the king; I have to eat like a king. "Now you are strong, like a bear," says my mother, "I wonder if you know why that is", she would ask me. "It is because you fought with a stubborn child who back then didn't know what was best for him," I answered. My father started teaching me how to fight with swords and spears in the daylight and when the night came he would teach me how to read and write, and not just any kind of writings. He taught me how to understand other languages, unspoken in our realm. One day I asked him why I have to know about all this. He told me, "My son, one day my kingdom will be yours. No one knows what the future can bring at your door, but as a king, you will need to protect your people first. When the dark days come, and they will, kings will have to unite in order to defeat their common enemy. Our realm is not the only one in this vast world. There are so many languages as realms. Kings and people will listen to your words differently when you speak to them in their own tongue. They will respect you and if they respect you they will follow you."

"Do you think Dolong will teach me how to speak other tongues?" asks Elidoc, becharmed.

"He would be more than pleased. He can teach you many things about this world, and the worlds you can't even imagine exist." "He can show me how big the world is?"

"He cannot show it to you; you have to discover it by yourself, and see it with your own eyes, but for that you need to learn how to read and write. Like knowing how to fight can save your life; knowing this can save your life too."

"I will let Larsa know not to give me all the salad. I will ask her to keep it for when you'll come back."

Wirgos spurs on his horse and rides away laughing.

"See you soon, Elidoc, and don't forget what I told you." as he shouted, waiving his hand.

"I will try!" bellowed Elidoc. "You have to succeed!"

Elidoc watched from upstairs, until Wirgos disappears from view.

Troko's Failure

"Where is the one I named to be your leader?" asks Troko, to the three assassins. "He was taken prisoner by those who attacked us," says one of them.

"What?!" shouts Troko, his eyes full of hatred. "Who attacked you, and how could you allow it? YOU were supposed to attack and kill every one who came out of that cave! Not the other way around!"

"We were not expecting to deal with armed and trained soldiers. In fact, we didn't expect for anyone to come from that damned cave at all."

"Who were they?"

"We do not know. There were five in all, and were lead by an old man who was not dressed like the other four, he had poor clothes and wore no armor."

"They were on horses," says another. "They seemed to be expecting an attack; they were waiting for us, hidden beneath the trees."

"How many prisoners did they take, and where were they heading?" asks Troko.

"They took two, and we do not know if they are still alive."

"And the others? Where are they?"

"They're all dead or devoured by bats."

All of them look at Troko with fear in their eyes; they cannot see his face under his cape. His voice sounded like it was coming from a tomb. Troko, one of the best lieutenants in Karken's arsenal, was sent to spy and hire assassins to attack anyone who used the secret passages. He knew only wizards could cross them, and it is these wizards he was most afraid. Troko, this servant of the Dark Evil, once a child without ever knowing parents dedicated himself, from the depths of his soul, to faithfully serve his master, must now explain his inexcusable failure.

"Very well then," says Troko "you have to follow me; my master wishes to speak with you. He will wait for you in his fortress; just fallow the path that leads you south of this land. Do not make him wait for you; my master doesn't like waiting for answers."

With that, Troko leaves the cavern, and disappears into the darkness like a shadow. The three were looking at one other, wondering what will happen to them. If they run, maybe they will be alive for a few more days until Troko will find them and kill them for betrayal. What choice do they have? Maybe it is better to meet the master, and pray he will understand. Their only hope is the master still needs them, and spares their lives. They exit the cave to find three horses waiting for them. They ride south. The sky becomes darker and darker as they approaches Karken's realm. Dark forests with trees in twisted shapes, and leafless branches with no sign of birds nor beasts surround them. The road leads them into a cavern the horses seem to know intuitively. They are taken deep into the dark underground. Suddenly, a black fortress appears before them. Thick walls surround the squared watchtowers. The black stones from which the fortress was built glisten like the surface of a smooth, still pond, and are heavily guarded byweaponless soldiers dressed in black. The presence of the assassins seemed to go unnoticed. As they entered the battlements of the fortress, the guards of the gates stop them. One of them realized that despite the deep darkness they could see well around them. They are so deep underground but have light. A light that seems to came from nowhere and everywhere at the same time. Dismounting their horses, another guard guides them with his hand; showing the entry of the fore-court. They pass beneath a curved arch where another guard led them in with a wave from his hand. No one spoke a single word; the silence was terrifying.

"My Master is waiting for you," says a familiar voice, from the top of the stairs. "Follow me!"

They entered in what looks to be the throne hall. Same strange light is surrounding them, coming from nowhere as they pass under the vault of arches springing forth from the columns. At the end of the hall they distinguish a throne set in the darkness, and the silhou-ette shadow of a stern and impassive was seated on it. No face can be seen, only a pair of glaring eyes without any shape; eyes that neither human nor beast could have. As they approach the gigantic shadow, black throne appears clearly. Beneath the throne was a crystal floor, and around the carved man, horrible creatures were swarming, mak-ing high pitched, squeaking noises. It was if the Master brought his own bestiary right there, in that hall, to protect his throne.

At the back of the throne were four human statues, as tall as the columns of the hall facing the entrance. These statues represented four old men. Men with beards, splayed like wings stirred by a strong wind. Each one of them held scrolls that unrolled to their feet. At each side of the throne was one small, stone chair, and on them were sited two silhouettes that looked like the ones they had met when they entered the fortress. None of them were moving.

At the first sign of the Master, the creatures left the Throne Hall, through a hole in the ceiling. Silence fell, and the one who brought them to this place, approaches him. The Master raises his gigantic hand. It seemed to be made out of black smoke. While no one is talking, they all seemed to understanding each other.

"Come close! Do not be afraid!" says the Master.

His voice sounded so deep and grave resonating on the walls.

The three approached the throne and could not see any shape that defined the one they all call Master.

"Do you know who am I?" He asks with his grave voice.

"No, my Lord, we were told to come here and speak with you," says an assassin.

"Then you already met my lieutenant, Troko."

"Yes, my Lord; he hired us to guard the cave."

"Which you have failed to do!"

"We did not know who could come out alive; we were unprepared."

"Who are you to judge? You've been paid to kill, and you failed!"

The Master's eyes start glowing like fire into the darkness of the room. The light that surrounded them disappeared.

"Do you know who they are?"

"No, my Lord. We told your lieutenant we could not see them well in the dark."

"And they took two of you prisoners, didn't they?"

"Yes, my Lord; we are the only ones to escape; the others are dead in that damned glade."

"Damned indeed; and one of those two just happened to be your leader, wasn't he?"

"Yes, my Lord; our leader was taken prisoner; they have taken him to the East, across the stone bridge that leads into the lands of Zurob, the lord of the fortress."

", And that idiot knows your plans and he knows what you look like!" shouts the Master at Troko.

"Why didn't you follow them?" asks the Master.

"We would have, but those lands are well guarded and those who attacked us are friends with Zurob." answers one of the assassins.

"Only few in this world know those secret passages, and even fewer can cross them without being killed. One of them must have been a wizard."

"We did not see any wizards. They all looked like soldiers."

"Except one!" says another, "He was not wearing any amour, and he seemed to be their leader."

"You fool! Do you think all wizards have long beards, long gray hair, and carry a stick?"

The master's shapes grew bigger and bigger, and on the walls black smoke in shape of wings started to take form, surrounding the columns of the hall.

"You failed me! You failed me and you don't even know whom you have failed! Let me introduce myself, I am Karken, the king of the southern lands! The king of the army of shadows, I am the only true and rightful king of this entire world! You fools!"

The three assassins gather closely together; almost taking one into another's arms, when Karken spreads his formless wings to encircle them.

"Now you cannot tell me what you saw, but do not fear, because what you have seen there in that damned glade is engraved deep in your soul, and this is what I am looking for. I will know because your soul cannot lie nor hide anything from me! But for that you must die!"

From the top of his throne with all his greatness, Karken descends like a thunderbolt made of shadow mixed with smoke and fire. He enters into the bodies of the three assassins like a vortex through heir mouths, ears, eyes and their noses. Their bodies start shaking like a great fever stroked them. Suddenly they levitate. The horrible creatures of the dragon sorcerer swarm them in endless circles, preparing for a gorgeous feast of the bodies of the three assassins. Those monstrous creatures took them to be consumed into the depths of Karken's fortress.

"That was Maedyv!" shouts Karken. "These fools let him escape!"

"I beg you pardon, Master," says Troko, "how would you like me to repay you for this great mistake?"

Slowly, Karken returns to his former shape; he sits on the throne, taking a book in his left hand, and reads from it.

"Master, I am waiting for your command."

"Wait!" shouts Karken as he continued to read from the book.

After a while he let the book on his knees and asks Troko, "What news do you have from the others?"

"No one had been seen crossing through the other secret passages," answers Troko.

"Of course not; they've been warned by Maedyv! That sneaky wizard has his own spies! He will not make the same mistake again!"

"What should I do then? Should I leave the passages unguarded?"

"You will need more than the help of the common folk! You will need to recruit among our own soldiers!"

"But we cannot move in the daylight, my Lord, and the people are afraid of us! The only ones who could serve us are the thieves and mercenaries."

"Well, then, you have to choose wisely among them who is worthy for this job! Pay them more if you have to!"

"Yes Master, I understand. I have to retire the others and go by myself. This way I will not attract too much attention."

"Do what you have to, I didn't name you Lieutenant for nothing."

Troko turned and left the throne hall. He is not pleased by his own incompetence and hates himself for his incompetence.

"Wait!" shouts Karken, "One more thing!" "Yes, Master?"

"Be aware of the wizard, Maedyv, he has his own spies, and beware of the falcons that fly in the sky of the northern lands. They are meant to see our kin and report to the Master Wizard."

"Then I will move only at night," says Troko.

"That will not help; they patrol those borders unflaggingly. Move always under the trees, in the shadow; even at night, and avoid the light of the moon."

"I will listen to your counsel and I will do as you command."

A doubt that his secret plan was unveiled has started to grow inside of him. Should he warn his Master? No, he will wait! For now what he has are only rumors and nothing more. The prisoners that Maedyv took didn't know enough to unveil his plans, he thought.

"General!" he shouts at one of the soldiers, seated at the right of the throne on the small stone chair.

"Yes, my Lord."

"What is your army condition?"

"They are training restlessly, and the new ones that you brought are helping build weapons."

"Very well then, I want you to build an army I can be proud of."

"Master, I just have one question." Says the general.

"What is that?"

"How will we cross the borders of their realms? They carry heavy spells and we cannot cross them."

"We have to make them get out of their realms and fight them where their spells cannot reach us. Leave this matter to me; you watch upon the soldiers, make them be ready as the time will soon come to see what they are made of."

"I will watch over them myself," says Karken's general, "to be assured they are ready when the time comes."

"I will count on that," says Karken, as he resumes reading dark spells from his book.

Knowledge is Power

You must look amongst your men and choose only those who are worthy to keep watch over all of our roads, says the Master Wizard to the Captain of the Guards. We cannot risk letting the enemy enter our lands unseen," says the Master Wizard.

"Yes, my Lord," says the captain, "I will put four of them on each road that enters our lands."

"They should not be dressed like soldiers; you have to conceal them, no sword or other weapons that could betray them."

"I understand. They will look like common folk, but they need to protect themselves."

"Use only two of them to watch the roads, and the other two; hide them somewhere in order to protect the others. Put two bowmen to watch their back. Do not forget, they have to use higher grounds in order to better control what is below them."

"Should we guard the villages, too?"

"I do not think they will pass through the villages; they will not risk being seen. Do not forget, Captain, Karken's spies cannot move by daylight, so tell to your men to not sleep at night and not to make any fire that could disclose them."

"What if Karken manages to hire common folk that can cross our borders and report back to him?"

"Indeed, for that, your men have to watch who is entering and who is getting out across our borders. We cannot know who is who anymore."

"I suggest my men have to stay low and observe from the distance every stranger that enters our lands."

"Good thinking Captain. We cannot ask every person that comes through here who they are. If we do that we will raise questions and the enemy will know we have increased our security. Karken will know we are up to something, and I do not want him to become suspicious. We cannot afford that, at least not for now, until we are ready to fight."

"Yes, my Lord. I will supervise that myself. It will be like nothing ever happened, and as if life here just follows its normal course."

"Remember, the enemy is always watching us." "And always listening."

"Indeed, do you have any news from Maedyv yet?" asks the Master Wizard.

"No, my Lord; that falcon from the Zurob's fortress was the only message from him. I hope he is already in his fortress."

"I hope so, as well Maybe we should use... what did Maedyv call them?...Oh, dead spies."

"Dead spies, my Lord?"

"Yes, dead spies. They are among common folk and their only mission is to transmit false information to the enemy's spies."

"It could be wise from our part, and I know just the right ones to do this game of deception."

"Well, then, you have to use them."

"I will and I must leave now if you allow me, my Lord."

"Yes; leave. You have so much preparing to do."

With a bow, the captain leaves the house of the Master Wizard. On the stairs, Elidoc is descending slowly, helped by his mother.

"There you are," says Master Wizard, "I was looking for you."

"You will give me another potion of your magic potions?" asks Elidoc sadly.

"Oh, no, my child, not this time. It is only two times a day, and you have already taken both; remember? Only if you feel ill, then maybe I will give you something to make you feel better."

"Master Wizard, can you put some honey in your potion? It tastes horrible."

"Forgive my son, my Lord. He is always complaining," says the mother.

"Elidoc would you please stop whining?" she begs.

"Why? I just asked if he could, mother."

"That's all right," says the Master Wizard, "he is just a little child, and children of his age have so many questions. I don't mind if you ask me questions, child. I will even encourage you to do so. By asking questions, you will get answers that will help you better understand the world around you."

"So I can ask you all kinds of questions if I want?"

"Indeed, and I hope I will have the right answer for you."

"I know you will."

"And how do you know that?"

"Because Wirgos told me you know everything," says Elidoc, with a proud tone in his voice.

The Master Wizard chuckles.

"Oh, my child, no one can really know everything. If I knew Karken would deceive us all, I would have prevented it, but I did not know."

"Yes, but Karken is an evil, and Dolong told me that no one can know from where the evil may come, and where he can thrive."

"You are a smart, little boy."

-"And what else has Wirgos told you?"

"I cannot tell you more because that's our secret, and I promised him to..." suddenly, Elidoc stops speaking; biting his tongue.

"What did you promise him?"

"Nothing. I promised him nothing."

"Alright then," says the Master wizard, laughing. 'If it is between you and Wirgos then, it's not my business."

"I just told him good bye when he left."

"Oh, you were awake then?"

"I found him sitting at the window, talking with someone, but I didn't know who it was," says the mother. "Where is Dolong?"

"He is in the dungeons, as he is every morning, still searching for those writings."

"Wirgos told me you can teach me how to draw all the languages," says Elidoc.

"Yes. I will if you would like. And it's called writing, Elidoc. Drawing is something totally different," says the Master Wizard.

"I think it will do him good," says the mother, "he's bored staying all day in the room."

"Did you take your magic potion this morning?"

"Yes I did, you promised me that it will make me strong and tall," answers Elidoc.

"Yes, indeed, but you have to eat the food that Larsa gives you as well."

"I will be a little hard for him," says the mother. "Eating was always a problem."

"Well, then, we have to find a solution for this problem," says the Master Wizard.

"Mother, did you asked him?" whispers Elidoc.

"Alright child. He wanted me to ask you, my Lord, if you will allow him one day to visit the village to see if he can meet children his age so he can play with them."

"And this is what are you keeping so secret?"

Elidoc focused his eyes to the ground not looking at the Master Wizard.

"Let me think about it. I will let you go with Larsa, but I have one condition." Elidoc smiles with joy

"What condition?"

"You have to behave and eat the vegetables, and also you have to study and learn how to read and write."

Elidoc turns his eyes to the walls, thinking.

"Why do all of you have the same condition?"

"It's not even a condition, Elidoc; that's what all good children do," says the mother.

"But it is so hard to behave, and ... I miss my grandma's chicken."

The master Wizard and his mother laugh.

"Very well then, as soon as you can walk without help, which should be soon; you and your mother will go into the village and stay there as long as you wish. One thing I will ask from you," says the Master Wizard to the mother.

"Yes my Lord."

"Under no circumstances you will tell them who you are and where you came from."

"What I should tell them if they ask? There is no way to avoid the question."

"Tell them you are the sister of Borysth, the Captain of the Guards, and Elidoc is his nephew. Yes... tell them that, and I am sure that they will ask no further questions."

"I will do as you say, my Lord, but may I ask you why so many secrets?"

"Assassins hired by Karken, attacked Maedyv on his way home. He send us a message to beware of any strangers that cross our borders."

"Is he all right?"

"Do not worry about Maedyv, actually he attacked them in the end, and took two of them prisoners. That's how he found out who hired them." "You say we cannot trust the people from the village?"

"I am not saying that; the people know each other and we can be sure that they will not betray us, but word travels fast and the enemy is always listening. I will put guards on each road to be sure who is coming and what matters bring them here."

"Do you think we will be safe?"

"Yes, we are safe. I am not worried about that. What I am worried for, is they will find out who the boy is, and I don't want to risk that."

"But why, what do they want from him?"

"I don't know for certain, could be revenge, could be even an excuse to start a war, but let's not speak about these things. You have not to worry, these walls are well protected and there will always be a guard with you. Remember, you are the sister of their Captain. They fear Borysth."

"Maybe it is not a good idea to leave these walls?"

"As long as you do as I say, there should be no troubles. Besides, you two need to get out and see other things except these cold walls and my guards. Elidoc, tell me, how are you feeling now?"

"I am fine, just bored because I have nothing to do in my room."

"What if we take a walk to my library, it's here in the house. I will show you some books that have drawings, and you may look through them."

They walk through the hall and the Master Wizard opens the library door. The library was gigantic, with countless books sitting on wooden shelves. Two floors of books with a wheeled ladder to reach the highest shelf of books, the shelves are arranged around the walls and some perched in the middle of the room. Large, stained glass windows brought a colorful light into the room, mystically transforming it into a glowing prism.

"Awww, so many books," says Elidoc. "Did you read them all?" "Yes, child, I read them all, and I wrote some of them too."

"And I have to read them all too?" asks Elidoc, daunted by the endless shelves. "No, Elidoc, it will take you more then a lifetime to read them all."

"Where are those with drawings?"

"They are here, somewhere. Let me see if I remember where I put them. Take a seat at that table, so you can look through them."

He took the wheeled ladder and start looking for the books.

"Oh, here! I found something you may like," he says as he descends the ladder. "What it is about?"

"It tells the story of this world. Let's put it on the table so we can enjoy its pages." "It looks so heavy. I never saw a book before. And it is so thick."

"Indeed, my child; all books are heavy and thick. Some of them are so thick that you may thing they are indestructible."

"The covers are thick too, and why they are covered with leather and what is that? Metal?"

"Yes, they have wooden covers and are covered with leather because we have to protect them. You see, my child, you think a book could last forever, because it is thick and has covers made of wood, leather, and some of them are even covered with metal, but you see, a book is very fragile. The time wears it, the rodents love to chew on them, and even our hands could harm them."

"Our hands? How?"

"See, when you don't wash your hands before touching a book all the things that your clumsy fingers touched are left on the pages and with time that destroys them. There are books in this room that we will touch only with cotton gloves. Those are very old books that have been here for hundreds and hundreds of years. So you see my child, we protect them not only against ourselves, but against nature too. If we did not do so the majority of these books would no longer exist."

"And what happens if a book cannot be saved?"

"That's a very good question. If a book is too old, or was used very hard, then we have to rewrite it. We copy all pages and make a new book."

"So that's why I have to learn how to write?" "No, my child, not only for this reason."

"But why, then, why do I need to write? Isn't it easier if I only learn to read?"

"You see all these books? If no one knew how to write they would never exist. Sometimes we cannot express our feelings, except only by writing them down. When we write, a part of our soul is bound to those letters. The page becomes a part of us. The books come to life. If no one knew how to write, then how would we learn about things that we don't know about, things we've never seen in our lives? How we learn about places and people that are long gone? Imagine what would happen if Maedyv didn't know how to write? Imagine if he could not write that message to warn us of the danger. By writing that message, he saved our lives and protected us from terrible things."

"Now I understand why Wirgos told me that one day this could save my life."

The master Wizard starts turning slowly the pages of the book. The child looks with interest at all those colored drawing represented beast and trees that he had never seen until this very moment.

"Are these animals real? I mean they really exist?"

"Yes, Elidoc; they exist, but not in this realm. They are from the land across the sea."

"Sea? What is a sea?"

"A sea is like a very big lake," and showed him a map with the Great Sea. "But here is small," he says.

"That's why we call it a drawing. Imagine a lake so big that it will take you weeks to reach its opposite shores."

"Weeks!?"

"Yes, child, weeks, and that's if the weather is good."

"You need a big boat to cross the sea?"

"Yes, a very big boat. You cannot go alone across the sea; there are great storms and waves bigger than the Great Hall."

"And on the shores are there beasts?"

"Yes, on those shores and inside the lands. It is almost the same as it is here. They have their realms, their Kings and Lords, and their evil too.

"And all that is in this book?"

"In this one and the other books," says the Master Wizard, turning slowly the page. "You have to know you will not find all your answers in these books, Elidoc." "But there are so many? Why can't I find my answers?"

"Sometimes you have to seek your answers from this world, and the books can only lead you there. You have to go there by yourself, you have to go in places no book can take you."

"Where?"

"Into the real world, but to do that you need knowledge. If you have knowledge no obstacle is invincible for you. Knowledge is the key, and the book is the map to help you find what you are looking for. The rest depends on the power of your soul."

"My Lord," says the captain of the escort, "this is as far as we are allowed to go. Across that stream are the borders of Lord Taiss. You will not have any trouble crossing them."

"Thank you, Captain," says Maedyv, "tell your Lord that I thank him, and we will meet again soon."

"I will tell him. Ride safe my Lord," says the captain, as he turns his horse and starts riding back to the fortress, followed by his soldiers. Maedyv followed him until they disappeared into the thick forest.

"Well, that's it, now we are again on our own," he says to his guards.

"Who is this, Taiss?" asks one of the soldiers. "Should we worry about him?"

"We don't have to worry about Taiss; he will guarantee safe passage for us, if we will meet him. But I don't think his lands are guarded like Zurob's. He is one of those that do not believe in war, unless the war is at his gates. I don't expect to meet any guards on our way home."

"Should we pass through the villages?"

"We have to avoid them," says Maedyv, "Karken may have put his spies in those villages too, and we can risk being seen."

"Hide your amour well and conceal your weapons. From now on, we have to look like common folk, even if we are taking the back roads. Our home is not far from here."

The guards wrapped all metallic parts of their armor in clothing, so no noise would be heard when they ride. They watered their horses, and one by one crossed the stream, following Maedyv.

After a while they found the road that lead to the fortress of
Taiss, and with a slow pace they rode until Maedyv turned left to a
new trail. The trail led them near the southern borders of Taiss's
land, and although that makes their trip a little longer, they cannot
risk being seen. No one should be trusted after what happened in the
glade of the damned forest. Soon the sun sets over the western lands,
and horses gave sign of tiredness.

'We have to give them a break," Maedyv says, "We have to stop
at the nearest stream and take care of them."

They water their horses, and a few hours later are on the road
again, riding through the darkness of the night. Maedyv and his
guards get out of the woods and take a steep mountain trail where
they are forced to dismount their horses and take the mountain on
foot. The trail is full of thin rocks with sharp edges that could damage the horse's hooves so they went slowly and always watched the
step of their horses took.

"If the secret passages were safe, now we would have been almost
home," says Maedyv. "Well, it looks like we have no choice but to
cross this mountain."

Soon after they left the trail, in front of them appeared a sea of
ice. Deep crevasses are all over the place. They are so deep no one
can see the bottom. The sunlight makes them glow dark blue and
make the snow shine like a mirror, blinding them and their horses.

"We have to protect our eyes, and the horse's too," says Maedyv,
as he ties their eyes with a cloth so they could not see. "Do not
worry, they will follow us."

"What about us," asks one of the soldiers? "We cannot see where
we are heading, and we risk falling into the deep of the glacier because we can't see where we step."

"We have to tightly close our eyes too, but we should make a
small cut, a small hole where our eyes are, so you can see through it."
says Maedyv. "If not, the glitter of the ice will blind us."

The soldiers follow what Maedyv had instructed, and now they
advance; crossing the glacier safely. All of them breathe very hard

because of the thin air of the mountain heights, but soon they reach the edge of the glacier and see their land far away in the distance.

"Finally, we are out of this struggle!" says Maedyv. "From now on, we are safe."

They descend the mountain and cannot feel fatigue anymore. Their home is a few hours away. The descent was smooth this time.

"There is our home," says Maedyv, when he saw his fortress. "I hope no one missed me," he said smiling.

His fortress was stuck on a mountainside with steep walls and a double gate. The first gate was build with two feet of thick oak beams, bolted to an iron frame. It closed behind them as they passed. The second one was built with iron bars and opened only when the first one was perfectly closed. The riders entered into the fortress court and soldiers on guards took their horses.

"Where is your captain?" asks Maedyv. "Send him to me!" he orders a soldier.

He took the stairs that led into his room to look into a pile of scrolls from one of the shelves.

"You send for me my lord?" the Captain asks.

"Oh, I didn't hear you come in," said Maedyv, "yes, please take a seat."

"Tell me what happened while I was gone."

"Nothing unusual, my Lord."

"What about our borders? Did you notice anything out of the ordinary?"

"I'm afraid we are on the brink of a war," says Maedyv. "Our old enemy has built an army under our noses and we have been so blind and we didn't see it."

"What enemy, my Lord? We have no enemies around here."

"Oh, we always have some kind of enemy," says Maedyv. "And the worst are those we cannot see; this one is Karken."

"Karken? He was supposed to be defeated." "Apparently that's not the case."

"His spies were waiting for us at the secret passage into the northern lands. We took two prisoners. We now know a spy of Karken's hired them to kill everyone who came thought that passage. I am sure they are watching the others too."

"Should we worry about the safety of our borders?"

"We have to, and we have to do everything secretly so no one will notice that we reinforced our guards. We need to know about everyone who crosses our borders."

"I will precede right away, my Lord."

"Wait! One more thing!" says Maedyv. "Do you know where Tykas, Kelrem and Nysgar are? When did you see them last?"

"They are in the village of Loend, my Lord, at least that is where I saw them last. Should I send word for them to come?"

"No, I will go myself, there's no need to hurry. You have more important matters to solve."

"As you wish.", says the Captain, as he leaves the room.

As soon as the captain closes the door behind him, Maedyv searches in the leather satchel he brought from the Master Wizard's realm.

"Ahh, here you are!" he exclaims, when he found the crystals he used to trap the poison from the Elidoc's body. I knew I would need it."

He puts on his old cloak and ran through the door, shouting to a guard.

"Where is my horse? I need it, quickly! Open the gates!" he shouted, and the heavy bar gate followed by the wooden gate opened; one after the other.

He rode through the forest so no one could see him. Even in his own lands he can trusts no one. He rides until he reaches the village of Loend and heads straight to the tavern where the three that he needed would be. As he enters, no one recognizes him. He crossed the tavern's main hall until he reached a table where three were drinking ale.

"Bring some ale to our friend," says one of them to the barkeeper. "And do not take your time."

"Thank you, Tykas," says Maedyv. "I really needed one."

"What brings you here," asks Kelrem, "I have a feeling it isn't good news." "He always needs us when things start going south," says Nysgar, smiling.

"Well, Nysgar, this time you are right. Things are really going south and south are where I want you three to go."

"Now I am really confused," says Tykas, "but I think that I've been drinking too much."

"A war is coming as we speak," says Maedyv, "and we have no time to waste."

"What?" Asked Kelrem, "What war are you talking about?"

"I am afraid that it is not," says Maedyv.

"All right then, say it!" Nysgar exclaims.

"I need you to go into the southern lands, near the fortress of Karken the dragon sorcerer."

"Tykas spit all his ale when he heard these words." "Karken? Do you want us to go into the Karken's fortress?"

"Near is sufficient. Into it would be better, but I cannot ask this of you, you could be killed as soon as you cross the dark gate."

"Dead indeed," says Tykas, "we cannot get even close to that domed entrance! Actually, they will smell us as soon as we enter the forest. No way can we make it to that point."

"You are right," says Nysgar. "No one has ever made it out alive from that fortress. You had sent many to watch over that place and we never saw or heard of them."

"I agree with you both," says Maedyv, smiling.

"Wait!", interrupts Kelrem, "I have a feeling he found a way to help us...didn't you?" he asks Maedyv.

"Indeed, this time you will succeed to enter that cavern and approach Karken's fortress."

"Sounds interesting, but how you will do that?"

"I will show you, but tell me, Tykas, have you seen any unknown faces in this tavern? I want to be sure we are not watched."

Tykas looks a closely at each face.

"It looks like we are among friends here, but tell me, why are you afraid of being watched?"

"On my way back we were almost attacked by Karken's spies. We managed to escape and take two prisoners."

"That's a hell of an escape," says Nysgar. "For sure they didn't expect you to come out from those woods."

"They had no idea what they were doing there, and what the purpose of that cave is."

"How did they attack you, yet you took two prisoners? Something escaped me." "They were not very skilled, as we heard them coming in the forest at night." "You slept in the forest?"

"Yes, we did; we hid under the trees so the blood sucking bats could not see us. We managed to enter into the Zurob's lands, and there I asked them questions. They were supposed to kill every thing that came from the cave. But they did not know who hired them. They described it to me; it was one of Karken's spies. He hired common folk, so we must be aware now."

"And we are staying here, drinking ale and rusting in this village. So when we can go?" Nysgar asked impatiently.

"I don't think you heard, but a while ago, a boy escaped from Karken's spell." "What? That is not possible." says Tykas.

"He escaped being taken by Karken because his mother brought him to Dolong. Dolong brought the child to the Master Wizard. The Master Wizard sends word for Wirgos and I to join him as soon as possible in his fortress, but we did not know why. When we got there he told us how Karken's strength had grown, and he needed help from all of us in order to save the child. We stopped the spell, and took the poison from his body. He is now safe. He's interested in we know of his plan.

Truth is, we don't know much."

"And that's why you want us there; to see what he's up to?" says Nysgar. "Precisely!"

"You said you have something that could take us into the cavern unseen? What is it?"

"When we saved the child, the only way to take the poison out of his body was to catch it in a crystal so it cannot be spread. I brought those crystals with me, and as long as you have them, Karken's soldiers cannot smell you. It will be like you are one of them."

"Seems crazy, but it may work."

"Well, we have only one way to find out," says Kelrem.

"And what exactly do we have to look for, once we get there?" asked Tykas.

"You should observe how many soldiers he has, and the way they train. You will know if they are ready for war or not."

"Now you know, in order for us to see what he has, we have to enter his fortress?" Nysgar says.

"Only if you can; do not risk your concealment."

"Hmmm, I don't think they train in plain sight; they should be deep under the fortress, or somewhere they can hide."

"There you go, he's awake now," says Nysgar, "his brain is working again." "So what, then?" Kelrem asks.

"No matter what happens, do not disclose who you are. If you think that it is impossible, stay away from the gates."

"All right then, we have the crystals, we have our target, now we need some of their clothes." suggests Nysgar.

"It's simple," says Tykas, "we kill three of them and it is done." "They cannot be killed so easily, I have never seen one of them dead."

"Yes, they can be killed, but not with ordinary weapons," says Maedyv. "You need weapons made of metaur."

"Made of what?" Tykas asks.

"Metaur. It is an alloy forged by our old allies from over the sea. It is made of gold and an unknown metal. That metal was brought in our world by the falling stars. It is a knowledge long forgotten by common folk."

"I understand. So, how can we get those weapons?"

"I have a few of them hidden in my fortress. You will have them tomorrow, before you leave. I will bring them to you, so no one will know that you are gone."

"Sounds good. Can't wait to see what those special weapons can do."

"One more thing," says Maedyv, "you have to go there on foot, disguised as poor peasants, so no one will give you any trouble. Do not enter the taverns, you don't know who is listening or watching."

"We understand. Do not worry. The only thing I am concerned about is if your poisoned crystal will work to conceal us."

"Alright then, I will meet you in the Forgotten Glade, first hour of the morning. Be careful, and check that no one follows you."

"We will be there," says Nysgar.

Maedyv rises from the table to leave the tavern in the same way he entered; unnoticed. He rides back to his fortress and enters in his house. "Now is time to dig out the weapons of old" he though. He pushed a bookshelf and underneath, a rectangular, white, marble stone.

"I though I'd never have to break this sealed stone, yet here I am. I wonder if there will ever be an end for all this?" he asks himself.

He hit it hard with a pickaxe, around the edges of the stone. Small chips of marble flew all over the library.

"It is much harder than I expected. I forgot how thick this stone is. It was not meant to be broken. These are the only weapons that could kill Karken's soldiers. After many strikes, the stone breaks in two, diagonally, falling into the hole beneath.

"Finally!" exclaims Maedyv, as he descends to his cache. The cache stretches under the entire library, filled with shelves made from intricately carved holes, deep within its walls. Each shelf overflowing with ancient relics and weaponry, He advances into the dark cache, holding a lit candle lantern in his left hand, searching each relic tediously. Deep in a corner, he finds them hidden in a wooden coffer, covered with a tattered linen cloth. Here they are; the weapons of old age were no longer hidden. He slowly opened the coffer and the rotten wood disintegrated. Many centuries have passed since he buried them. He takes apart what's left from the coffer, awaking centuries of war and sorrow. Under the pile of rotten wood, he unveils swords, daggers, battle axes, maces, and flails covered with cloths. From those, he chooses three daggers, and arrowheads made from the magical alloy. He looks at them with the feeble light coming from his candle lantern. They were in perfect condition.

"Well it is time to do what you were made for; fighting the Dark Evil, once again."

He puts them on the table and cleans the mess made by breaking the marble seal stone. No one should know about his cache, not even his closest guards. There's no one that Maedyv can trust in his own fortress. Not in these uncertain times. He can breathe easier now, he has the tools his spies need.

In the last light of the setting sun, he pulls a dagger from its scabbard, studying its magical blade. Veins of gold, woven into a dark, grey metal, intricately designed patterns made the double-edged blade seem majestically fabricated. His simple cross guard was made of silver steel; the handle from a stag bone. The pommel ended with a pointed spike meant to crush the skulls of an enemy. He sheaths the dagger and admires the arrowheads. Their three blades are right twisted, and made of the same alloy, tips made of hollow steel. The blades are toothed upward, toward the tip, making them easier to penetrate flesh, and mutilate bone. The twist of the blades, along with the fletching, forces the arrow to spin as it flies, making the shooting as precise at long distance, as short range. With a deep breath, Maedyv packs the weapons into his leather satchel, and hides them behind the books. He is finally prepared...for anything.

It was still night when Maedyv left the fortress. He rode across the forest until he reached the Forgotten Glade. Tykas, Kelrem and Nysgar were already awaiting him; hiding in trees so if they were followed, they would be unseen. Maedyv approaches.

"Did you bring everything?" asks Nysgar. "I have all you shall require."

"And the crystals?"

"Yes. You also have daggers and arrowheads. Use them wisely; only when you need them."

"Do not worry. We'll be back in a few months, to report directly to you." "If we are not dead," says Tkyas.

"Now leave. I will check to see if we have been followed. Do not forget, stay low and always watch your back."

Maedyv turns his horse and rides back to the fortress. The three spies disappear into the thick woods, heading South to Karken's realm.

Spies

"Elidoc! Where are you hiding?" shouts the mother.

"I am in the library!" he shouts back. "And I am not hiding."

The mother enters the library to find Elidoc sitting at a table with his face in a thick book.

"What is this, Elidoc?"

"Well, I cannot understand the language, but after looking at the drawings, I think it tells the story of those people who live across the sea. I wish one day to go there to see all those mountains and animals."

"What animals do they have there? We have the same here, don't we?"

"Oh, no, Mother! Look!" he says as he turns the pages and shows her the animal drawings. "See this one? This one lives only there, across the Great Sea, and this one too. The Master Wizard told me it's very dangerous to sail across the sea. Strong winds and huge waves, taller than the Great Hall will tear your boat to pieces. And you need a big boat."

"Are you not afraid to cross the sea?"

"Now I am, but Wirgos promised to teach me how to fight, Mother, and I will not be afraid anymore. Please do not tell him I am afraid. Let it be our secret."

"Wirgos promised you that? You are just a child." "We made a deal, Mother, but that is our secret."

"If it's your secret then I will not ask you about it anymore."

After a few moments of contemplation, Elidoc finally gave in, and said, "Fine I will tell you, but do not tell to anyone else!"

"My lips are sealed! But it's all right; if you think I should not know, then don't say it."

"We made a deal before he left. He promised if I will behave and eat the food Larsa prepares, then he will teach me how to fight with a sword, and shoot a bow. He told me that when he returns I will be strong enough to lift that sword."

"Then you have a good reason to do what he asked from you, and honor your word."

"And he told me to take the Master Wizard's medicine too; he said that this one is the most important."

"I am glad to see he likes you; I never thought a wizard like him would want to teach you how to fight."

"He promised me Mother."

"Then you need to leave that book and follow me into the dining room; it's time for lunch."

"Already? I thought it was still morning."

"No, Elidoc, morning was a while ago, and Larsa has already put your food on the table."

"Let me guess, fish again?"

"Let ME guess, you want to know how to fight?"

"I would have been better off if I wouldn't have told you what our deal was."

"And what if Wirgos will ask Larsa if you behaved and ate the food she prepared? Did you think about that?"

The two of them leave the library and head to the dining room. The Master Wizard was already there, waiting for them.

"So how is the book, Elidoc? Do you understand it" the Master Wizard asks. "I like the drawings, but can't understand what is written."

"Do not worry; with time you will learn that language too. When you read and write well in our language, we will take another step forward."

"You told me we will go into the village as soon as I can walk by myself." "Indeed, I said that and you will, I think tomorrow with Larsa, if she agrees."

"Of course, my Lord, I will take them with me; they need to get out and see other folk, not only the guards and the fortress walls," Larsa says.

"Alright then, tomorrow will be a great day for you child. I hope you enjoy it." "I can't wait to got there," he says, with his mouth full of greens.

"Do not forget what I told you; once you are in the village," says the Master Wizard to the mother, "it will save you and us from trouble."

"I will not forget, my Lord," says the mother, "I told Elidoc too, so he knows." "Very well then, lets enjoy our meal and thank Larsa and Kolnet for this lunch."

"I'm done!" says Elidoc, with his mouth full of food. "May I go back to my book?" he asks his mother.

"Well that was fast? Are you alright, Elidoc?" asks Larsa.

Elidoc nods his head, and leaves the dining room. His mother is thankful for the return of her son's health, and all they will experience tomorrow.

"I see that he's getting better and better," says the Master Wizard.

"Yes, my Lord, he is regaining his strength, and I am so happy he likes the books. He was in the library the whole morning."

"He learns fast, I must to admit. Tomorrow, I will send my guards to escort you. He's still weak and if he's not feeling well, they will bring him back, so you have not to worry about carrying him."

In the library, Elidoc is turning the pages, wondering about the drawings of the book, and thinking about the day of tomorrow; how the other children will accept him in their village. For them he is a stranger. He spends the rest of the day looking through the many books that the Master Wizard has in his library. So much of what is in them he can only dream of, and even more he cannot even comprehend.

"There are so many languages in this world" he thought. "I wonder if one day I will know them all. I have to, because Wirgos told me if I am able to cross the sea, I have to know what people are saying to me. The Master Wizard said I have time."

He puts the heavy book that he finished to his place on the shelf and leaves the library. He is tired, and his eyes are hurting. Elidoc climbs the stairs to his room, and falls asleep on the bed.

"Mother," says Elidoc "it's the morning; we have to wake up! If not, Larsa will leave without us."

"Oh, child, it is still night outside, go back to sleep. Larsa will not leave without us. Even for her it's too early, and the children from the village are sleeping too."

Elidoc pulls his blanket over his head, as he cannot fall back asleep. "Why does it take so long for it to be morning?" he thinks.

After a while Elidoc hears that someone is beating slowly at the door. "Mother! Wake up! I think its Larsa!"

"Oh, you just don't want sleep."

The mother gets out of the bed and opens the door. It was indeed Larsa.

"Breakfast is ready, my Lady; I want you to wake up Elidoc so he can enjoy the whole day in the village."

"I am already awake!" shouts Elidoc, from under his blanket. "I think he was awake the whole night," says the mother.

"Very well, then, we will leave when you are ready.," said Larsa as she left the room.

"You know what you have to do now, don't you?" asks the mother.

"Yes, I have to take that stinky magic potion, and then I have to eat breakfast." "There you go, so let's make it quick and leave to the village early."

Elidoc jumps from the bed and waits for his mother to give him the Master Wizard's medicine. He takes it without breathing and almost runs down the stairs to eat his breakfast.

"Where is the Master Wizard? Asks Elidoc, "is he coming with us?" "He is with the wizard, Dolong, in the dungeons," answers Larsa.

"They are still searching for those writings," says the mother. "I wonder if they will find something soon."

"I want to go in the dungeons too," says Elidoc.

"I don't think that's a good place for a child," says Larsa. "I was there yesterday to bring Dolong some food. He was there until night time."

"But it's like the library?" Elidoc asks. "They have books there, don't they?"

"It is not like the library, it is more like an old prison transformed into... how should I call it... storage. They keep all the archives the Master Wizard thinks don't belong in his library. It is a mess of old papers and books and it's dark and quiet. You need a lantern if you want to see."

"Dolong told me no one is allowed to go there except the wizards," says the mother.

"That's true. I cannot go deep into the tunnels; he was waiting for me at the entrance. But I spoke to the guards and they told me what it's like on the inside. Creepy places, those undergrounds are."

"Maybe one day they will let me," says Elidoc.

"Why you want to go there?" asks his mother. "You have all the books you need right here in the library."

"The Master Wizard told me I couldn't find all the answers I'm looking for here in these book and that's why I should never stop searching. He told me there are books that should never see the light of day, but I don't know why."

"Well, if the Mater Wizard told you that, then there is a reason," says the mother. "My lady, your carriage is waiting for you," says a soldier from their guard. "Oh, there we go," says Larsa. "Go ahead, I will follow."

Elidoc jumps from his chair, running to the front door. "Slowly, my son, you are not strong enough to run."

"No, I will not," he answers, jumping in back of the carriage.

"We have to wait for Larsa," says the mother. "She knows the village better than we do."

"I am right here," says Larsa. "I can see Elidoc lost his patience."

The four guards mount their horses, and ride to the fortress gate for the first time since they arrived. It seems so long ago, these past few months. Elidoc gazes in amazement at the Great Hall; an enormous matriarch, keeping watch over the entire fortress. The paved streets of the fortress make their ride shaky, but as they pass through the gates, the gravel smooth's into grass. They pass under the waterfalls, and are soon in the fields of the Master Wizard's realm. The convoy crosses the narrow packhorse bridge and soon Argam Village appears. Townsfolk work in the fields, while others fish in the river nearby.

"Mother, may I go fishing with the children of the village?"

"First, Elidoc, you have to meet them and make some friends, then we have to ask the Master Wizard if he allows it."

"Why every time I want to do something, we have to ask him for permission?"

"Because the Master Wizard knows better what is good for you, and if you can do it or not. You have to understand Elidoc, your body is still fighting what's left from that poison, and even if you don't notice, you are still weak."

"Fine. I will ask. Maybe, when Wirgos returns, I can ask him to take me fishing."

"You can ask him that too," says the mother, smiling, "but until then you have to behave, remember?"

"We are almost there," says Larsa.

They cross the bridge at the Northern entrance of the village and soon they are in the village market.

"You can go and play there," says Larsa.

Larsa and Maryia laugh at the sight of Elidoc so happy. Two guards dismount their horses to keep watch over Elidoc.

"He is well guarded; nothing can happen to him," assures Larsa. "We can go into the market; I need to buy our food." The other two guards follow closely.

The children nearby notice Elidoc, and invite him to play their game of rocks and crystals.

"Where do you live?" asks a child. "I have never seen you before." "I live in the fortress," he answers, "with my mother and my uncle." "Who is your uncle? A soldier?" asks another.

"Yes, his name is Borysth," says Elidoc.

"Borysth? The Captain of the Guards?" asks another, through wide-open eyes. "Yes, that's him," says Elidoc, proudly.

"Is your uncle here?"

"No, but I think he may come later. His soldiers are here, outside."

"Can we see their swords?"

"I don't know, but I could ask."

They watch in wonder, amazed and so proud to have such a friend. Elidoc takes a deep breath, approaching the soldiers.

"Excuse me," he asks one of the guards, "may I ask you something?" The soldier looked at him surprised.

"Yes, child, what is it?"

"I know I've made a mistake to show off in front of my new friends, and tell them that you are my friends," says Elidoc, stuttering "but...I told them that you can... maybe show them your sword?"

"Tell them to come here, child."

Elidoc ran to his new friends, to tell them what they all longed to hear. A guard draws his long sword, "You may touch the sword, but not on the edge. Without a word, the children touched the magical sword one at a time, and Elidoc instantly became their new leader.

Hours passed so fast Elidoc didn't realize it was almost evening.

"Just a little more time, Mother, please?" begs Elidoc. "I do not want to ever leave."

"We will be back again soon."

"When you will be back?" Asked one of the boys. "Soon!"

He took his mother's hand as they slowly started toward the carriage. Elidoc breathes slowly and shallow, something is taking the air out him.

"Are you alright, my son?" "I'm fine, Mother, just tired."

It is evening, and the village market is full of people. Some just returning from fields and gather together to eat, and enjoy each other's company. Suddenly, a young woman from the neighboring village approaches, bending her knees, and taking Elidoc's small hands into hers. The mother looks at her, wondering who she is, and what she wants.

"Do not be afraid, child," she says, closing her eyes. "You have to know you are a magical boy."

She let go of Elidoc's hands and slowly disappears in the crowd. "Are you alright, my Lady?" asks one of the guards.

"Yes, she just spoke to my son, but I don't know who she is."

"She is a girl from the Village of Strebo, just across the Emerald River,"says Larsa. "I know her. Her grandmother died when she was young, and her grandfather was the Captain of the Guards before Borysth. He is also dead, but how, I do not know. Do not be afraid. She means no harm."

"What did she say to you, Elidoc?" the mother asks.

"She said I don't have to be afraid; I am a magical boy. What does she mean by that?"

"I think she knows who you are, and you are the only child to survive Karken's wrath."

"Let's not say that name here, "says Larsa. "We do not know who is watching us."

Slowly they leave the village. Aside from Elidoc's new friends, who are still watching from their wooden castle, no one seems to notice their presence.

They enter the fortress with the sun setting behind them, throwing red and purple over the realm.

"Mother, I don't feel well."

"You have to get in bed as soon as you finish your dinner, and have taken the medicine."

"Alright. When I will stop taking it?"

"Do you feel you are taller and stronger than you were yesterday?" "No, actually I feel weaker, and now my head is hurting."

"Then you will stop taking it when the Master Wizard says to stop."

They enter the house and head to the dining room. Kolnet has already prepared dinner for them.

"There you are!" says the Master Wizard. "I was wondering when you would come back. How was your day, my child?"

"It was better than I imagined! Now I have new friends!"

"I can hear by the tone of your voice something is different."

"He is not feeling well," says the Mother.

"Come, child, let me take a look at you."

Elidoc approaches, taking a seat next to the Master Wizard. Taking the child hands into his, the Master Wizard looks at each carefully, then at his eyes.

"Just take your medicine, and go to sleep, my child. The medicine is most important now."

The mother and child leave to their room. The master Wizard knows Elidoc will need his blood cleansed. The poison of Karken was too strong, and too much time had passed on their journey. Unfortunately, there are sicknesses even the Master Wizard cannot heal.

After a while Maryia rejoins them for dinner. She looks troubled.

The Master Wizard does not delay in telling her, "Do you remember when I spoke to you about how his blood was affected by the poison, and we have to give him medicine in order to cleanse it?"

"Yes, my Lord, I remember."

"Well, it looks like the poison is still in his blood. I am afraid we have to find someone that can give us his own blood, to replace Elidoc's. "I can give him my own," says the mother.

"I am afraid that no one from this realm can have the blood he needs. We need someone who comes from the ancient race of giants."

"Race of giants?"

"They lived a very long time ago, even before the Light of the Alburn Star come to this world. They lived across the sea, deep into the mountains."

"They are monsters?"

"Oh, no! They look like us, but three times larger. I think they are the ancestors of all of us, men and wizards alike."

"Where are they now? We can get to them? You speak their tongue and maybe they will help?"

"It is not that simple," say the Master Wizard. "They are all gone."

"Gone? Where? You can find them, can't you?"

"They are all dead, none of them are still alive. Their descendants have mixed between them for the millennium, and their blood line had been lost."

"Then...my Elidoc..." the mother cries.

"There is one left, my Lord," says Dolong, entering the dining room. "My Lord, there was a royal bloodline the line of King Dorbald. For generations they have kept their bloodline as pure as they could. His great grandson is the only one who's left. His name is Armizeg, and he was one of the greatest warriors, not only of the realm, but of the all lands across the sea. The reason you have not known of him, is that he has been protected by generations of family. I cannot remember how long ago, I meet a wizard from across the sea. He came to our world to seek crystals in the Bald Mountains caves. He knew of me and our paths crossed before, I helped him find what he was looking for, and he told me the story of his lands and Armizeg.

"And how did he cross the sea?" asks the Master Wizard.

"He paid with gold," answers Dolong. "In those mountains they have so much, Kings can buy all the realms and armies he wishes."

"Not this realm," says the Master Wizard.

"Not all realms are ruled or protected by wise kings or wizards, my Lord," says Dolong.

"Yes, the kings are greedy," says the Master Wizard. "The realm from which the wizard come is different."

"Were they who discovered the metaur? They are the only ones who have the knowledge to make that alloy and forge weapons out of it. I remember their blazon too. It was a wolf head with its mouth open on top of a stick, and when the wind passed through its mouth he howled. We called them Getaes."

"Yes, my Lord!"

"So much time has passed since then. I am not sure if they remember our alliances or us. Too many generations have passed, but one thing is certain; if we will fight Karken again, we will need those weapons. Please continue your story and forgive me to interrupting you, Dolong."

"So he paid with so much gold they were waiting for him to come back. They told him of me and where to find the crystals he was searching for."

"How could he trust them? They are thieves and mercenaries of the sea."

"They are what their employer wants them to be. If you pay them enough, they are loyal as long as the contract is valid. Once they fulfill their contract, they will forget about you."

"What did I say, thieves and mercenaries," says the Master Wizard.

"The wizard told me the townsfolk from there are not cherishing the gold the way the others do. For them, the gold is the only metal to keep the evil away, and the only way to kill him. He told me that they have a fortress built in a mountain that is very hard to access, yet easy to defend. They have no enemies because no enemy dares fight them. They are taller and stronger, but they are not the giants their ancestors once were.

"Yes, I remember how they look. They fought with us and crossed the sea into their ships but I never saw their realm and the fortress that you tell me about."

"What the wizard told me after that was even more interesting. Actually, their fortress is built only to deceive their enemies, what is below that fortress is where their secrets lie."

"Have they built tunnels to escape?"

"Yes, and an entire city, underground. Even the castle of their king is there. Imagine, my Lord, the entire fortress and the villages of your realm, all underground."

"It would take centuries, and has to be built in secrecy."

"The giants built it in order to protect the generation to come from evil and enemies. The giants were those who discovered the gold in those mountains, and built all those tunnels underneath. They found a way to mix gold with the strongest metal in this world, brought to us by the falling stars. They created the metaur."

"I cannot even imagine how it looks. I desire to see that city."

"Maybe we will all have the chance to see that wonder," says Dolong.

"And what about your warrior," asked the master Wizard. "What is his name again?"

"Armizeg, my Lord. Armizeg is the only true descendant of the old race of giants. Armizeg had two children; twin boys. Karken took them both into his realm. Armizeg did not know who he was dealing with. His children were taken in the shadows, and soon after that his wife was gone, too, form the sorrow of losing her children. She died from heartache. Armizeg had lost everything and renounced the throne. The last one to see him was the wizard who told him the story about Karken and the old wars that his ancestors fought."

"And where is Armizeg now?"

"He lives like a hermit, hidden in the mountains, where no man dares to enter. It will be very hard to reach him."

"The fact that Karken took his children could help us in this matter," says the Master Wizard.

"I ask your permission to go there, when the time comes," says Dolong.

"I agree, you have to go there. Perhaps this time the wizard will help you to find what you are looking for."

The mother was listening to them, without saying a word. She was very confused about what Dolong was saying to the Master Wizard.

"This means that there is someone who can help my child?" she asks.

"If Dolong is right, then yes, there could be someone, but we don't know where he is, and if we can find him we don't know if he will come to us."

"When can we leave?" asks the mother. "We? You want to go and find Armizeg?"

"Yes, my Lord. I think that he will listen to me. He remembers how his wife was broken, after Karken took his children. I can convince him to save Elidoc."

The Master Wizard took a deep breath. Should he let this woman go to the untamed lands across the sea? She just discovered a whole new world after many years of not leaving her village. Maybe this adventure would be too much for her, and this world too big and ruthless. At the same time, she could be the only one to bring Armizeg.

"If you go, you both will need the skills and diplomacy of Maedyv to accompany you. He is the only one who speaks their language, and you also need an escort."

"My Lord," says Dolong, "I suggest traveling as few as we can, maybe four or five. If we must have an escort, people will start asking questions."

"You are right, so there are already three of you and you need two more. I will ask Borysth to give two of the best men he has."

"My Lord, do you know when Maedyv will return?" asks Dolong.

"Do not worry, there is hope."

New Friends
and a New Hope

"Maedyv and his spies are always hiding in the shadow behind the enemy. I wonder if they feel safe in their concealment," Wirgos was thinking, while he rode. "Now he tells me we must not cross the secret passages because the enemy is already there. And what if Maedyv is wrong? What if the enemy knows we know about the passages? Maybe now it's safe. No, I'm not crazy enough to take such a foolish risk," he thought.

Taking the long path, Wirgos had lengthened his ride by weeks. Without an escort, he had to be more aware of danger and avoid any contact with people. Even the horse he's riding is not his.

"What if Karken has no clue about the boy? Then how and why was Maedyv attacked?" he contemplates.

Five days he slept in the trees so no danger could take him by surprise. His horse is not of the finest, like the one he left in the fortress. The mission can be a success one only if he stays hidden. As he rides, he questions how many allies they still have. If Karken attacks now, there is no chance to win this war. In these times, they are weak and unprepared. If Karken knew, he would take advantage. He cannot let this happen. He must talk to their old allies and restore their alliances. The kings and lords of the old age are long gone and now the young ones are quite ignorant. How will the new kings answer to his call? Now he understood why the Master Wizard was not allowing for history to be forgotten in his realm. The new kings should know this so they will not make the same terrible mistake of their ancestors. Their own goal is to gather more riches and more land. Their struggle for more power is an endless battle. How can they forget what the true mission of their reign is? The mission to protect this world and the people against evil is most important. He hopes the legacy of the old kings passed among their heirs; that it was written for generations to come, so they will not forgot what their ancestors have fought and died for. He crossed the lands to the West, and entered into the kingdom of Partogos. He never talked to the new king but he was a close friend to his great grandfather. He doesn't know if the new king had even heard of Wirgos, the wizard who watches over the Western lands, or his kingdom. He got out of the forest road and the castle of the King, Partogos rose far in the horizon.

"No! This is not happening to me!" Wirgos shouts angrily.

The kingdom of Partogos was surrounded by an enormous meandering river flowing South, between a mountain range, and a forest. The river provides a natural defense from attackers that might come from all the corners of the world. Wirgos has never traveled this way, he always used the secret passage, and now he cannot pass inside the meander where the castle was, because it's the only bridge that crosses the muddy river is at least 200 leagues to the North. He looks hopelessly at the muddy river, and has no idea how he will cross, except to take the Northern road. Night approaches quickly, and he is forced to prepare camp for the night.

"I hope Maedyv was right; if not, I will never forgive him. Now, instead of sleeping on a real bed, and eating good food, I have to sleep in the forest. Another night in the trees."

The sun sets over the mountain, and clear skies allow the light of the stars to sparkle into the river's water. Slowly, Wirgos falls asleep on a thick oak branch, his arms dangling low.

It is now almost morning, and the first light of the sun lights the mountain ridges. "What was that noise?" he asks himself.

Slowly, he descends the tree he was sleeping in, and approaches the river's shore, hiding in a bush. In the darkness of the morning, he distinguishes a boat, close to the opposite shore. It's a rowboat. "Who could it be? No enemy would come with only one boat. Could be spies?"

He decides to wait until sunrise. The boat comes, his direction; now he can see clearly it is a fisherman. "Should I ask this man to help me cross? How can I be sure I can trust him?"

Doubtful thoughts crossed his mind. He didn't know what to do. Instinct told him he should take the long path, but his stomach said otherwise.

"Oh, why not! Only Maedyv trusts no one, and I'm not like him. He is the one who always has a bad feeling about everything and everyone. Anyway, this fisherman doesn't know who I am."

As he was fighting with his own thoughts the boat drifts away. He mounts his horse and rides to the boat.

"Hello there!"

The fisherman steers his boat to the shore. "What brings you here?" he asks. "Are you lost?"

"I am not lost, but I took the wrong path, and now I'm here, stuck on the wrong shore."

"Where are you headed?"

"To the castle, to see my brother. He's an officer in the King's Army, and our father has died, so I must bring him the news."

"I am sorry for your loss. How may I help you?"

"Can you offer me a passage to the other shore, asks Wirgos. The bridge is too far from here, and it will take me days to reach it."

"You are on the wrong side of the river, and I cannot tell if you can cross that bridge."

"Why is that?" asks Wirgos.

"The bridge was destroyed last year by floods"

"Do you think your boat can hold me, and my horse?"

"I don't think so, but if I take you first, and then your horse, we can manage." The fisherman approaches the boat to the shore, and Wirgos boards.

"I don't think my horse will listen to you, it will be better if you take him first."

The suborn horse would not board the boat. Wirgos is getting more and more annoyed by the stubbornness of his horse.

The fisherman started laughing as he saw this entire scene of Wirgos and his horse. Slowly the horse puts his heels unsurely into the boat.

"Very good! Now I hope we can push the boat back into the river."

After a few attempts Wirgos wanted to give up and take the long path.

"Let's try something else," says the fisherman.

He puts mud under the keel, and they managed to push it into the river. The fisherman jumps into the boat and starts rowing.

"See you soon!" shouts Wirgos.

"I will be back as soon as the horse is on the shore."

"What a day," says Wirgos, "and my journey is not over yet! I hope the king will listen to me."

After a while he sees the fisherman coming back for him with his keelboat. He jumps into it just before he hits the muddy shores. The fisherman rows back to the place where he left Wirgos's horse.

"Tell me, good man, how I can pay my debt to you?"

"You came, bringing sad news for your brother. There's nothing to pay for." "Tell me, if I may ask, how is this new king of yours?"

"New king? He's been our king for fifty-two years now."

"I didn't know that such a long time had passed since the old king died." The fisherman looked wonderingly at Wirgos.

"How old are you, may I ask?" "I am sixty-two."

"You look more around fifty," says the fisherman.

"That's because I eat only vegetables. So, tell me more about your king. How is his reign? Is he a good king, like his father? He gave us a life of plenty and happiness. Maybe you will have the chance to meet him when you are in the castle. He often disguises himself like a poor man and lives among common folk to see and hear the need of his people. After the spring flood, many of those who lived by the river, like me, lost their homes and their beasts. We had lost everything. The king gives us the means to rebuild our homes and gives us the beasts that belonged to the castle."

"Well, that's a good king; he cares more about his people than about his own wealth. That is rare to find these days."

"Indeed, our people are lucky."

As they talked, they reached the shore of the river, and Wirgos's horse was neighing when he saw his master.

"There you are, I bet you missed me, didn't you?" "You know the road from here?"

"I think so, the other one I knew, too, and as you saw, I didn't end up so well. It would be better if you could please tell me which way should I go, so I will not make the same mistake again."

"You take North, across the forest, and in a short time you will see a path; take a right until it joins the road. From there you take another right until you see a small village. You follow that road until you reach a crossroad. From there you take a left. That will get you out of the village. Keep left, and in no time you will see the castle."

"Thank you. You are a good man."

"Good luck. I am sorry for your loss. It could take you days to arrive, be patient."

They booth waived and said goodbye again. The fisherman continued to cast his nets, while Wirgos disappeared into the forest. He rode through the rugged forest tirelessly. The village the fisherman told him of was now in front of him, but Wirgos passed through without stopping. He followed the fisherman's directions after the crossroads, and he reached the road, which takes him to the castle. On top of a rugged hill, above the village, was the castle of the king. With its round, white towers and walls, the castle was lit like a beacon from the midday sun. An elongated building was in the center of the castle, furnished with numerous towers and turrets. From afar, he could distinguish the balconies and the sculptures embellishing the building. The entrance to the castle was through a gatehouse, flanked by two spiral stair towers, guiding him directly into the courtyard. A few soldiers in shining armor guarded him, on the walls he could see enormous war machines resembling crossbows, mounted on wooden tripods. Near the machines were stockpiles of arrows. By their sheer size; are meant to be shot from those machines. No one stopped him, nor asked him any questions. So many people were moving back and forth, through the gate. From the heights of the castle gate, he now could see the broken bridge the fisherman told him about. It looked like they were rebuilding it. Just next to it, a narrow boat bridge was thrown across the river to provide temporarily access to the castle. As he crossed the courtyard, he found himself in front of the elongated building, near the Throne Hall. On both sides of the entrance two pair of guards, Wirgos dismounts his horse, and approaches the entrance. The guards crossed their spears, blocking the wooden door. A gatekeeper appeared from inside the building.

"Who are you, and what are your affairs here?" he asks.

"I am Wirgos. I come from the Northern lands to speak with your king," he answers.

"In three days from now, you may return."

"I cannot wait three days. Please tell him that Derron sends me to check upon your king's legacy. And tell him as quick as you can"

The gatekeeper disappeared on a small door, hidden behind a statue. Wirgos waits impatiently.

"Should I tell him the truth? That I am the wizard of the Western lands? No, I cannot tell who I am, not to a gatekeeper."

"My king agreed to see you now."

They pass through the same door out of which the gatekeeper came, and after they cross a narrow hall, they were in the Throne Hall. This sumptuous hall with a massive chandelier hanging from the ceiling seems to occupy the whole building. Forest scenes with warriors fighting, were painted on the walls. They were framed with oak paneling, and decorated with carvings. On the floor lie a carpet made of red silk, with gold embroidered trimmings. The throne was covered with blue silk, and embroidered lions, swans, and lilies. In the far corner of the Throne Hall was a fountain. A silver lion surrounded by swans. The tall, stained glass was covered with curtains made of violet colored silk, magnificently embroidered in gold, with leaves, tendrils, and peacocks.

"Where is your king?" Wirgos asks the gatekeeper, looking at the empty throne. Wirgos was staring at the fountain, and did not hear the king approaching him.

"What troubles brought you here? I am sure Derron didn't send you all the way here, just to see how I am. Who are you?"

Taken by surprise, Wirgos struggles to find words.

"Dark times are coming our way, but I cannot speak here." "Follow me."

The king pushed open a marble door, and they entered into a short tunnel. At the end, they entered a small, dripstone cave. Large glass windows with uninterrupted view of the mountains were at the end of the cave.

"This is my refuge," says the king. "Now no one can hear, or interrupt us. You may speak freely."

"My King," says Wirgos, "I am the wizard of the Western lands." "And why didn't you tell who you are? Why such secrecy?"

"My presence here should not be noticed by any of your people. This secrecy will define the success of my mission. I came to you in these dark hours to seek an old alliance that your great-grandfather made with us. The times of old evil are back again, and with sadness, I have to tell you the world is on the brink of war."

"A war? Against whom? We have no enemies here?"

"Against Karken, my Lord, the dragon sorcerer."

"Karken? I know the stories of the old wars. My ancestors wrote them. They wrote Karken was defeated, and all his army was destroyed. Tell me what makes you say this, and what Derron has to say about it?"

"Karken was defeated, but not killed. The Master Wizard sends me to gather our old allies, to defeat Karken, once and for all."

"I remember the words from the book."

"Yes, my Lord. We need weapons made from metaur," as he draws his short sword. "This is one of the weapons of old, forged by Getaes people."

"All my life I never imagined that a time like this would ever come."

"My Lord, these weapons were forged by the people across the sea. Not many are left in these lands. Karken's spies bought them from those who fought the wars."

"How did you figure out the Karken is preparing a war?"

"A boy was saved from his spells not long ago. The Master Wizard, Maedyv, the wizard of the Eastern lands, and myself, fought to undo the spells, and take out the poison form the boy's body. Karken's strength has grown all these centuries. He has deceived us all. The boy saw in his dreams, what Karken is planning, he saw his army of shadows training for war."

"I never thought someone could escape Karken's wrath."

"Neither did we, that is why this should be kept in secrecy. If Karken finds out what we are up to, he will attack us now, when we are weak and unprepared. He has sent his spies, and is recruiting assassins among common folk. We should be very careful."

"And this boy, where is he now?"

"He is in the Master Wizard's fortress. He's well protected. The spells lying upon those borders are impeaching the enemy, crossing into the realm."

"A few of our village children have recently gone missing. No one knows what happened; they disappeared overnight. A lot of sorrow has been brought upon my people.

"I understand your pain, but if we cannot stop Karken, there will be no people and no kingdoms because he wants all the power. The whole world will be submerged into darkness."

"I know what we risk; I will start preparing my army, slowly, so no one will notice. I will send word to Derron when we are ready. One thing I ask..."

"Yes, my Lord."

"I wish to meet the child. Is there a way he can come here? I can send an escort for him."

"I am afraid that his health will not allow him to travel such a great distance, and the enemies are searching for him relentlessly."

"Then I will pay a visit to the Master Wizard. I must see this child. He can bring hope to my people. Will you stay here for a while and rest before you continue your mission?"

"I am afraid time is against us, and I've already wasted enough of it on the roads and hiding in the forests."

They headed to the exit of the cave, but this time the king pushed a glass door, and they were inside another tunnel.

"From here you have to go alone, I cannot risk being seen with you. This tunnel will lead you into the garden, behind the Throne Hall. Take a left, and you cannot miss the courtyard. Your horse will be waiting for you."

"Thank you, my Lord."

"No, thank you for bringing hope into my heart. That child should be protected whatever the cost. I hope I will meet you at Derron's. Good luck. I hope the other kings will answer to your call like their ancestors did."

"I hope that they are all wise like you," Wirgos was thinking, as he was walking through the tunnel.

When he mounted his horse it was almost evening. Now he had to cross the boat bridge and continue riding West until reaching his realm. He decides to take a detour to the South, to see how far Karken's power has advanced poisoning the minds of the rulers of those lands. A risky thing to do, but he had to know.

Allies and Alliances

After days of lying in the bed, weak and helpless, Elidoc felt well again. He had again immersed himself in the books of the Master Wizard's library. The food had no taste to him, so he had not to worry what he ate. Dreams about the far lands across the sea were growing in his mind, and all he read now was about the people that live on there. Some of the books describe them being wild and uncouth, barbarian-like; while others were described as being civilized and very good craftsmen. They were renowned beekeepers and had a taste for fine wine.

"I remember Wirgos and the Master Wizard talking abut that metal from which the magic swords are crafted, but I cannot find any words about it in the books," he thought. "They were once allies, and fought against Karken, so why do some of the writers see them as barbarians? I guess I will not find everything about them in these books. Like the Master Wizard said, I have to go by myself to find it." He closed the book and slowly fell asleep.

"Elidoc," said the mother, awaking him, "it is time for lunch."
"Again? But I am not hungry."

"Remember your bet with Wirgos; I don't think you want to lose it."

With little strength, Elidoc rises from the chair, and with a slow pace, follows his mother into to the dining room.

"How are you feeling, child?" asks the Master Wizard.

"I am fine," answered Elidoc "with no strength in his voice."

"Do not be sad, you'll be fine. I heard the children from the village are waiting for you to come back," says the Master Wizard.

"I want to go back, but last time I was there, I ran too much, and now I am sick again. I should listen to my mother."

"You have to understand that even if you feel well, your body is still weak. That's why we both need to work on how to make you strong again."

"My mother told me about that but I don't want to show my friends that I cannot do what they can."

"I know you and your mother miss your village, your home, and all your friends."

"How do you know that?" "I am wizard, remember?"

"Tell me, child, what have you found interesting in those books?"

"Well, the more I read, the more confused I get. The books are supposed to enlighten me, and help me know the world they describe, but I read one thing in a book, and in another one I find the opposite, so in the end I don't know what to believe. Which one is telling the truth?"

"My child, that's how the books are. You don't have to believe every word that is written in their pages. The more you will read, the more you will know how to find the truth. Remember, sometimes the truth needs to be protected and for that it has to be hidden in lies."

"So, I don't have to believe the words of the books anymore?"

"That is up to you. You have to choose what you believe in. This knowledge will help you."

"You should go outside and play in the garden if you want. The fresh air and the sun will help you feel better."

"I will take him," says the Mother, "he has to take a break from reading." "But mother, now I want to discover how the people across the sea really are."

"Maybe one day you will meet them, and see the truth for yourself, "says the Master Wizard. "We cannot know of what the future is made of."

After the lunch, the Master Wizard returned to the Great hall. Elidoc and his mother were taking a walk in the garden of the fortress. It was a cloudy sky and the sun was shining between their passages. The birds and plants of the garden are continuing their lives without the worry. Elidoc and his mother sat on a bench talking about old times, about their friends, and what they will do when they go back to their house. The mother cannot tell him yet that she will have to leave across the sea. She doesn't want to trouble her child. Elidoc lies on his mother's lap as she passed her fingers through his hair. The child was sleeping peacefully, while the sun played on his cheeks. Suddenly, she realizes that Elidoc's hair is falling out in clumps. Her fingers were filled with it. She looks scared at Elidoc, not knowing why. Slowly she tries to wake him up, without any success. Elidoc's body shivers, and a cold sweat drips from his forehead. She takes Elidoc into her arms, and at a fast pace, heads to the Great Hall for the Master Wizard. One of the guards at the entrance saw, and ran to help her.

"Please, my Lady, let me to help you carry the child."

With a trembling voice, the cries, "We were in the garden, when suddenly, he started shivering and had a cold sweat covering his face. I need the Master Wizard."

"He is in the healing room."

The three of them almost run the whole length of the Great Hall, entering the healing room.

"My Lord!" shouts the guard, as soon as he passed the door. "The child is ill!" The Master Wizard gets up and runs toward them.

"Quickly, put him on the table!" he said. "When did this happen?" he asks the mother.

"Not long ago. We were in the garden, and he fall asleep in the sun. Without any warning, he started shivering and I realized my hands were filled with hair falling from his head, My fingers were filled with his hair," she wept.

The Master Wizard put his hand on Elidoc's sweaty forehead, whispering indecipherable words. He turned to a table from the far corner of the room and prepares a potion. He mixes herbs in a small cauldron with bubbling water, dropping powders into the mixture. Now and then he reads from a book, always closing his eyes before turning the page.

"I had prepared something to bring his fever down," he says to Elidoc's mother. "We will see if it works."

"But why he is now so ill?" she asks. "Is it because he was tired from playing in the village? I told him he should not run because he's too weak. He didn't listen to me."

"No, it is not because of that. I told you before, his body is in a continuous fight wit the poison. No matter how long he will rest, he will be always be tired."

"And why is his hair falling out?"

"I was expecting that to happen. I didn't want you to know it because I was waiting for the right time to tell you. The medicine I made for him is producing this side effect. I know it is hard to believe, but this is normal."

"I wonder if after all this pain he has to endure, and this entire struggle, if he will be the same child he was before all this happened," says the mother crying. "I'm starting to lose hope he will get out of it."

"All I can tell you is your son will be like this for quite a while. One day he will be just fine, and the next day he will be ill again, like you see him right now."

"What can we do then? You told me he will be fine."

"You must understand; this takes time. He is the only one to ever escape Karken's witchcraft, and that's why we don't know yet what the consequences will be. What I do know; destroying little by little, what's left of the poison, and at the same time repair the damage it has done inside of him, is not easy. I do not know how his body will react to my medicine, so I give it to him little by little to see how he reacts."

"I understand, she said so he will lose all of his hair?

"It will grow again, when he is finished with the medicine. He will be as normal as you knew him before all this."

"Poor child. He will not want to play with his friends anymore, because they will laugh at him."

"Children don't understand what it is to suffer and to be ill."

"Your medicine is working in him quickly. He isn't sweating anymore. The fever is almost gone. Do you have any news from Maedyv? I think we have to find the warrior Dolong was talking about, and quickly."

"He should be here soon," says the Master Wizard. "You will have to leave as soon as he says. Are you sure you want go with them? I have to tell you; it will be very dangerous. Now with Karken's spies spread all over these lands, you must trust no one."

"What choices do I have, my Lord? Elidoc's life depends on it. I prefer to be useful there, than stay here and do nothing."

"What is this all about?" Maedyv asked, entering the Healing Room? "I was waiting for you in the house for a few hours. Larsa told me to find you here. What happened to the child?" he asked the Master Wizard, seeing Elidoc lying on the table.

"The poison weakened his body, and now the medicine makes his hair fall out," answered the Master Wizard.

"I am so sorry," says Maedyv, with sadness. "I know this would be a dreadful burden to carry, and for a mother, even heavier. Do not lose your hope, he will be fine in the end, we just need to let time and our knowledge do their work."

"Thank you for your kind words," the mother says. "I hope it will be as you say." "Tell me, why did you send for me?" Maedyv asks the Master Wizard.

"I need you to go across the sea, to those who forged the weapons made of metaur. You will have to convince them to forge them once again, and see if they are willing to fight beside us, against Karken's army. I know this is not an easy task, but we really need them. Without those weapons, we have no chance against Karken. You will also have to take Dolong and Maryia with you."

"What? That place is not for a woman!"

"She knows the dangers. You have to find Armizeg, and..."

The Master Wizard was interrupted by Maedyv's laughing. "Are you serious? Armizeg? Do you know who he is?" asks Maedyv.

"I know everything Dolong told me about him," says the Master Wizard. "Dolong told you?"

"I see his name is familiar to you. Do you know him?"

"I do know who he is. But I knew him well, when he was only a child. His father was a good friend of mine, and for some time we both shared information about enemies around their borders. And I knew his grandfather, too. His ancestors were our allies in the old wars. I hope they still know the secret of making that metaur and forge weapons out of it."

"So you will be among friends there," says the Master Wizard.

"They don't have any friends, at least not anymore," says Maedyv. "They have been forced to live underground. They get out only to watch over their crops and beasts. No one had told them they had to paid tribute to Karken with their own children."

"The old king knew this," says the Master Wizard. "How could they not know?"

"It seems the books written by those who fought in the old wars were lost. The legacy of their ancestors didn't withstand the wrath of time. Now the line of their kings, the true one, is broken. Armizeg, the last descendant of the giants has taken a hermit's path. He lost both, his children and his wife because of Karken, and for over a century now, he has been living in the forest. No one had seen him, and honestly, no one knows if he is even alive."

"He comes from the race of giants," says the Master Wizard. "He should live for hundreds of years."

"Yes, indeed; he should live for hundreds of years, IF he is not killed by a men or a beast."

"Tell me, Maedyv, why you are so afraid of him?"

"I am not afraid, I just don't know what you want from him?"

"Elidoc needs him; he needs his blood. This is crucial for the boy's survival. I have done everything I can, and now I need help. I need Armizeg."

"Now it's becoming more and more complicated. First we have to find him."

"Maedyv, I am afraid you have to convince him to come here," says the Master Wizard.

Maedyv looks at Elidoc, wondering how it could ever be possible to save this beautiful child's life.

"Alright," he answers after long contemplation, "if he will not kill us, we have a chance to speak with him, and we will beg him to come here for the boy. Let's pray Arming remains alive after all these years."

"This is why you have to take Maryia with you; I think he will listen to a mother who suffered as much as his own wife did."

"I see; and what about Dolong? How can he be useful to me?"

"Their wizard owes him, and he is the last one to see Armizeg. Find the wizard, and he will find Armizeg."

"How can I go there and protect them. I was attacked by Karken's assassins, and could easily have been one of his prisoners."

"I will give you two of my best warriors, and the finest weapons." "When shall we leave?"

"As you think you're ready."

"We will leave tomorrow morning," says Maedyv, through a deep breath, "but there are conditions."

"They will do as you say; do not worry. You know those lands better than anyone."

"Alright. My Lady," he says, looking to the mother, "you have to prepare yourself for a long ride, and weeks of sailing across the sea. Bring only what is absolutely necessary."

"I will, my Lord."

"Maryia, please know you will need to conceal yourself as a man, as women are not welcome in places we will pass. We will require the assistance of people who despise women, and would kill you if they knew your true identity. Lars will bring you proper clothing, but you will need to appear as a man at all times. Do not ever let anyone we pass know your identity, and do not speak unless you must."

"Yes, my Lord. I shall do just as you require."

"Master Wizard, we will need sufficient amounts of gold to pay our way." "I already have Larsa filling a satchel for your needs."

"Make five equal bags. Each one of us will have one. Now it is time for us to go, I need to rest in preparation for our trip. We leave in the morning before the sunrise."

"I will," says the Master Wizard, "now, you have to leave, my Lady. Elidoc is fine now."

"May I see him before I leave?" she asks.

"Of course, he will sleep in your room. I will bring him as soon as he awakens. The medicine makes him sleep for quite a long time."

Maedyv and Maryia left the Healing Room by the side door, while the Master Wizard prepares another dose of medicine before sending orders to the others, announcing their journey.

"Where is my mother?" Elidoc asks upon awakening.

"She is at the house," answers the Master Wizard. "She brought you here because you were not feeling well. Your body is still weak, my child, and as I told you, you will be in pain for several more days. Child, your mother leaves tomorrow, for a long journey. She has to go over the sea to bring you medicine. Do not worry about her; she will return soon."

"Can I go with her?"

"I am afraid you are too weak for such a long trip. She will go with Maedyv and Dolong."

"Can I go and play with my friends from the village?"

"You may go with Larsa when you feel stronger. Elidoc, you know there's still poison in your body, and because of this fight for healing, your body is weak, and the poison is causing enough damage, your hair is falling out. This is the time for you to be as strong as you possibly can; not just physically, but strong minded as well. Fight the poison's damage, fight to get well."

"I will be bold," Elidoc said with determination, and tear-filled eyes.

"Do not worry about your hair. It will grow again. This is just a stage of the entire process."

"Then how I am supposed to play with my friends?" he asks, crying, "They will all laugh at me."

"It will not last a long time, dear child. Tell them you are preparing to become a warrior, and for that you need to shave your head."

"The warriors do that?" Elidoc asked, encouraged.

"Yes they do! They shave their heads before every battle."

"There are fierce people living across the Great Sea, far in the North. Their lands are covered with ice and snow. All of them have their heads shaved."

"Do you think they will believe me?"

"Elidoc, they may shave their heads too," says the Master Wizard smiling. Elidoc smiled as he wiped his tears with his sleeve.

"May I see my mother? When does she leave?"

"Yes, we will go right away, so we can dine together. They are leaving in the morning."

In the realm, evening arrives peacefully. The fresh air from the mountains makes Elidoc shiver. A guard covers him with his cloak as they continue on their path. At the Master Wizard's house, the other two guards take Elidoc to the dining room, to dine with his mother.

"Elidoc, my son, how are you feeling? I heard your friend Wirgos will be back soon. How are you doing with your bet?" asks his mother.

"Really? I can't wait for him to return! I will ask Larsa to make him a big salad with plenty of fish!" he says, jokingly.

The mother turns to Larsa, "Thank you for the clothes for the voyage. I look like a soldier in them, but I should pass as a man."

"Exactly as you should look," says the Master Wizard.

"Maedyv said I should have a sword, but I need to learn how to use it."

"Maedyv will teach you on the road to the sea. I hope you will never have need to use it."

"The art of disguise is hiding in plain sight," says Maedyv, entering the dining room. "We have to avoid crowded places, and not attract attention."

"Where's Dolong?" asks Maedyv.

"He's in the library," answers Larsa. "Should I tell him to come for dinner?" "Only if he wishes," replies Maedyv.

"My Lady," says Maedyv, "let us enjoy the last real meal for the days that will come. A long and perilous road lies ahead of us," he says as he lifts his goblet of wine.

"The sea is not for everyone," says the Master Wizard to the mother. "I hope you will be fine on the ship."

"Remember, my Lady, once on that ship, you do not say a word."

"I will do as you say, my Lord. I have never traveled on a ship before, not even on a boat."

"It's alright. For now, let us enjoy one another."

Elidoc slept that night, cradled in his mother's arms. Maedyv quietly enters the room.

"My Lady," he whispers, "it is time."

She looks at Elidoc, and slowly, without a sound, she descends from the bed. She exchanges her clothes with those given to her by Larsa, placing her bag over her shoulder. She approaches the dreaming child with tears in her eyes, softly placing her lips upon his forehead, with a lifetime of affection in one kiss. In front of the house, Dolong and Maedyv await her, speaking with the Master Wizard. It was still night, but morning soon approaches.

"This is your horse, my Lady. I choose it for you. I know this horse well, and he will not give you any trouble; he will protect you with his own life," says the Master Wizard.

"Would you please tell Larsa to keep an eye on Elidoc?" she asks, trying not to cry.

"We will take the greatest of care of this boy, my Lady. Do not worry. Think about your journey and what you will tell Armizeg to convince him to save Elidoc."

"It is time to leave," says Maedyv. "The sun will soon rise and we have to pass through the village prior."

With a short pull on his horse's bridle, Maedyv rides ahead, followed closely by Maryia and Dolong. They keep a slow pace, not disturbing the silence lying upon the city fortress. The soldiers of the night watch open the gates, and bow their heads in honor.

As the riders turn the corner, they see two silhouettes mounted on horses. "Good morning, my Lord. My name is Cythun, and he is Dytes."

"And now we are five," says Maedyv. "We must hurry, the sun will soon rise."

Maedyv and his party leave the mountain of the fortress, and head into the village. They cross, riding swiftly, and are quickly on the forest road, leading to the borders. Behind them, the sun is rising over the realm, once again bringing life to the land. Maedyv makes a sharp turn out of the road, and they are instantly in the glade.

"Before we continue, starting now, no longer address me as "my Lord". We will call each other by our given names. Dytes and Cythun, you have to escort and protect us until we reach the sea, then beyond, until we reach our destination. Tell me Dytes, what is your best skill?"

"I am the best bowman of these lands," answers Dytes.

"In that case, you will need to change your arrow tips with these", says Maedyv, throwing him a pouch of metaur tips. Dytes looks at them closely.

"I am speechless. I never imagined seeing one of these in my life, let alone shooting them."

"You must use them wisely, this is all that I have," says Maedyv.

"I do not know what to think about this falcon above, but since we left the fortress, that falcon is always upon us, and it is not the Master Wizard's."

"He is mine," says Cythun, "he will watch our road for us."

"You are also a falconer?" asks Maedyv.

"I know how to read tracks of man and beasts as well." "Do you know how to fight with a sword?"

"I know how to fight with any weapon."

"I see," says Maedyv. "I am thankful Borysth send you two with us."

"Maryia," says Maedyv "from now on, your name will be Nather, and you will answer only to this name alone. Next time we stop, Cythun will teach you to fight with a sword. We must speak as soldiers. From now on, we are on the mission to find the captain of the pirates, Vingoth, he is recruiting for his ships."

"Maedyv, one more thing," says Cythun, "under any circumstances do not call them pirates. We should call them privateers."

"How do you know about that?" asks Maedyv.

"I was not born on these lands; my family was killed by them, and they brought me here. I managed to escape, and Borysth took me under his wing to the Master Wizard's fortress."

"So you are born on the lands across the sea," says Maedyv. "Good, then you are going home."

"I have no home. I was only five, and as much as I've tried, I can't remember it." "So you know Vingoth?"

"When I see the one that slaughtered my family, I will remember. If you will allow, I will take my revenge."

"Is there anything else we should know before we continue our journey?"

Not one more word was spoken until the sun set that evening.

The Five Riders

"In a few hours we should be at the borders of the damned forest," says Tykas. "I know," says Kelrem, "I hope Maedyv's trick will work."

"Odd we have met no one on our way," says Nysgar. "I wonder if is it because we carry these poisoned stones, or perhaps because we are close to Karken's realm?"

"Those are crystals," says Tykas, "not stones. Let's cover our heads and continue on our way. We have to see what Karken's up to, and we must do it fast."

"How will we know where to go?" Tykas asks.

"We follow the smell of death and pestilence. We cannot miss the cave. From now on, we must keep out mouths shout. No more words."

The forest changes rapidly in front of their eyes; the trees become leafless, and no song of bird can be heard from within. In front of them, on each side of the road, marking the borders of Karken's realm, two pillars carved in black stone arose from the ground, surrounded by a thick blanket of dust. They walk, one behind the other, with Tykas leading their way into the unknown. Behind them, Kelrem notices their steps leave no mark on the dusty, ashen road. He also notices an uncomfortable and strange stillness in the mysterious woods. It feels they are being watched. Suddenly Tykas signals, they are being watched by Karken's guards, and there are many of them. Without raising their heads, they continued to walk toward the entrance of the cave. They pass unnoticed and reach the entrance. No guards in sight.

"If we go further, we must change our clothes," whispers Kelrem, "let's hide inside and wait until some of them pass. We have to kill them fast and without sound, if necessary."

They enter into the cave. The smell of rotting flesh brings waves of nausea over each of them.

"We will get use to it," says Kelrem, "but now we have to find a place where we cannot be seen. We have to let our eyes get used to the darkness. It will take a little while."

Carefully they follow Kelrem until they find a small pit, carved by water flowing from the cave ceiling. With their heads still covered by capes, they draw the daggers from the scabbards, covering the metaur blade with the mud from the bottom of the pit, preventing them from sparkling in the dark. With their knees bent, they patiently await their victims. Outside, the night is falling. On the path that descends into the cave's darkness, they see movement. Karken's soldiers are taking their shifts for the night watch. They are moving in groups of two, with a significant distance between them.

"If they are moving the same on the way back, we should not have any problem killing them," says Tykas. "The only problem is hey are moving by two and we are three."

"I think it's better only the two of us go into the fortress, says Kelrem. "Then, if something happens to us, the one who is left outside will warn Maedyv."

"I do not want to be the one who will tell him we have failed," says Tykas. "We shall not fail."

"Here! Take these arrowheads. Out of the three of us, you're the best one with a bow."

"But I don't have a bow," says Tykas.

"Then it's time to build one, and arrows." says Kelrem. "Wait! Look! The guards have bows!" says Nysgar.

The soldiers that had been on watch are now entering into the cave, heading toward their fortress. None of them smell the three spies hidden in the pit, at least not yet.

"How many were there?" asks Kelrem.

"Fourteen," says Nysgar. "Eight of them have already passed us."

"Be ready, and do not make noise. When you hit them, hit them in the heart, and close their mouth with your hand. It is the only way to kill them. Do not take your daggers out until they are dead. Let the metaur does its work." "The last two should come at any moment now."

"I hope they have good bows," says Tykas, squeezing his dagger's handle in his hands.

"Now, be ready. Let them pass us."

As being thrown by some unnatural force, the three spies jump at the same time on the back of the two guards. With a fast move, their daggers pierce deeply into their bodies. They cross their legs around them so they cannot move; the guard's bodies spasm as their brains are deprived of oxygen. Tykas and Kelrem pull them out of the sight. Nysgar diligently keeps watch.

"What is happening to them?" asks Tykas, seeing grey smoke rising from the dagger wounds.

"They are dying," answers Kelrem. "Their soul are at free at last."

The bodies blacken, and in short time look like they have been taken out of a fire. "What sorcery is this?" asks Tykas, scared. "I have never seen anything like this."

"And you never will again," says Nysgar. "This is Karken's witchcraft, and why Maedyv and the other wizards want to put an end to it. If we fail, and Karken attacks them, all living will be like these two poor souls."

"Now they are dead," he says, putting his foot on one of the dead's chests. Under the weight of his foot, the body shatters into ash.

"At least we don't have to hide their bodies."

"Hurry!" says Kelrem. "Nysgar, lets put on their clothes; we are already late."

The two got rid of their own clothes and put on those of the Karken's guards. With a fast pace, they rejoin the others, keeping a safe distance between them.

From the distance, hidden in the darkness, Tykas, armed with a bow, follows. As they approach the fortress, the surroundings are lit by a green light coming form nowhere and everywhere at the same time.

"So not everything was in the dark after all" says Nysgar to himself.

Hidden in the dark, Tykas watches Kelrem and Nysgar enter through the gates of Karken's fortress.

"I hope you will not be discovered" he says. "The future of the world depends on you two."

"Those who have finished their watch!" shouted an officer. "Join the other for training! Leave your weapons aside and follow me!"

"What now?" asks Nysgar.

"We will follow them." whispers Kelrem. "Just keep your head down, and move like they do."

The soldiers descend down the road that leads beneath the fortress foundations. They enter a tunnel lit with the same strange light that surrounds this entire place. A gigantic hall opens before them, with spiral stairs descending even deeper underground. From far, they can hear noises made by blades, muffled by indistinct murmuring. In front of their eyes, Karken's soldiers trained.

"Follow me, quickly!" whispers Kelrem.

They hid inside a crevice in the wall of the enormous hall, watching intently.

"Look! They use swords! Real swords, and they are hurting each other," whispered Nysgar, amazed. "Look! Did you see that one near the left corner? The sword just passes through him, and he's unharmed! Regular weapons have no effect on them."

"I saw that! Maedyv was right; if we want to defeat them, we will need weapons made of metaur." says Kolnet.

"This is an army poised for battle," says Nysgar, "and I don't know what you think, but they look like they are ready for war."

"Indeed they are," says Kolnet, "we have to warn Maedyv."

"How many do you think there are?" Nysgar whispered. "I think it's over forty thousand of them alone, in this one hall."

"And we do not know how many are in the fortress," says Kolnet. "We have to find a way to get out of here. Maedyv have has be warned before it is too late."

"We cannot go out now, they could see us. We must wait until they finish, and then they will have to come out. That's when we go out, too."

"Now I understand why we didn't see many soldiers on the surface; they are all here, underground."

"This rock has a strange feel," says Nysgar, touching the cave's wall.

"It is salt. We are in the bowels of a mountain of salt," says Kolnet tasting the rock. "That is why the air is so hard to breathe, and how they could build such a gigantic hall with walls so smooth."

"How do they fight here, without eating or drinking? Since we have been here, they all fought without resting."

"They are the undead, and the undead need nothing that living beings require to survive."

"Look! I think they are coming out!"

One by one, and without any noise or orders, the soldiers climb the spiral stairs to the surface.

"We wait for the last to pass, and then we join them. We move in the same fashion as we did when we came. Remember, no words."

Nysgar points his finger at their feet, and then at his ear. The soldiers made no sound as they walk. Kolnet nodded, signaling he understood what Nysgar wanted desperately to say. Finally, the last one passes in front of them, and they join them on their way to surface. In the forecourt they start splitting formation in a chaotic manner, continuing their specific tasks. Under his cloak, Kolnet watched the soldier's signs, and the way they communicated with one another.

In that chaotic movement, Nysgar seizes the opportunity to get out of the fortress. Head down, Kolnet signals the guards, raising his left hand, pointing only his thumb and index finger. As a discrete sign of the gatekeeper, the heavy iron bar gate rises, and they pass through unstopped. Moving slowly, as Karken's soldiers move, they take the road that exits out of the cave. Watching from his den, Tykas sees them.

"Something is wrong with their pace," he thinks. "Those two have to be Nysgar and Kolnet!"

"Tell me, what did you see there?" he asks impatiently.

"Well how can I put this into words?" says Kolnet. "If Maedyv is right, Karken's army appears ready to march for war."

"What army? I barely saw but a few guards on the walls."

"They are all training deep underground, so no one can see them."

"You didn't see all those thousand of soldiers in the courtyard, just before we came out?"

"Thousands of soldiers? No, I saw only a few, and you two, when you passed thought the gate!"

"I can't understand all this," says Nysgar. "They were all right there, it's impossible not to see them."

"Could it be that Karken's spells protect his fortress from outside eyes? I think we have to leave this damned cave before the sun rises, and they figure out that two of them are missing."

"I don't think they will figure that out anytime soon; there are too many to keep track of in such a short time."

"Even better then; this allows us to get out of this dying realm."

The three of them exit the cavern, taking the road to the borders of Karken's realm. Suddenly, Tykas realizes they are not dressed the same. He makes a sign to Kolnet to make him aware of the situation.

"Let's try a new trick," whispers Kolnet. "You have to walk between us, like we are escorting you out. Take off your cape, and walk like a man does."

"Why do you think it will work?" Tykas asks in fear.

"It will. Karken has been hiring spies and assassins among common folk, and it's not unusual they have to be escorted out of the borders. This would avoid any of them having an interest sneaking around, and maybe seeing thing that should not be seen." adds Kolnet.

"Just shut up and listen for once!" Nysgar angrily said through gritting teeth. "Do it quickly!"

"Leave your bow with Nysgar; no one from the outside of this realm is allowed to carry weapons."

"And how do you know that?" Tykas asks.

"When we came out from the underground, I saw two men that looked like thieves entering the Throne Hall. None of them were carrying weapons."

"How do you know that it was Throne hall?"

"There were too many guards at the entrance, and hidden among those columns, the sun was rising behind them, and they saw the two pillars that marked the borders of the realm."

"I know what you are thinking," whispers Kolnet. "Do not speed your pace, and Nysgar, don't look around; we are under watch."

Slowly they passed through the pillars still keeping their pace for more than a league. Kelrem looks around assuring they have not been followed, and then jumps into the road of the forest, followed by Tykas and Nysgar. They bury the clothes they took from Karken's soldiers and head straight through the forest until they reach another forest road.

"We have to use shortcuts this time," says Kolnet. "Maedyv should be warned as soon as possible."

"If we had horses this would be much easier," says Tykas.

"Indeed, but we must make it with what we have. I hope Maedyv is waiting for us."

The three spies didn't know Maedyv has left his realm, already headed to the seashores. The time for the three to serve under another master has come. Their next question remains; should they trust him?

INTO THE REALM
OF SHADOWS

"**I**t's time to wake up," Maedyv said to his riders. "It's almost morning, and there's no time to waste. We will rest once we are on the ship, headed East."

The riders arise slowly; the morning laziness still upon their faces. The mother didn't sleep most of the night;, the noises of the forest reminded her of the journey she took with Elidoc and Dolong and how they had passed into the mountain cave. Such a long time had passed since then, but for her, every small thing she encounters brings back haunting memories.

"Let's have a hearty breakfast, and if the horses are not tired, we will skip lunch," says Maedyv. "Eat well, and water the horses before we go. Maryia, I told you on our next stop, Cythun would teach you how to fight with a sword, but I saw you were tired after riding the whole day. Do not worry you have time to learn. Many breaks are ahead of us, and we have to be well rested in order to keep up with our schedule. If we are one day late, the ship will leave the shore without us, and we have no other means to cross that sea."

"I thought we would meet them in the harbor," says Cythun.

"That was the plan initially, but we cannot allow ourselves to be seen. They will wait for us hidden in a cove. This is our agreement."

"How did you make the deal?" asks Dolong.

"Zurob made the deal for me. I sent word for him before we left the fortress. He knows Vingoth, and I trust him."

"What if Vingoth will not trust him? Did you tell him how much he should pay Vingoth?"

"We will pay him when we are aboard his ship. This way he'll wait for us. A pirate remains a pirate."

"Privateers," says Cythun, "if you will call them pirates we will be all in trouble."

"Indeed, I already forgot about it. We will call them as Cythun says. He spend quite some time among them, so he knows better."

"Tell me Cythun, what does your falcon see?"

Cythun whistles with a tone only known his falcon. His falcon descends from the sky, landing on his forearm. He whispers in the bird's ear as if he was a human being, stroking the shiny feathers.

"The road is clear," says Cythun, "at least for the next ten leagues."

"Alright then, let's not waste time. If we encounter any surprises, we will take a break in the Forest of Valades," says Maedyv. "Those woods are so dark, even our enemy does not dare enter."

"And what about us?" asks Dytes. "How can we know if it's safe?"

"You have two wizards here," says Dolong. "I know those woods well, and they are protected with spells against our enemies."

"I hope those spells still work, those spells were made in the age of the old wars against the Dark Evil. Now times have changed, and we cannot trust that our old tricks still work."

"There's only one way to find out," says Dolong.

"Indeed, follow me. I know a short path to Valades," says Maedyv.

They gallop East, into the woods. They ride without the comfort of a path or trail, guided by Maedyv. From time to time, he turns his head to see if they are all still following him, and that none of them gets lost in the thick woods. A deer jumps from out of nowhere, frightening them when they pass near their sleeping spots. Maedyv leads them until they all reach a narrow forest road. A cedar forest lies ahead of them, and the road covered with a treed canopy forms a green tunnel around them. They slow their pace, when Maedyv makes a sign to Cythun to approach.

"Your falcon is still there?"

"He never left us," answers Cythun. "I can see there hasn't been anyone before us on this path. The ground is undisturbed, and I see no trace of man."

"The soldiers of Karken are not men," says Maedyv. "They are undead, and they leave no traces behind them when they move."

"I don't know what they look like, but no matter what; undead or human beings, they will always leave a trace."

"I hope you are right, and we will not have any surprises on the road," says Maedyv.

Cythun nodded, and took the lead, riding ahead on the trail. From far, he heard a dog barking. They all stopped and listened in silence.

"What's wrong?" whispers Maedyv.

"I heard a dog barking, far in the woods," says Cythun. "Did you hear it?" "No, I heard nothing," says Maedyv.

"Could it be a hunter, or could there be a house? It is a few leagues ahead of us. I do not know this trail, so I cannot say what there is or isn't on our way."

They slowed their pace to a trot. Cythun, ahead of them, could barely see in the distance. Suddenly, he turns his horse, and gallops toward them.

"I smell smoke," he says to Maedyv. "I think there is a house in these woods. What do you think we should do?"

"Go ahead and see who is living there. Do it so no one can see you. A long time had passed since I have been in these woods, but I cannot remember of any house on the way."

Maedyv watch Cythun ride, as he disappears from sight. The smell of smoke becomes stronger, and Cythun slows, approaching the house. Hidden in the woods was a small cabin made of logs, nestled in the middle of a glade. It could be seen from the trail, and through the trees. Cythun ties his horse to a tree, and slowly approaches the

glade for a better view. It had a turf roof, and he could see holes between the logs, filled with moss. In front was a porch with an old
bench next to the front door. Not far from the cabin was another
building, more elongated; perhaps a barn. Between them, a hand dug
water well with stone edges, and a tiny roof, sustained by two,
wooden beams. Near the well was a wooden trough, but no animals
to be seen. A dozen beehives scattered near the edge of the glades.
The door to the tiny cabin opened, and a dog ran outside. An old
man followed, moving slowly with the help of a wooden stick.

"What is it, Obert? What did you smell?" asks the old man.

The dog barked in the direction of Cythun's horse, then ran circles around the tiny cabin.

"Oh, you silly dog, there's nothing here," says the old man.

Cythun draws back slowly, walking beside his horse, mounting
only after they are far from the glade. They soon join the others
awaiting them.

"It is a cabin with a barn, and an old man and his dog." "Did
you see anyone else?" asks Maedyv.

"No, no one."

"Then we should ask for shelter, the night is falling quickly."
"We have to find some food," says Dolong.

"Let me handle this," says Dytes, disappearing into the woods
with his bow.

The four of them follow Cythun, and are soon in the glade, approaching the cabin. The dog barked viciously.

"Good evening sir," says Maedyv. "We are five riders, lost in
these woods, seeking shelter."

"Five? I count only four of you. Perhaps my sight has gotten
much worse than I thought."

"The fifth will come later; he is hunting for our dinner," says
Maedyv. "Where are you headed?"

"To the sea," says Maedyv. "We took a trail, and are lost. Fortunately, we heard your dog, so we headed here hoping you could show
us the right direction."

"You just follow the trail you came on, until you reach the old windmill. From there, you will see the road splits into two. The left one will take you to the sea. It's a two days ride, if I remember it correctly."

"Thank you," says Maedyv. "We leave at first light. I don't think we are the only ones who get lost here, are we?"

"Not many riders are using this trail. If everyone knew it's a shortcut to the harbor, many people would be crossing my land. Last time I saw someone here was two years ago. Forgive my poor homestead I wasn't expecting any guests. You and your horses may stay in the barn, and there's some hay in there, so you can sleep dry."

"It will be more than enough. You don't raise any livestock here?"

'Oh, no. That was a long time ago. I am too old for that. I barely take care of my bees and myself, and of course, Obert, my dog. But come, come. I have some rabbit left; Obert caught it this morning. And maybe some honey, or honeycombs if you wish."

"Thank you for your kindness. We have our own food, and if you want to join us we will be more than pleased."

"Thank you. I will join you just to exchange some words, and hear some news from the world, if you don't mind. I talk with Obert most of the time, but sadly, he cannot talk back. Please leave your horses in the barn. It will rain soon, so you better hurry."

"Thank you again," says Maedyv. "We are very grateful."

Dismounting the horses, they leave them at the wooden trough where Cythun pours water for them.

"There were a lot of holes in the barn walls, but it has a good roof," said Maedyv, entering the barn. "At least we will sleep in a dry place tonight. Find yourselves a spot to sleep, I will go outside and wait for Dytes to come."

Outside, Maedyv looks at the grey clouds that are gathering upon the woods, bringing the rain in with them. Without being heard, Dytes exits slowly from the forest bringing a doe on his horse.

"For a moment, I thought you were lost," says Maedyv, when he saw him coming.

"I almost did, by following this doe, but in the end, I got it. So, what is the situation with the old man? How is he?"

"He's a good, old man who lives here alone with his dog. He let us to sleep in his barn," says Maedyv.

"That's good. We will sleep dry tonight. A heavy rain is coming this way."

"Did you see any traces up there where you were hunting?" asks aedyv.

"Not at all. It's like no one is passing through this woods. Even the beasts were not afraid of me. This is a sign that no one hunts them here."

"Then we should have a peaceful night. Bring your horse inside as soon as you finish with the doe. We will prepare it inside the barn. There's plenty of space for a fire."

Dytes hangs the deer on a tree and skins it. He takes the hide away, stretching it over a tree stump.

"The old man will be happy to have the hide, it will keep him warm in the winter," he thought, scraping the fat and flesh from it with his knife.

"You have to be a good hunter," said the old man, approaching Dytes without being heard.

"You scared me, sir; I didn't hear you coming. I can say I was lucky that no one hunts them in these woods. They were not scared of me, so it was an easy hunt."

"I used to hunt when I was still able to draw my bow," said the old man. "Now I live only with honey and rabbits that my Obert catches for me."

"Here, I will leave you this hide. It will serve you well when winter comes." "Thank you. I had to have some old frames in that barn."

"I will make you one as soon as we finish with supper. Come join us," said Dytes.

"Thank you, young man", he said, leaning on his wooden stick. "It's been a long time since I had people to talk to."

"Then you will enjoy our company." He throws the deer over his shoulder, followed by the old man, with a hand on his stick, and in the other, the deer's hide. His dog was running around them, enjoying the last minutes of daylight. In the distance they saw lightning strikes approach, followed by a big roaring thunder.

"It will be heavy rain this night," says the old man. "The roof of this old barn will hold so you can sleep well."

"We will after we eat, and besides, we are well guarded," he says, looking at Obert.

Inside, the mother, Dolong and Maedyv were gathered around a fire that burned in what was once the old man's forge. Their horses were in the back of the barn, unsaddled, and Cythun was rubbing them with hay.

"Cythun!" shouts Dytes, "Come! Give me a hand to put this doe on the stick!"

Cythun left the horses, and headed toward the fire. Raindrops started falling on the barn's roof and soon the rain was pouring outside. It was like the sky unleashed all the waters upon that barn.

"I told you it would be a heavy rain," said the old man, smiling to Maedyv. "I hope this barn will hold."

"It will. This is not the first one, and not the last one of rains for this year."

"Tell me," says Maedyv, "Why are you living here alone? Why don't you move in a village or near the harbor?"

"Well, I have no family in the villages. My wife passed away twenty years ago, and we had no children. Besides, who will want to take care of an old man? I will be only a burden for them. No, I am fine here. Here is my home."

The mother looks at him with sad eyes and doesn't say a word.

"May I ask you why are you heading to the harbor? There are bad people there. Pirates, I hear", said the old man.

"We are waiting for our master to come from across the sea," says Maedyv. "He should be there in three days from now."

"Oh, if you follow the road I told you about, you would be there in two days at most."

Dytes and Cythun turn the deer above the fire, and the others stare with hungry eyes. Soon they cut the meat that was ready, and share among themselves. They all eat, until one by one, fall asleep in the hay. Only Maedyv has his eyes open, listening to the rain falling on the barn's roof.

"The old man will be happy with the frame I've made, so he can tan that hide," says Dytes to Cythun.

'Poor man," says Cythun. "I hope I will not finish like him."

"Why's that? He said he's happy here and the life in a village has no meaning to him. And yes, he is right, at his age, he would be a burden for anyone to take him and care for him. It is better to finish your life in a place that you love, then in one you cannot find your place."

"You may be right, I think that time will tell as we get older what is best for us, or what's not," says Cythun.

"There is that windmill that the old man said we will find." "Or what's left of it," says Cythun.

"Tell me Cythun, what does your falcon see?" asks Maedyv.

Cythun whistles the signal, and his falcon descends onto his left hand. "No enemies around here, I think we are good."

"That doesn't mean we should let our guard down. We are in the open and can't know who is watching us," shouts Maedyv, riding quickly.

Soon they arrive at the ruined mill that looked abandoned for tens of years. Perched on top of a hill, the time and the elements had no mercy on the wood. Now it looks like a broken skeleton in the middle of a grassy meadow. They took left and in a few leagues they are again in the forest. A stream flowed on the side of the road and they take advantage of it to water the horses.

"The sea is close now," says Cythun. "How can you know that?" asks Maedyv.

"I feel the air has changed. It has a salty taste to it," says Cythun. "I smell nothing," says Dytes, taking shallow breaths with his nose.

"Very well. If you can smell the sea, soon you will have plenty of it. The night is coming ahead of us; we have to find a place to pass the night. If we keep this pace, tomorrow will be in our way to the Eastern lands, across the sea."

"If the pirates will keep their word," says Dolong. "They will, or they will not be paid," says Maedyv. "What we will do with our horses?" asks the mother. "We take them with us on the ship," says Maedyv.

"That ship must be big," says the mother, "to take our horses and us across the sea."

"Yes, and on our voyage you will see things that will challenge your imagination."

"There, among those spruces," says Cythun, "there's a good place for us to camp."

"Good, then," said Maedyv, heading towards the place Cythun showed him. "We will camp here and this time we will be on our guard."

"We are always on our guard," whispers Dytes to Cythun.

"Well, maybe that's the reason we are still here and alive," he says, smiling to Dytes.

They tied the horses to the spruce trunks as they lie down near the trees.

"Come," says Cythun to the mother, "I will show you how to handle that sword of yours. Take this stick."

"But, how am I supposed to handle my sword if you give me a stick?"

"Well, if we start straight away with the sword, you will cut yourself, and we can't afford that. First, you learn how to hold that piece of wood, and then we start training with real swords. Now remember, your sword has a double edge blade, so you wont be worried which side is which. They both will cut the same. Now you can use two hands to hold it, if you don't carry a shield of course like in our case. Now, you lift it above your shoulders and strike to the right, and then the opposite side."

The mother repeats what Cythun shows her, and she seems to enjoy it. After many repetitions, Cythun stops her. She is exhausted.

"Alright, now let's take a small break," he said. "You see, your sword had four parts, your blade; which you will use the most, then the guard that will protect your hands, the grip, and the pommel. In a fight you can use the pommel, too. Especially this type," says Cythun, putting his finger on the pointy pommel. "Now let's try something else. Take your 'wooden sword' and lift it above your head, just like this," he said, showing her the position of the sword. "Now strike! And one, two, now pierce! Three. Good. Repeat!"

The mother does what Cythun asked her to do, again and again, until she was breathless.

"Let's stop here. You should train by yourself when you have some time with your own sword."

"But you told me that I risk cutting myself," she said.

"Not if you have a good grip, and do as I showed you. You have to become more familiar to its weight. It is heavier than this piece of wood. You choose a tree and you train like it was an enemy. Then we can pass to another level of training."

"I will," she said. "But we don't have much time. We ride the whole day, and once we are on that ship I don't see where I can train again."

"I understand, but you can practice those movements in your mind too," says Cythun. "Just imagine you are fighting, and then when you find the time you'll see how easy it will be. It's all about training."

The mother takes her sword, and goes among the trees, training as Cythun showed her. From under the cloak, Maedyv was watching her with sad eyes. He hopes they will not encounter any enemy on this trip and none of them will be forced to fight.

Maedyv took the first watch, but until the middle of the night none of them were asleep. In the morning, everyone was awake before sunrise, and in silence they continued their journey. It was late afternoon when the mother heard for the first time, the sound of the sea.

"What is this noise?" she asks Cythun. "Am I the only one who hears it?"

"No, my Lady. I mean Nather. We all hear that sound; it's made by the waves that break on the rocks. The sea is not far from us."

Indeed, it is not far. In front of them the forest opens into a stony plain, and far in the distance they can distinguish the deep blue color of the sea, separating from the sky. The trail joins a road passing in front of them.

"Which way now?" asks Cythun.

"We take a right," says Maedyv.

"I thought we are not going to the harbor, and to the right is the road to it."

"We will not reach the harbor. A few leagues from here there's a protected cove. Your privateers are supposed to wait for us there."

"They are not my privateers," says Cythun indignant. "Soon it will be dark. We should hurry."

"No," says Maedyv, "we have to be there after the nightfall. No one should see us when we board the ship."

"But we have to lift our horses on that ship, and the night will make this very difficult," says Cythun.

"We have until morning to get to sea. Hope the wind is on our favor." "And the tide too."

They ride at a slow pace, headed South. The mother is gazed by the sea. She has never seen such a large expanse of salt water. Slowly she approaches Cythun.

"May I ask you something?" she says. "Sure," says Cythun.

"Those pirates you talk about, who are they, and why they are living at sea?" she asks Cythun.

"No one really knows where they come from. Maybe once they were simple fisherman, maybe they were thieves and mercenaries since the beginning of the world. Who knows? But I remember their entire world is build around the ships."

"They have no homes?" asks the mother.

"No, they live and die at sea, or on their ships."

"For thousand of years they had claimed the sea, they have gathered the power to brave the vicious storms and waves. They attack all

known kingdoms scattered on the coast, unable to defend themselves, There greed and their life on board the ship has made them
ruthless fighters. We cannot trust them; no one can trust them. But
amongst them, they live and die by their own code. A pirate will always trust another pirate, and often they join their forces when the
prize is big enough for all of them."

"Why can't the wizards convince them to fight against Karken?"
she asks.

"They never go too far from their ships inland. They called it
land sickness. That's why they built harbors. If they get sick of the
sea then they have a steady land that is not far from the sea."

"Strange people they are," says the mother.

The night had fallen upon them, and a sky covered by heavy
clouds hid the light of the moon. They had arrived in the dead of the
night, but they could not see any ship in that darkness.

"Watch out! The cliff is steep here!" says Maedyv.

Suddenly, the bushes move, and a dozen silhouettes appear in
the darkness. "Which one of you is the one called Maedyv?" asks one
with a grave voice. "I am Maedyv. Who are you?"

"The captain is waiting for you at the shore. You must dismount
you horses and walk in front of them. The path is steep, and if one
of you falls off the cliff, he will be dead before his body reaches the
sea."

They follow the directions of the pirate, and slowly descend on
the trail to the beach.

"Where is the ship?" asks Maedyv.

"It is there, you will see it soon."

At the shore, there were four boats with men on them. A tall
man approaches, holding a candle lantern in his hand. He lifts it and
looks at them with curiosity.

"You have to be Maedyv," he asks Dolong. "No, I am Maedyv,
he is Dolong."

"I met with your friend, Zurob. He said you would pay us to
take you and your people across the sea. Now we kept our deal and

brought the ship here. It's strange you want to keep all this in secret, but it is not my business as long as I get paid."

"May I ask, who are you?" asks Maedyv, to the tall man. "I am Vingoth, the captain of the ship."

"I will pay you six bags of gold. Half now, and half when you bring us back on the same beach that we are now," says Maedyv.

"Fair enough. Bring them to the ship!" He shouted. "And take care of their horses, too."

"How you will lift the horses on your ship?" asks Cythun.

"You will see when time comes; my men will take care of that, you don't need to worry."

They board one of the boats, and a few men push it from the shore. The men inside plunged the oars deep into the water and rowed as one. With a booming voice one of them yelled, giving them the rowing cadence. The darkness was so thick they had not seen the ship until they reached it. Its hull was built with mighty oak, and they can see one mast but they could see no sail on it. They climb a rope ladder until they reached the deck of the ship. The men on the deck move in silence, preparing a sort of rope with pulleys attached to it. Two of them were hanging on the boom of the main mast trying to attach a big pulley at its end.

"With this we will lift your horses, one by one," says Vingoth. "You will see it is not such a big deal," he said, with pride in his voice.

"Follow me, I will show you your quarters. The men prepared them in the last moment. Usually, we keep our barrels with water and ale, but if not they will go under deck."

On deck at the stern was a bridge where the rudder was, and just under it were their quarters. At the stern was Vingoth's own cabin, and on each side they had prepared cabins for them.

"You must decide how you will share this space," he says, "there are only two cabins, and you are five. It should be enough space for all of you."

"We will handle it," said Maedyv. "The three of you go to the left," he said to Cythun, Dytes and Dolong. "Nysgar and myself, we share the one on the right. Let's put our stuff inside, and wait for our horses, maybe they will need our help." The mother followed him. Maedyv closed the door behind them.

"Do not worry, my Lady; remember what I've told you. You will sleep here alone. I will spend the night on the bridge. I cannot trust them, and besides, I never sleep," he whispered, smiling.

The mother nods and puts her bag on the bed below. In the night they saw their horses brought over by two boats. Two boats were attached together with wooden planks at their bow and stern, with one horse in between, and men rowing only at one side. This makes it one stable boat of the two were capable to transport heavy on loads. The horse was lying in a net made of thick ropes, preventing him to fall into the sea. As they approach the ship, the men on deck throw a thick rope with four ends attached to the big pulley on the mast's beam. After passing through the big pulley, the rope descends to the ship's deck, passing through another pulley. At its end were eight men waiting for orders. Those in the boats attached the fours ends to the net where the horse was and those on the ship started pulling. The horse was lifted out of the water, hanging in the air attached to the rope. Others were turning the beam, and in no time their horse was below the deck. As soon as the horse was lifted, the two boats disappeared in the dark. They did the same with the rest of the horses and then they lifted their boats on the bridge, attaching them with ropes to the railing.

"Prepare to weigh anchor! All hands hoist sail!" yelled the man with a booming voice. Vingoth was on the deck near the rudder, supervising all his men.

A square, black sail appeared out of nowhere, scrolling off the mast's boom.

"Knock it off there! Pull those ropes all at once!" The orders started flying across the ship, and the men were obeying them in a mechanical manner. The great black sail cracked as the Western wind lashed against it. The ship slips away from the cove and soon they disappeared into the darkness. Now Maedyv was relieved, he could not see the shore anymore. Their ship was getting more and more speed as its hull crashed through the waves, spraying water across the deck. Cythun's falcon lands on his arm.

"Is that your bird?"

"Yes, it's my falcon," says Cythun, caressing its feathers. "And where do you plan to keep him here?" asks Vingoth.

"Most of the time he will follow the ship," says Cythun, "and he will rest on it when he's tired."

"I thought he would sleep with you in a cabin," says Vingoth. "Maybe he will, if we catch a storm," says Cythun.

"Well, then, as long as you keep him out of my sight I don't care where the bird sleeps. And one more thing, if I see him making his needs on the deck, I will have it for dinner, with potatoes and wine," said Vingoth, smiling and raising his eyebrows.

"Don't worry, you won't even notice that he's here."

"Release the foresail!" yells Vingoth. "Give her more speed!" The man with booming voice repeated the command, and the men released the foresail. Maedyv and Cythun were outside watching and asking themselves how those pirates are moving so fast on a ship that swings in all direction. It was so dark they could not even see the foresail on its mast near the bow of the ship.

"Hold that rope! Give her more from the port side!"

"If the weather is with us, in three weeks we should be on the other side," says Vingoth to Maedyv.

"Are there are chances that it will change?" he asks.

"This time of the year the sea is unpredictable. Long time ago we were almost sunk by a hurricane," says Vingoth.

"A hurricane? "Asks Maedyv. "I never had the chance to see one."

"And I hope you never have," says Vingoth. "It's a storm like you can't even imagine, with huge waves and heavy rain that broke apart our sail and destroyed our mast. I lost twelve men to the sea that day. We barely made it to the shore with only our foresail and the oars."

"Then I prefer not to see such a storm. We have to reach the shore safely."

"If you are hungry, and I'm sure you are, I can order some food for you," says Vingoth.

"No, it's fine, leave this for tomorrow. We are tired after that long ride."

"As you wish," says Vingoth, climbing the stairs to the bridge platform. "Soon it will be morning. I hope my crew will not disturb you with their daily duties."

"Do not worry about us. They are so tired they will hear nothing." "Very well then, enjoy your trip on this mighty ship."

Maedyv left the deck and entered the cabin when Cythun, Dytes and Dolong were. They were all asleep in their beds when Maedyv woke them.

"What? What's happened?" jumps Dytes, scared.

"Nothing happened, calm down. Not yet, at least."

"I was sleeping so well," says Cythun. "The swinging of the sea makes me feel like I am in a swinging crib. I never thought it would make me fall asleep so quickly."

"I am sorry to tell you that we must be on our watch," says Dytes interrupting him.

"Indeed. You are learning fast. Maybe after this you will join my guards," says Maedyv.

"I cannot do that, I have an oath to keep."

"Tell us your plan," requests Dolong.

"What plan?" asks Cythun. "What plan do we need on this ship? It's only them and us."

"Do you know them personally?" asks Maedyv.

"No but..."

"Do you trust them enough to put your life in their hands?"

"No."

"Then we have to be on our watch. We have to protect Maryia, and if I am not here you should watch that no one enters that cabin. If they know that she's here we are all doomed."

"Maybe if we pay them more?" asks Dytes.

"I am afraid not all things can be bought. And this is one of them," says Maedyv.

"What if we see someone wanting to enter in that cabin? What if it's Vingoth? It is his ship."

"In that case you have to be clever," says Maedyv. "Distract him with something else until she's undercover. She knows what to do. A few minutes is all she needs. Then yes, you can let him enter. We should not make him suspicious about her or us."

"He is right," said Dolong. "Even here we have to watch each other's backs. After all, they are pirates hired by us, not our friends."

Cythun and Dytes nod, bringing their swords close to their bed.

"I will be outside most of the time," says Maedyv. "If you cannot find me, then I am below the deck where our horses are. If you have nothing to do or if you get bored then take a look at them. Prepare them for our trip to the Eastern lands."

"I have a feeling these three weeks will be the longest ones," says Dytes, nodding his head.

"That is the least of my concerns," says Maedyv. "We have to convince Armizeg's peoples to forge those weapons we need, and convince him to come with us."

"First we have to find him," says Cythun.

"We will find him; it will not be easy but we will find him. Their wizard owes me and he will lead us to his hideout."

"I still don't get it," says Dytes. "Why would he renounce his throne and almost all his life?"

"Maybe one day you will understand him," says Maedyv, "but for that you have to get married and have children, and lose them," said Dolong. "You cannot understand Armizeg if you didn't lose what he lost."

"I will take the first watch," he said going out on the deck.

A sunrise like Dytes never saw in his whole life was in front of the ship's bow as they sail to the East on the endless sea. He takes a deep breathe of the salty air. Stealthily he's observing the mother's cabin, and Vingoth at the same time. The captain of the pirates is looking toward the horizon, not even bothered by Dytes's presence on the deck.

Pirates of
the Great Sea

"I've heard Wirgos is on his way," says Elidoc, happily.

"And who told you that?" asks the Master Wizard. "I just received his message a few moments ago."

"Folmart, the falconer," he says. "He told me Wirgos would be back soon."

"I see you have made some friends here," says the Master Wizard. "The guards like you, and Borysth is taking very seriously his uncle role."

"Is that bad?" asks Elidoc.

"Oh no, it's not bad at all. It is s good to have friends." Elide asks, "When I grow up, may I have my own falcon?"

"Now you want a falcon too? You want to be a true warrior. Yes, you can have a falcon, but I have to tell you; he must chose you to be his master, and you have to take care of him. Do you think you can do that?"

"Sure I can!"

"Then I should talk to your friend, Folmart about this. You have to go with him in the mountains and find yourself one."

"Why should we go in the mountains? He had falcons here, at

the fortress." "You have to take an eyas from his nest, and get him used to your presence." "What is an eyas?"

"It's a baby falcon. You know when a falcon is born they have no feathers. Their bodies are covered with white down, and they are so helpless in their nest, not all of them will live to an adult life."

"I didn't know that," says Elidoc, with sadness.

"That's why you should take care of the one who choses you to be his master, but until then we have time to prepare. Now tell me, how is your writing?"

"I think it is well."

"So you are not so sure about it?"

"I am sure about it," responds Elidoc, strongly.

"Well, then I will need your help. If you want of course," said the Master Wizard, flipping through an old book.

"I want to help you, too. What is that?"

"Alright, then, I want you to help me to rewrite this book. It is an old one, and the writings are beginning to fade."

Elidoc admires the book, imagining how he will help rewrite these pages of history.

"You can take your time," said the Master Wizard. "Here This will be the new book. For now it has only empty pages inside, but with your help, this could be a true representation for the people who one day will need it."

"And should it be exactly like the old one?"

"As exact as it can be, yes. Do not miss any word or letter." "I understand. What is this book about?"

"I am sure you will discover that for yourself. You will like it."

The child takes the two books, places them on the writing table, and carefully opens the old, slowly beginning to copy the words into the new one below. The Master Wizard looks pleased, and without any noise, leaves the library. He enters the dining room where a soldier awaits him.

"My Lord, there are three men at our gates. They are looking for Maedyv.

"Who are they? Did they give you their names?"

"No, my Lord, They told us Maedyv knows them, and one of them gave us this dagger so he will know who they are."

He took it with care, and slowly draws the blade. Like seeing a ghost, he sheathes the blade.

"Bring them to the Great Hall; I'll be waiting for them there."

The soldier leaves the house quickly."

"Those could only be Maedyv spies" he thinks. "I wonder if they will tell me what they know". He takes the dagger, fleeing the house, headed toward the Great Hall. In his right hand he holds the dagger.

"If Maedyv gave them such a blade, it means he trusts them. Now I have to make them to trust me."

"Our Lord said to let them enter!" shouts the soldier to the guard from the gate. "Let them pass!" shouts another from the top of the wall.

The heavy gate opens slowly, and Kelrem, Tykas and Nysgar enter the fortress.

"Follow me," says the soldier. "My Lord is waiting for you in the Great Hall."

Without saying a word, the three spies follow the soldiers on the streets of the fortress city.

They enter the Great Hall and the statues with the angry falcon piercing their eyes, frightened these three.

"I wonder if one day we will be among all these warriors," asks Tykas.

"Not even in your wildest dreams," says Kelrem. "They fought in the battles of old, not like us."

"But we fought just a few weeks ago, with Karken's soldiers," says Tykas. "Well, we almost got into a fight."

"We don't even have a real name, and we fight only hidden in shadow, and covered by deception."

"So you say we are some kind of useless warriors?" replies Tykas, with sadness, as he peers into the eyes of the carved falcon.

"No, you are not useless warriors," said the Master Wizard, as he enters the Great Hall. "You are warriors who the victory or defeat of all other warriors depends upon. If we don't know what the enemy is doing, or what his forces are capable of, we have no chance to stand against him."

"Where is our Lord, Maedyv, asks Kelrem.

"I am afraid he's not here," says the Master Wizard. "He is gone across the sea on a new mission."

"Across the sea? He never spoke of this. He said to would wait in his fortress."

"We will wait for him to come back," says Tykas, preparing to leave to return to the fortress.

"He will be back here in a month or two."

"What?" says Kelrem, angrily. "We don't have a month!"

"You can tell me what you want him to know. I know you were in Karken's fortress. What do you see there?"

"We work for Maedyv and him alone," says Kelrem. "And even if you are his superior, we still cannot tell you."

"I see Maedyv has trained you well, but you have to understand, we both have the same enemy, and the same mission. I know Karken has rebuilt his army and he wants to attack us in secret. Maedyv sent you there to see what his forces are."

"Yes, you are right," said Kelrem wrinkling his lips. "We were into Karken's fortress and we saw his armies. We counted over forty thousand soldiers. They were training relentlessly, and they are ready for war. Karken is also recruiting mercenaries among common people. We saw them entering the Throne Hall."

"How did you reach his fortress, and remain alive? No one before you has succeeded."

"Maedyv gave us these poisoned stones," says Kelrem, showing him the crystal. "Each of us had one."

"Of course! The crystals with the poison from Elidoc's body! Disturbing news you bring. If Karken will attack us now, we have no chance to fight back."

"I don't think he will do it soon," says Nysgar. "His generals are not ready for a war. Not yet."

"Maybe we have some time to gather our old allies. I wonder how many will come to arms," said the Master Wizard.

"Not many," says Wirgos, entering the Great Hall. "But those who will, are the finest warriors these lands have."

"I was not expecting you to come so soon," says the Master Wizard.

"I used the secret passages; they are unguarded, but I cannot guarantee all are."

"It means Karken knows we are aware of his plan. We will not use them," says the Master Wizard.

"Better not, we cannot take chances," says Wirgos. "Who are you?" he asks the three spies.

"They work for Maedyv," says the Master Wizard. "They are the only ones who had been into the Karken's fortress and come out alive."

"Maedyv spies," says Wirgos, laughing. "No wonder you are still alive."

"That's not the reason," says the Master Wizard. "They counted around forty thousand trained soldiers. It could be more."

"The King, Partogos, will come with twenty five thousand," says Wirgos. "As well as Hydal who promised us twelve thousand. That should be enough."

"Against Karken? It's never enough. We need weapons to fight his armies."

"For that we need to cross the Great Sea, and convince those barbarians to forge them, once again," says Wirgos.

"Maedyv is crossing it as we speak, and they are not barbarians."

'Well, at least they fight like barbarians. But if we had them here, we could attack Karken in his damned nest."

"If, Wirgos, but unfortunately this is not the case."

"Armizeg will came for sure," says Wirgos, "we just have to ask him."

"He is not their king anymore. He is now living like a hermit, hiding deep in the mountains."

"What? Why? He is the right king!" says Wirgos.

"Karken's wrath reached those lands, too, taking his loved ones from him. His children are now Karken's servants, and his wife died from heartache. He has nothing left to fight for."

"But his people? They too have children. He should protect them."

"They are now living underground, they are well protected against any enemies, not only Karken."

"Why did Maedyv go over there? We don't know their present king," asks Wirgos.

"We have no choice. I count on Maedyv's cunningness to convince their king to forge us those weapons."

"Where is Dolong? Still searching for those writings? I didn't see him in the house."

"He is with Maedyv, and Maryia, too."

The Master Wizard told the whole story, explaining the reason why Dolong and Maryia are with Maedyv.

"Poor child," says Wirgos. "I had promised I would teach him to fight."

"He is fine now," says the Master Wizard. "He is in the library, copying a book." "So he kept his promise? Now I have to eat my salad," he says, laughing. "What are you planning to do next?" asks the Master Wizard, to the three spies.

"We go back, and wait for our master," says Kelrem. "You have no need for us here."

"There will be always be need for you," says the Master Wizard. "I can offer you shelter and food, if you wish to wait here for Maedyv."

"We thank you, but we have to watch over our own lands, too," says Kelrem.

"Very well then, I thank you for your confidence. Allow me to give you horses to return on. There's a long way ahead of you."

"We accept that with gratitude," says Tykas.

"Guards!" shouts the Master Wizard.

"Yes, my Lord," says the soldier.

"Send word to Borysth to give three horses to these three brave men, and some food too."

"We thank you, my Lord," says Kelrem, leaving the Great Hall.

"Wait! I think this is yours," says the Master Wizard, handing him the dagger.

Kelrem bowed, taking the magical dagger. The three spies leave the Great Hall, with Tykas still gazing at all the statues.

At the gate, Borysth was waiting for them with horses.

"Three horses, and some food, just as my Lord ordered. He told me to give you whatever you need. His orders are my commands."

"We are fine. Thank you for everything," says Kelrem. "Ride safely", said Borysth "and hope we meet again."

Kelrem nods, and passes through the gate, followed by Tykas and Nysgar.

"If it was not for Maedyv, I would stay here," says Tykas, looking back at the gate.

"You can ask Maedyv to release you, and you can move here. Maybe the master Wizard has a job for you," says Kelrem.

They head West towards Strebo Village, leaving behind the fortress city.

"Let's surprise him," says the Master Wizard to Wirgos, "he's been waiting impatient for you to return."

"Very well, I will wait in the dining room," says Wirgos, taking a seat at the table.

The Master Wizard enters slowly into the library, finding Elidoc sleeping at the writing table, his head lying on his arm.

"Elidoc, wake up," whispers the Master Wizard.

"Oh, I fell asleep," says the child, barely opening his eyes. "What is it?"

"I have a surprise for you," says the Master Wizard, smiling. "Come. Let's go into the dining room."

"What surprise?" asks Elidoc. "Let me guess, more fish and salad?" "Not that kind of surprise. One I am sure you would like." "Alright," says Elidoc, as he gets up from his chair.

Moving with uncertain steps, sleepy Elidoc heads towards the dining room. Suddenly his eyes glare with happiness at the sight of Wirgos sitting at the table.

"You are back!" yells Elidoc, running toward Wirgos.

"Yes! I am! Now, calm down, so you will not get ill again. Sit down child, and tell me what's happened all this time I was gone."

"Well, I don't know were to start," says the child. "Start from the day I left," says Wirgos.

Elidoc tells him about his visit to the village, and his new friends; how the Master Wizard taught him to read and write. He tells about the day he felt ill, and how his mother left the fortress with Maedyv and Dolong, and that the Master Wizard promised him a falcon.

"I can help you with that," says Wirgos. "I know a good place where you can find your falcon."

"But I have to wait a few more years, until I grow up."

"Do not worry; time will go by fast. First, we have to train, because the mountain is merciless. Once Armizeg will return, you will feel better; you will see."

"Now, you have to teach me to fight, and to eat your salad," he laughs.

"All this time, I had hoped you forgot about it," says Wirgos. "Tomorrow, I will ask the carpenter to craft us a few wooden swords, so we can start our training."

"And then we can train with real ones?"

"Yes, then when you know how to use the wooden one, we can train with the real ones. Go and tell Larsa I am back, and to take the chicken out of the oven," said Wirgos, smiling at Elidoc.

The child enters the kitchen in search of Larsa, but found only Kolnet preparing dinner. He told him what Wirgos requested, and he gave Elidoc a carafe with wine.

"Until then, tell him to appease his hunger with this wine. I am sure he will like it," says Kolnet, handing the carafe to Elidoc.

"Tell me more about your trip," asked the Master Wizard.

Elidoc lies his head on the table, moving only his eyes, waiting for Wirgos to begin his story.

"I almost forgot," he says. "Partogos wants to see the child. He doesn't believe we saved him from Karken. He will come here to see Elidoc."

"He cannot risk being seen, coming in here," says the Master Wizard.

"I told him, but he said he would come alone. Do not worry, he will disguise himself so well, even his guards won't recognize him."

"Why is that?" asks the Master Wizard. "Is he a friend of Maedyv's?"

"I didn't ask. He wants to see for himself; the life his people live, and their needs. He's a good king, like not many kings these days."

"Then I will tell Borysth, so he can come here with no trouble."

"Despite the fact his city was almost destroyed by the flood, and Karken has taken his tribute from those poor souls, he still offers us help," says Wirgos.

"Did he know about Karken?"

"Yes, he did. His ancestors had written the whole story in a book the future rulers had to learn from."

"Now, that's a good thing. See, Elidoc, why we need books in our life?" says the Master Wizard, looking at the child.

Elidoc nodded, and without lifting his head from the table, answers, "I want to tell Wirgos how many books I have read since he was gone. I want to learn the tongue of those who live across the sea, but I have to wait for Maedyv."

"And why do you want that?" asks Wirgos.

"I want to go there, when I will be older. I want to see the whole world. The Master Wizard told me I will not find all the answers in the books, I must find them myself."

"Maybe we will go there together."

"Really? Really?" asks Elidoc, finally lifting his head from the table. "You would do that for me?"

"I will, if you will come and ask it when the times comes. In ten years from now, you will be a strong man."

"Strong and wise," added the Master Wizard.

"So, tell me child, what will you do when you return to your village?" asks Wirgos.

"Mother told me my old friends would not recognize me. The Master Wizard said my hair will fall out, too, so I don't want to go back."

"It will grow back, do not worry about that. Plus, you will see, when you go across the sea, you will meet warriors who shave their heads all the time. Only warriors shave their heads, not common folk. You can tell yourself you are a fearful warrior," encourages Wirgos. "Elidoc, you have to know I will always tell you the truth. You have the right to know what is happening to your body, and at the same time, you need to know what this world is all about."

"Tell me; are you still afraid of the dark?" asks the Master Wizard.

"Not anymore, I descend the stairs myself, in the middle of the night," says Elidoc with pride.

"You see, little by little you will get rid of all your fears, but to accomplish that, you must know the truth about them."

"Dinner is ready," says Kolnet, entering the dining room. "We have chicken today," he says, looking at Elidoc.

"Yeah!"

It felt like it was his birthday, when he but suddenly looks at the Master Wizard, sadly.

"I am not allowed to eat that chicken," he says to Kolnet.

"This time you are allowed," said the Master Wizard. "A few times a year you can eat chicken. It will not cause you any harm. Elidoc one good meal doesn't heal you, just like one bad meal doesn't harm you either."

"Well, it seems as we have no choices, but to eat what Kolnet provides us," says Wirgos, taking the whole chicken on his plate. "Fortunately there's plenty!"

Elidoc takes one too, and the Master Wizard looks at him discouragingly, as Wirgos laughs hysterically.

"Elidoc, relax; eat slowly. You have plenty of time, and chicken!" Elidoc nods without slowing.

Outside, the sun was already setting, and a full moon was shone over the realm, casting a soft, yellow light over the beautiful fortress's white walls.

Troubled News

"Good morning," says Vingoth to Cythun, when he saw him on the deck looking after his falcon.

"Morning," nods Cythun, looking at the sky. "How far are we from the shore?"

"In two days, we should be in the fjord, and from there we should stay for half aday until you will be able to go inland."

"I thought you would leave us on the shore, not on a fjord," says Cythun. "And what is a fjord?" he asks Vingoth.

"A fjord is where the sea enters the land through steep mountains and cliffs. From there, you will have just three day's ride to your destination. If I leave you at the shores, you would have to ride for weeks."

"I see," says Cythun, stretching his arm so his falcon can rest upon it. "I think there will be a storm approaching us soon," he said, looking into his falcon's eyes.

"Yeah, I can see that too, and I don't need a bird to tell me that," said Vingoth. "We have a few hours of peace before it will hit us. You can take your bird into your cabin with you, it will be a big one."

"How do you know all this?" asks Cythun.

"After living a life at sea, you learn how to read the clouds," says

Vingoth, looking starboard, far in the horizon. "You will know the difference between those, which bring the rain or the storm and those who don't."

Cythun looks in the same direction, not fully understanding what all those black clouds means.

"We should prepare then," he says. "What should we do, Vingoth."

"Well, there's not much you can do; you have to know the ship first. Do not worry; my men will handle it; they are well experienced. But if you want to be helpful, just close tight all the doors and hatchways, and stay inside or you will be swept away by the waves and lost into the sea."

Cythun enters his cabin, awakening Dolong and Dytes.

"A storm is coming," he says. "We have to prepare ourselves. Where is Maedyv?"

"If he is not with Nather, then he is somewhere at the bow of the ship. I will go find him," says Dytes, leaving the cabin.

"Well, what should we do in a storm at sea?" asks Dolong.

"We should close tight, all the doors and hatchways and..."

"And what?" asks Dolong.

"And stay inside," says Cythun.

"But we have only a door," says Dolong, puzzled.

"Then we will close it, and stay inside," says Cythun, putting his falcon on the top of his bed.

Dytes was looking after Maedyv, finally finding him lying at the base of the foremast.

"Cythun said a storm is coming."

"Since when is Cythun a seaman?" asks Maedyv, getting up slowly. He looks south at the horizon, over the water.

"Indeed, it will be a big one. Let's go inside, and let the crew handle this. We don't have to stay in their way."

Clouds that were of a dark slate color come toward them from the South. Vingoth yells with his booming voice to the crew preparing for the coming storm.

"Let them loose! Fold it more! Leave the foresail! Come 'on, move a little faster before we are in the midst of it!"

Few words were spoken between the men on deck, aside from what the second in command ordered. Less then an hour after they finish dressing the ship for the storm, the sea ran higher and higher as the water became dark as night. The strong wind grew worse. The ship plunged into the waves. The water poured in throughout all the deck openings, threatening to heave off everything on board.

"Hold it steady!" shouts Vingoth. "What are you doing here?" he asks Maedyv.

"I prefer to stay outside, than in that small cabin."

"Then take this rope and attach yourself to the railing if you don't want to get lost into the sea," as he tosses the rope.

"I said let them loose! More! That's fine! Now tighten it well!"

The ship was plunging madly into the waves, with each drive rushing over the bow, burying the entire bow under water.

"Everything is secure on deck and below," says Vingoth's second in command. "The hatchways are closed, and the ship is holding well."

Vingoth nods, looking South at the storm that seems to grow with every passing minute.

"We changed our course Northward as much as we could!" he shouts to his second in command. "Put two more men on the rudder!"

The second disappears under the deck, searching for another two.

The ship was driving into huge seas, plunging into the waves covering the bridge with water high up to a man's chin.

"Do not be scared, storms are a normal thing at sea, and these men are skilled," Maedyv assures the mother.

"But I can't swim," replies the mother.

"You don't have to swim. We will get out of this soon. Now think of something else. I will go to see how the others are."

The mother locks the door behind him, and sits on the bed, terrified. Suddenly, Maedyv finds himself floating in the air as the ship was raised up, and then plunged below the water again. He lands in Vingoth's cabin door, hurting himself.

"Next time, watch what you say about getting out safe from the storm," he thinks, getting up slowly.

Throughout the night it stormed violently with snow, hail, sleet and rain, beating upon their ship. The clouds clear away at sunrise, and now the wind is fair. The crew is already up repairing damages on deck. Some make new rope, while the others sew the main sail. The rain pours steadily, and Maedyv heads outside the cabin, climbing on the rudder bridge.

"Well, we are all fine, at least my men are. Do you have any losses?" he asks Vingoth.

"No, not this time," he says. "We were ready for it."

"Have you been here all the night?" asks Maedyv.

"That's where a captain should be in weather like this. I cannot leave my crew alone fighting against this unmerciful sea. It requires good skill and watchfulness to steer a ship in a gale of wind on a heavy sea. A little carelessness and the waves might sweep the decks or take the masts out."

"I heard you when you told to change course. Does this mean it will take us longer to reach the shores?"

"This storm saved us time. Tomorrow morning we should be near fjord. As I told you before, do not worry; leave the sea in the hands of those who live on it."

"I hope you have winter clothes. In the northern, it is always cold, even if it's not winter."

"Yes we have," says Maedyv. "How long will you wait for us?"

"I'll give you a month. It's more than enough time to reach the barbarians and come back."

"I don't understand why everyone is calling them barbarians."

"They are fearless warriors and ruthless riders. Their horses are so big and strong that one can pull this ship alone to shore. Good craftsmen they are, but I've heard they don't have a king anymore."

"When did you hear that?"

"Two years ago. Their true king left the throne and let his most trusted men to be a... I forgot the word..."

"A regent?" asks Maedyv.

"Yes, a regent. And they are still waiting for their king to return."

"I didn't know about that," says Maedyv, puzzled. "Do you know where their king is?"

"I heard he lives in the Black Mountains, but I am not sure if someone had seen him in the last tens of years. Why do you ask about him?"

"I didn't know he abandoned his throne. You know more than I do about those barbarians."

"Barbarians, yes, but once they were all united, and had no enemy." "Do you know the name of their king?"

"I don't. As long as they leave the sea to us, what they do and who they are is of no concern to me."

"Fog ahead," yelled the man from the crow's nest.

"Reduce the main sail!" shouts Vingoth to his second. "All men on deck!" The second repeats the command, and soon the men were at their posts.

"We are closer to the shore than I thought," says Vingoth. "The storm pushed us towards the land. We have to be careful with this fog if we don't want to hit a reef or a rock."

With the wind down, the ship now lays in a dead calm in the midst of a thick fog during the whole forenoon. Cythun goes out from his cabin, followed by Dolong and Nather. They find the ship lying perfectly still, enclosed in the thick fog, surrounded by a smooth sea. On the ship was total silence. Maedyv is perched at the bow, looking at the water when suddenly he sees a long, low undulating movement rolling under its surface, slightly lifting the ship without breaking the smoothness of the sea.

"Be silent," whispers Vingoth from behind, "do not disturb them." "What are they?" asks Maedyv, turning only his head back to Vingoth.

"We called them Ketos," says Vingoth, "sea monsters. They are so big and powerful they can break this ship into pieces with ease."

"I crossed the sea a long time ago but I've never seen them, until now," says Maedyv, with eyes agape.

"They live only in the frozen North, in cold, icy waters," says

Vingoth. "They came in these parts only to mate, returning after in their sea of ice."

"Indeed," says Maedyv, "the water is warm, and no storms in that part of the sea," as Maedyv listens to the slow breathing of the mighty creatures.

"There are storms there, too; even bigger than the one we just passed through. It was there that I lost more than half of my crew. This time of the year could be even hurricanes over there."

Slowly, Maedyv gets up and heads towards Vingoth.

"Tell me, how do you know where we are headed in this thick fog? You cannot see more than thirty feet around the ship."

"Come, I will show you how," says Vingoth, headed to the bridge where the rudder is located. Maedyv follows, watching at the Ketos, how they pass under their ship like he was playing with it. On the bridge near the rudder was a wooden bucket half filled with water. On the surface of the water a thin, rectangular piece of wood, pointed at one-end floats.

"Here," said Vingoth, pointing at the bucket. "This will always point to the North, no matter how the ship turns. We need no sun or stars to know our heading."

"What is this," asks Maedyv? "a magic piece of wood?"

Vingoth laughs, forcing himself not to disturb the creatures of the sea. "Look closely. See, on that piece of wood, there is a small stone." "What is that?"

"It's a stone called magnate. Those who gave it to me live in the Northern seas. In those parts, there's much water and many mountains without forests, so they came here to harvest wood for their ships and homes. We met them once and made trades. They gave me this stone, and this crystal," he says, showing Maedyv the crystal from his pocket.

"I understand the use of this stone, but why do you need the crystal?" asks Maedyv.

"With this crystal, I see where the sun is, no matter if its hidden in clouds or if there is fog, so I know where we are on my map."

Maedyv looks at him, puzzled.

"And how can this crystal show where the sun is. May I take a look at it?"

Without saying a word Vingoth handed him the translucent, square shaped crystal. Maedyv turned it on all its sides without seeing any sun.

"Let me show you," says Vingoth, taking the crystal in his hands, raising one of its sides toward the sky.

"Now you search for the sun," he says, turning it in place, still looking at the crystal. "When the stone is in the same line the sun is in, a red beam of light will pass through. Here!" exclaimed Vingoth. "Can you see it now?"

Maedyv looked at him, astonished. He now understands why Vingoth is the greatest captain of all. He has tricks some would consider magical. No breeze, and the sea surface is completely unbroken. The crew is now asleep, waiting for a soft wind to come. Maedyv heads toward the cabin where Dolong, Cythun and Dytes relax.

"Vingoth says it will be cold where we are going."

"The winter is now close by," says Dolong. "In the realm of the Master Wizard, we forgot how it feels."

"Not in mine," chimes Maedyv. "We have winter clothes, though, so we should not worry."

"Did Vingoth say how far we are from shore?" asks Cythun.

"He said the storm brought us closer. We are not far. They await the wind to spread the fog; then we will know for sure."

"Land on the starboard!" yells the man from the crow's nest.

All run onto the deck, looking at the starboard side. A breeze, smelling of rotten seaweed pierces their nostrils. The fog has dissipated, and they can now see for miles. Far in the horizon, they distinguish peaks of a grand mountain.

"The fjord entrance is between the two mountains," says Vingoth, from the rudder bridge, pointing into the horizon.

"I can see only one peak," says Maedyv, shading his eyes with his large hand.

"You have to spend more time at sea to be able to see that far," says Vingoth. "Life on land weakens your sight."

Cythun enters the cabin, placing his falcon upon his arm. He whispers in the bird's ear, and the bird flies off in the heights of the sky. Cythun follows with his eyes, until the falcon disappears from sight. The ship turns starboard, heading toward the mountains. As they sail closer, the mountain Maedyv saw becomes two mountain peaks.

"I cannot see where we pass through," Maedyv says to Vingoth. "Wait, and you will see. They will open when we get more South."

He was right. In front of them, the sea pierced into the land between those two mountains that now look like two pillars of a gigantic gate.

"Fold the foresail and prepare the oars," says Vingoth to his second. The men repeated the command, yelling. As they approach the entrance, the mountains seemed almost hanging over them. They were green and well wooded. A slow breeze was in the fjord; not enough to push the ship with a desirable speed, so they row hard. As they enter deeper inland, the mountainous landscape opens in front of them.

"A few leagues from here should be a fisherman's settlement. We will stop there, and you will continue your trip," says Vingoth. "Prepare your men, there's no time to waste. You have to be on shore before dawn."

Maedyv nods, leaves the deck and heads to the cabins.

"We are almost there," he said to the mother. "Put your winter clothes on, and forget nothing behind."

Soon all of them were on the bridge, waiting. On the right side of the fjord they saw columns of smoke rising undisturbed into the sky.

"The settlement is still there," says Vingoth. "They have a dock, so your horses will be on land sooner."

As they approach, Vingoth gives docking commands to his second.

The second in command shouts them with his booming voice to the crew. They open hatches where the horses are, and one by one, lift them in the same manner they boarded. Out of nowhere, a dozen of children appeared on dock, looking curiously at the horses now on deck. Near their ship were fisherman's boats; long and narrow, full with nets and ropes. The men inside stopped their work to look at the newcomers.

"We have to meet their village chief," says Vingoth, "he knows better these lands."

From the village side, a few men followed by children approach. Vingoth nods his head toward them, letting Maedyv know the chief was coming their way. Like a mountain goat, he jumps from his ship, heading toward them, followed by Maedyv and his men. Vingoth was speaking with the chief in a language none of them understood. Moments later, the chief smiled, pleased.

"What did you tell them?" asks Maedyv.

"I offered them twenty bags of wheat, and five barrels of wine," says Vingoth, "so they would let us stay here for a month."

"But we will not have enough food for the return."

"Do not worry; I brought these especially for this trade; gold has no value to them. They can't eat gold."

"Will you ask him if he knows of the Getaes people?"

"You mean the barbarians? I will ask him. Maybe he can answer your questions."

They took their horses to the land where Cythun and Dytes were preparing for the road. The chief of the village approached and spoke in his native tongue. Cythun and Dytes look at each other in confusion.

"He says you should sleep here this night," shouts Vingoth. "He will prepare a house for you. Leave the horses in the care of his people."

The chief of the village was gesturing to them to follow him into the village where their houses are. Vingoth and Maedyv were the last to arrive. The houses were built out of clay and stone, and roofs made out of turf. One of them was painted white, while the others left in raw clay. They had a wooden door held by hinges with animal tendons. In the middle of the house was a stove with an oven also built out of clay and stone. Around it were the beds made out of uncarved wood, and in a corner were heir-fishing tools. The windows had no glass on them, only wooden shutters.

"He invited us for dinner," remarks Vingoth, "and we better accept. They will be offended if we say no."

"We do as you say. You know these people."

One of the women in the house served them fish soup and some bread made of ancient grains in a carved wooden bowl. The spoons were also carved from wood. Near the stove, hanging from a rope in the ceiling, smoked fish filled the room with the scent of sweet mesquite.

"Tell him we thank him for his hospitality," says Maedyv to Vingoth, which he translates in their native language.

The chief nods and smiles at Maedyv, asking Vingoth something.

"He wants to know where you are heading," says Vingoth. "The winter will be here in a few weeks from now and he thinks that you are not prepared."

"Tell him we will be back before winter comes," Maedyv tells the chief. "Tell him we are going to meet the Getaes people."

As soon as he heard of the word Getaes, the chief nods his head to Vingoth, speaking in his language. The tone of his voice made them understand he was worried.

"They called them Wolf Warriors," Vingoth tells them. "He said hey were living in an underground city, beneath the mountains, and it would be difficult to pass or climb to get to them. He said they have a lot of gold, he says a lot, a lot of gold, and silver and salt too."

"Yes, that's it! That's the place we are going! Ask him what else he knows about them."

"He says you have to ride South until you reach a great river with muddy waters, flowing to the East. Donnar, it's the name of the river. From there you have to follow the river on horse, or on a raft."

"Looks like we have to build a raft, too," he says, looking at

Dytes and Cythun. The two of them agree, and continue to eat their fish soup.

"What else?" inquires Maedyv.

"You should be careful if you ride near the river. Raging warlike people inhabit the Donnar's tortuous bends. Their bodies are covered with signs and scars."

"What about Getaes?" asks Maedyv. "Ask him to tell us more about the wolf warriors, as he called them."

Vingoth asks the chief. They could see the fear in his eyes and hear his salutary speech.

"They are ruthless riders, and they color their hair dark blue when they go to war. They never cut their hair or their beards. You won't find anyone among them who does not carry a quiver and a bow. You should fear their arrows with the yellow spikes."

"Yellow spikes? Why?"

"He says the spikes are yellow because they soak them in viper's venom." Cythun and Dytes immediately stop eating.

"Ask him if their scars and signs are from battle wounds."

"No, he said their marks and scars are inherited. It's a legacy passed from father to son for generations. No one dares attack them in their fortress; they are made by steep mountains."

"How does he know all this? Did he meet them?"

"Yes, a long time ago they hired him and his men to build many ships to sail on the river. He says the river flows into another sea. There is another one; the Getaes called it the Dark Sea, and one day they were attacked by those who came from the Dark Sea. They had warships and wearied iron armor."

"Who were they?"

"He doesn't know their names but the Wolf Warriors were ready to fight them." "And who won the battle?"

"The Wolf Warriors. They killed all of them and sunk their warships into the Donnar River. Now all the shores are watched. He said their leader was shrewd in his understanding of warfare and in the waging of war. He judged well when to attack, and chose the right moment to retreat. He says he masters well the ambuscades and pitched battles, and he knew how to follow up a victory and how to manage well a defeat."

"Did he remember what his name was?"

"He would never forget it. His name was Armizeg."

"When was that? Ask him," pleads Maedyv.

"It was more than fifty years ago. Back then he was in his youth, when he worked for them. Armizeg was a man. He said now he must be very old or long dead."

"He's not old or dead, but do not tell him," says Maedyv to Vingoth.

"Just be here in four weeks. After that time we will sail back with or without you," says Vingoth.

"We will be here in time. Now tell him we are tired, and if he wants to show us were we will pass the night."

"He says here, in this house. It is his house but he is happy to let you stay here. He has great respect for those who want to meet the Wolf Warriors. He wishes you luck and hopes you return."

As soon as they finish eating, the village chief, followed by Vingoth, leaves the house, so they can rest.

"What are you all thinking about?" asks Maedyv.

"He was nervous and scared when he was talking about those people, but at the same time he respected them," remarks Cythun.

"That means maybe, just maybe, we have a chance to talk to their king," includes Dytes.

"Their regent," said Maedyv. "They have no other king except Armizeg."

"It's so complicated," says Cythun. "Let's rest for the night because this could be our last night for the next few weeks when we have some time and can enjoy the shelter of a house and the comfort of a bed."

"He's right," remarks Dytes, "lying on his soft bed."

One by one all the other follow. Only the mother sat in front of the stove watching the fire.

"Do not worry," says Maedyv, "your son is alright where he is. If we convince Armizeg to come with us, you two can return to your village in a few months."

"I hope you're right," she says quietly.

"Now try to sleep; a long road lies ahead of us and we all must be rested. I'll go to see how our horses are doing."

The morning came faster than Cythun and Dytes expected. Slowly, they arise from their cozy beds and head outside. It is a cold and wet morning with fog lying on the surface of the water between the fjord's steep cliffs.

Maedyv was on the dock, speaking with Vingoth.

"I miss the warm mornings from our lands," says Dytes to Cythun.

"Oh well, now we are here and we must go further South. Maybe there, the weather is warmer."

"There are our horses," says Dolong, pointing in their direction.

Vingoth and Maedyv come their way and soon the village chief joined them. He speaks with Vingoth.

"The chief says he gave you enough food for two weeks. Smoked fish and salted beef are in the bags on your horse's saddle. He says you should avoid going towards the mountains and stay in the lowlands."

"Tell him we are grateful for his hospitality and we hope to see him again in a few weeks," says Maedyv, mounting his horse.

They took a faded path that led them over the fjord's cliffs, and into the forest. Massive thunderclouds crept slowly along the mountain ridges, breaking with shattering suddenness in a torrential rain. It rained almost all day; a cold rain that seemed to penetrate their clothes. The landscape in front of them made them think they were on the threshold of a forgotten world.

"Let's rest somewhere between those trees," says Dytes, "and let the rain pass. We are soaking wet."

"We have no time to waste," complains Maedyv.

"If we don't get our clothes dry, we will go nowhere because will all be sick," replies Dytes, shivering of cold.

"He is right," says Dolong, "we have to get dry."

A Maedyv look at them finally deciding Dytes has a point. He chose a place on top of a heavy wooded hill where they could make a fire without smoke giving them away. They made a round shelter out of branches and small logs covered with a thick layer of dead leaves and grass. In the center they leave a hole where the fire can breathe, and smoke can escape.

"We will not use green wood," says Maedyv. "Dytes and Cythun, find some dead standing branches. We stay here for tonight. I hope the rain will stop until morning."

They all gather around the fire to warm, and to dry their clothes still on their soaking wet bodies. The dinner was salty meat and spring water. Cythun mounts his horse to see how the land looks after all that rain. What he saw worried him. Streams that before would have been small enough for horses to walk or jump are now impassable, roaring torrents. They have to go upstream to find a way to cross, and they will lose precious time. He returns to the shelter and whispers to Maedyv what he saw. Maedyv makes a sign to get some rest. The next morning they head upstream, crossing the icy, cold-water streams, slowly advancing South. Quiet valleys and gently sloping hills lie in front of them. They are leaving the Northern lands. From now on, the weather will be mild, and even with colder nights, they will stay dry. The bearskins the village chief gave them will keep them warm.

The Land Across the Sea

"Elidoc, are you there?" shouts Wirgos, looking upstairs.

"I am in the library!"

Wirgos enters he library to find Elidoc perched on the writing table, writing new pages from the old book.

"I see you have a nice and precise handwriting."

Elidoc did not even turn his head, afraid he might make a mistake. "You think so?" he asks, leaving his feather quill pen in the inkwell.

"Yes, you know you can see the soul of a man only by looking at his handwriting?" "Really?" says Elidoc, wondering how.

"Well, you see, if your letters are small, it means you are shy and meticulous; if they are large and widely spaced, it means you have a lot of confidence and you don't like to be overwhelmed or crowded. You like to be free."

"And what can you tell about my handwriting?"

"That you are well adjusted and adaptable. See how you made this loop? It means you are also relaxed and spontaneous, and it's easy for you to express yourself."

"The Master Wizard never told me that," as he gets up form the chair.

"Well, maybe he wanted you to discover this for yourself. Come on, I have a surprise for you in the inner court."

"What surprise?" he asks, excitedly.

"I can't tell you. If I do, it will not be a surprise anymore, would it?"

He opens a small door, and then takes them in the inner court of the house. Elidoc looks at it, gazed."

"I didn't know this house has a court. These are all for me?" he asks, looking at the hay targets and wooden poles buried in the ground, cut in the shape of a human silhouette for sword practice.

In the wooden stand were a dozen swords. Elidoc ran at them taking one of them and points it at Wirgos. "Let's play!"

"I'm afraid all this is not for playing, but for training," says Wirgos, with a serious tone. "This could be your playground, if you wish to call it that," he says, smiling at the child. "Here, I made you a bow too. Try and see if you can draw it."

Elidoc takes the bow and attempts to pull the string, without any success. "I will make you another one. I see we have to take all this step-by-step." "Why did you make so many wooden swords? Which one is mine?"

"They are all yours," he says, laughing. "And I made so many, because in our training some of them will break. Remember what I told you the day before I left the fortress?"

"Yes, I remember. But I am still weak," says the child with sadness.

"That's why we have to train your body. If you will eat well, in a few weeks you will be strong enough to draw that bow."

"I can't wait to show to my mother when she returns," Elidoc says, as his eyes fill with tears. "I miss her."

"They will be back in no time. That's why we have to train every day so you can surprise them all. I can't wait to see their faces when they see you fight."

Wirgos takes a wooden sword and shows Elidoc the basic movements. The child repeats them until he is comfortable.

"You will come here every day and train as I show you. It will do you good to take a break from time to time."

"But I have to write that book, too."

"Do not worry," says the Master Wizard, entering the court, and hearing what Elidoc has said. "Remember what I told you once? That you have to train your mind and your body?"

"So, I can come here and play with Wirgos?" asks the child, grinning from ear to ear.

"If you name this 'playing', then yes, you may come here whenever you wish."

"Now, let's get inside; Larsa prepared lunch. Maybe you will gain some strength after you eat so you can draw that bow," he said, smiling at Elidoc.

They enter the house, heading to the dining room. Wirgos and the Master walk behind Elidoc, talking softly.

"Do you have some news from them?" asks Wirgos. "Not yet."

"I wonder where they are now."

"They should still be sailing. In a week they will be at shore," says the Master Wizard. "But who knows, maybe they will be back sooner than we expect."

"Do you know something I don't?" asks Wirgos.

"Well, I have a feeling they are already near the Getaes lands."

"But you said that they are still sailing, I don't understand."

"It's just a feeling I have, Wirgos, just a feeling," says the Master Wizard, taking his place at the end of the table.

"Yeah, I know how those 'feelings' of yours are," he says, pouring wine in his cup. "What are you two talking about?" asks Elidoc.

"About the five..."

"We are talking about Maedyv," said the Master Wizard, interrupting Wirgos.

"I hope he and my mother are fine," replies Elidoc, pointing his eyes down toward the table.

"And what about the others?" asks Wirgos. "You don't like them?"

"I do like them," says the child. "I hope they all are fine."

"They are," said the Master Wizard. "A few more weeks and

they will be here." "Did you find something new about those people?" asks the Master Wizard.

"No, I didn't have time to read any books. I want to finish copying the one you gave me and then I will search more," says Elidoc.

"Maybe you will not have to," says Wirgos. "If they will bring
Armizeg here, you can ask him yourself about his people. He is
their king."

"I don't think a warrior king would speak with a child like me."

"Oh you would be surprised. Soon a king will come here and
you know why?" "Why?"

"To see you," says Wirgos, smiling. "He said he would help us
only if he sees you. Now, see how important you are?"

"What king?" asks Elidoc, surprised.

"His name is Partogos. He rules over the Western lands, across
the Bended River." "And why does he want to see me? I don't even
know how to speak to a king."

"He wants to see the child that defeated Karken's witchcraft.
You don't have to be shy in front of him. Think about this; first of
all, a king is just a man, like the Master Wizard and I, and only after,
he is a king."

"Do not worry," says the master Wizard, "he is a good king, and
his ancestors were our allies since the beginning of time."

"When will he come?"

"Well, any time now. He will be disguised as a poor man," says
the Master Wizard.

"Now we have to eat fish and leaves, again," he says, looking at
Elidoc with a sad face. "The Master Wizard wants us to be in shape
like he is."

"He doesn't want us to be fat," says Elidoc, looking at Master
Wizard unhappily.

"Let's enjoy our fish," he says, mouth filled with trout.

With a quiet pace, Borysth approaches the Master Wizard,
whispering in his ear. Surprised, the Master Wizard makes a sign toward him by nodding his head.

"Speaking of the wolf," he says, "Partogos is here." "He's in the fortress?" asks Wirgos.

"Yes, he is outside the door. I told Borysth to let him in."

A tall man with shabby clothing entered the house. Stepping strongly, he approaches them and unveils his face.

"So, this is the child," he says, admiring Elidoc. "Until this day, I doubted your words. Forgive me," he says, looking at Wirgos.

"You should never doubt me," replies Wirgos. "Please, take a seat; you should be tired after that long voyage."

"I apologize I didn't announce my coming," he says to the Master Wizard. "Wirgos told me no one should see me coming here, so the child could be safe."

"Indeed. You did well with your disguise. I barely recognize you dressed like that."

"We've never met before today," he said. "How do you remember me?" asks Partogos.

"Oh, you were just a child back then. Three years old, I believe. I was paying a visit to your father."

"So, it is true what the book says, you are immortal," says the king, looking at the Master Wizard, amazed.

"All is true in the book of your ancestors," says Wirgos. "You should take it very seriously, and maybe you could defeat Karken's wrath that has come to your realm."

"Too much time had pass since Karken was there last, Wirgos. For man's kin, a century is too long to remember. No one believes history anymore."

"That is sad," offers Wirgos, taking a sip from his cup."

"I feel like a fool," says the king. "I should take that book seriously, and maybe I could fight Karken when he comes for the children's souls."

"I am afraid you can't fight Karken. He cannot be killed with your weapons." "Why is that? I read that he was defeated once."

"Defeated, but not killed. No man can kill a shadow." "Then how can we fight him?"

"With these!" says Wirgos, putting his sword on the table. "Maedyv has gone across the sea to make a deal with the Getaes people to forge us thousands of weapons made of this meteor. I told you about this alloy, my king, when we first met at your castle."

"I remember it, but how do we know Maedyv will convince them, or that the weapons will be made in time?"

"We don't. That's why we must deceive Karken, and not let his spies know what's happening behind their backs."

"Can you bring the other children back, like you did with Elidoc?"

"I am afraid nothing can be done for them; They are already in the shadow. But for the next one, Karken will have a big surprise. Thanks to Elidoc, we now have the knowledge, and know how to stop his witchcraft and poison."

"I know you will not be here a century from now," said Wirgos, "but your heirs will. And for them we must fight, and defeat Karken once and for all."

"Before I met Wirgos I didn't believe all this," said the king. "And now I'm looking at the one who survived evil's wrath. I know how hard it was for you, such a young child to come such a long way. A warrior soul must lie within you."

"You are right, my king," says Wirgos, interrupting him. "He is a fighter, and now he is learning how to be a swordsman."

"We will surely need people like you, but I'm glad also that you are too young for the war that's coming. There is no place for children there."

"I still cannot understand why we can't finish with him once and for all. There should be some sort of a spell or magic to kill him."

"I am afraid there's nothing we can do about this except keep him at bay, deep in his cavern," says the Master Wizard. "You see, he was once one of ours. He was the forth of the great wizards."

"There are things you cannot find in those books of yours," says Wirgos, and tells him the entire story about how Karken became evil.

Elidoc listened, almost afraid about how things turned out for Barkon. The Master Wizard looks at him; making a subtle sign meaning he had to return to the library.

"I beg your pardon, my King," says Elidoc, respectfully, "but I still have work to do in the library. I must leave now before night comes."

"Child, I wish to be, but I am not your king. You may call me Partogos, and it's an honor to have met you. May I ask, what is your work in the library?"

"He is copying an old book into a new one," replies the Master Wizard, "like your forefathers rewrote of yours."

"He knows how to write?" the king asks, amazed.

"Yes, he does, and now he is almost speaking two languages," says Wirgos, with pride.

"Child, I may need a man like you. If one day you will need my help, Wirgos can lead you to me."

"Well, for now he has to stay here," says the master Wizard, looking after Elidoc. "Do you think Karken is looking for him?" asks the king.

"Even if he is, he is never going to find him. The poison Karken's spies can smell is long gone from his body."

"Then why doesn't he return home?"

"Karken's poison has damaged his lungs and his heart, poisoning his blood. Elidoc in still in danger, which is why his mother is with Maedyv; to bring a warrior from there to cleanse his blood."

"Why a warrior?"

"We need strong blood. Blood," he pauses for a moment, "from the bloodline of giants. Only this can save him. He will be able to return to his home then."

"I understand. Poor child. Is there nothing I can do to help?"

"Get your armies ready; at any moment we will need them," says the Master Wizard.

"But how can my soldiers fight Karken without those weapons?"

"He didn't know, that's why we have to deceive him."

"When should I move my armies?"

"You will know when the time comes. I will send you a message. From there you will have to move fast."

"I will. Now I must leave before my people notice my absence. I don't want to disturb the child."

"As you wish, my King," says Wirgos. "Tell Elidoc I hope to see him again soon."

"I will. Wirgos, please safely pass the king trough the secret passage." "I will, even if it is guarded."

"I think Karken retired all his assassins. He knows we don't use them anymore."

"Even better then. It will shorten your trip by at least four days, my King. Allow me to advise you. After the first crossroads take the road to the left, not the one straight-ahead, if you want to reach the bridge to your fortress."

"Trust me," urges Wirgos.

"I can see you tried the one straight ahead. May I ask you where it leads?"

"Of course. It will take you two hundred miles south of the bridge, right to the mouth of the river."

"Left it is," says the king, covering his head with his hood. "I will wait for you at the gate," he says as he leaves the court.

"I will be there; do not speak with the guards," Wirgos says as he turns left and heads to the place his horse is tied.

"Thanks to Elidoc, we are now sure the king will stand with us," he thinks to himself. "This child has something that makes the others gather around him; men and kings alike. I wonder what his future will be when all this is over?" He mounts on his horse and heads to the fortress gate. A clear night with sky perfectly clear blankets he realm with silence and a palpable peace upon all creatures, big and small.

An Unexpected Guest

The forest lies all around them. Giant firs block out the sunlight, so even at noon they ride in twilight. Veiled by the sound of wind, they advance fast deep into the forest.

"Do you know where we are?" asks Cythun.

"I don't" replies Maedyv, "we keep South until the river. What does your falcon see?"

"Not much in this thick forest. No village lies ahead, to ask where we are," says Cythun.

"No need for that," says Maedyv. "Even here we should watch our backs. These forests are home to thieves and outlaws of all kinds. We have to cross as fast as possible."

"I didn't see any signs of them."

"Did you look in the trees, too?"

"Oh, it never crossed my mind."

"Do not look now!" he whispers. "We cannot know if someone is there or not. Pass the word, no matter what happens we should ride together. If they attack us first, they will try to split us up. Now Go!"

Cythun rides back, passing the message onto each one of them. "No one is here," says Dytes. "I always look in the trees."

"Just do what he asks of you," demands Cythun. "Even if no one is there, this is the order. Our duty is to follow him no matter where he goes, and we shall fulfill it," says Cythun, advancing toward the front of the column.

They enter into a valley protected by high mountains, shaped in the manner of a crown. For the first time since they were on the road, they see grazing ships spread all over. Far beyond the trees, Cythun distinguishes a human shape.

"The shepherd is right there," he signals to Maedyv, pointing in that direction. "We must ask him for directions."

"Very well, you go and speak with him, but don't waste time with useless words." Cythun rides toward him, and soon returns, pleased.

"Well? What did he say?"

"He told me after this valley is the Donnar River. We cannot miss it if we keep South."

"Did he tell you anything else?"

"To be careful if we take the Northern shore. After the first river bend there's a village of people. Most are outlaws, hiding there from the outside world. And they don't wish to be disturbed."

"So, we have no choice but to build a raft," says Maedyv.

"It's not a bad idea."

Maedyv nods, and sees a beaten path leading South. He takes it with a slow pace. They ride toward the river. Among the trees from the bank they distinguish the river quickly. As soon as they arrive on shore, they are hypnotized by its vastness. None of them never imagined it could be so wide.

Shading his eyes with his hand, Maedyv looks at the opposite shore in hopes he would see any human or beast, but his effort was in vain. The river is too wide.

"We will ride downstream until dawn," he says. We will make camp, and in the morning we will build a raft. It's a good thing the river is so wide; we'll avoid being seen. A few hours later they reach a cedar forest, and in the clearing among the trees, they make their camp. The cold is unusually intense, but Maedyv decides they should not make any fire, and instead all sleep covered by the bearskin the village chief gave them prior to heading South. In the morning they awake, covered with frost on theirs bearskin. Slowly Cythun and Dytes search for dead, standing trees, suitable for their raft.

"Fortunately, we brought our battle-axes," says Dytes to Cythun.

"I never leave without mine," he says, marking the tree to be cut. "How many do we have now? Twelve?"

"Yes, we need four more before we can start to cut them," says Dytes.

"I will find four more," says Cythun, "you go and start work on the cordage, that way we will not waste time. Put the others to work, too. We should be floating before down."

One by one Cythun and Dytes were cut the timber and bring it close to the riverside, pulled by their horses. They line the logs, leaving one side to float in water, tying them together with cordage made of tree bark. They spread leaves, twigs, and bark over the logs to prevent the horses from sliding into the water.

"We have to be able to steer it, too," suggests Maedyv, figuring they have no means to do it.

"Dytes, find a tree to make an oar. A big one," says Cythun, scratching his head, and looking at their raft.

"We will take of the horses," says Maedyv. "They have to be fed and watered before we are on the river."

They built a gigantic oar and attach it to a tripod made of poles to be attached at the raft's stern.

"Now, we are ready to sail. Let's bring our horses."

With the raft floating, they board their horses on the gangplank made of timber. Holding the end of a long pole, Dytes pushes the raft further into the river while Cythun moves the huge steering oar, forcing it to turn toward the Southern side of the river.

"We have to look for a place we can stay for the night," reminds Dolong. "Soon will be downriver, and we will see nothing."

"We will not stop for the night," says Maedyv. "We will have a full moon, and must take advantage of it. Do not worry; I will steer the raft."

"He is right," agrees Cythun. "After all the chief said about those who live on these shores, it is better not to sail in daylight, but we have no time to waste. It is a good thing this river is so big; it means no rapids or rocks beneath the water. I will help Maedyv to steer the raft during the night. Two pair of eyes are always better than one."

Cythun's falcon lands on the stern of the raft, looking toward them. "Did he find something?" asks Maedyv, curiously.

"Yes, downstream there's a settlement on the right side of the river. Who they are, we cannot know, not yet."

"How far?" asks Maedyv, looking at the sky.

"About eight leagues from here. Until we get there, it will be night."

"Then it may be better if we keep sailing on the left side. Once close to them, we have to lay down our horses and keep the lowest profile possible. Oh, how much I wish for a little fog right now."

"We cannot command our weather, unfortunately."

"Even if we could, it would be dangerous because we don't know what lies ahead on this river," says Maedyv, looking around the raft. "I hope it will hold."

"It will; do not worry. How do we know when we are on the Getaes lands?" "We have to guess; I never took the river route."

"And how we do that?"

"They will find us. Their borders are always watched."

"I hope they will not take us for enemies. At least if we can show them something, I don't know; how about a flag?"

"Do not worry, their enemies don't come with rafts but with warships, and hundreds of them. They will not kill us before they know who we are, if is that's what are you are afraid of."

"First we have to sail until we arrive," he says as he mows the oar in the water, slowly steering the raft toward the left. "We are about two leagues from the settlement. Dytes, Dolong, wake up," he whispers.

"I will help them. You take care of the raft."

Slowly, he starts talking to his horse, gently patting his crest. He lies down on the raft, breathing hard in his nostrils.

"We all have to lie down and avoid getting up on the raft until we pass that village, reminds Maedyv to the others.

"Dytes, will you help Cythun take the oar out of the water? The water flow will push us in the right direction, so we won't need it for some time."

Almost crawling, Dytes reaches Cythun and both pull the steering oar out of the water. In the distance they see lights on the opposite riverbank. No sound could be heard in the total silence of the night. The river pushes them slowly until the village is behind them.

"Look! There! The river is turning," says Cythun, pointing his finger.

In an instant, Dytes jumps onto his feet, taking the oar, and helping him push it into the water. Both of them steer the raft, just in time to avid crushing it on the river bank. The moonlight allowed them to see a few leagues in the horizon, and soon they distinguish mountain ranges.

"Wake up Maedyv, and ask him if those mountains are to be on our way," he says to Dytes.

Moving slowly and without making noise, he approaches Maedyv. "What is it? Do you need me?"

"Are you not asleep?" asks Dytes, taken by surprise. "I never sleep."

"There are mountains in the horizon, and I think the river passes through them."

"It means we are close to their lands," says Maedyv, getting up and looking in that direction. "We should be there by morning. Take a break, and get some sleep; you need it,," he says looking at Dytes's face. "I'll go and change with Cythun for the night."

Without saying a word, Dytes lies down on the raft and instantly falls asleep. "What do your tracker instincts tell you?" he asks Cythun.

"It will be a quiet night. No sign of man on the river; not until we are close to those mountains.

"And what about the shores?"

"There are a few villages, but not close to the water. The woods are so thick no one could see us even if they want to."

"That's good, but we still have to be vigilant. Go and get some sleep; I'll take the watch for this night."

"If you have trouble or need me, I will be right here."

The raft was floating quietly, pushed by the Donnar River's waters, taking them closer and closer to the Getaes Land. From time to time, Maedyv moves the oar, turning the raft's bow and avoiding getting too close to the riverbank. The night passes in silence, and as the sun begins to rise he sees the mountain range standing becomes wider. In the center he notices the water has more speed than near the shore, and slowly, he touches Cythun's head with his feet, waking him up.

"I think we have a waterfall in front of us."

Cythun jumps up frantically, looking at the water and rubbing his eyes.

"No, the river is deeper in the middle and that's why it's moving so fast. We will need two hands on that oar once we enter that defile. If the river flows straight this could help us sail faster. The mountains are too steep, so no villages will be in our way."

"I will wake up Dytes," says Maedyv, leaving the steering to Cythun. "Tell him to make some breakfast; it will be a long day."

Cythun steers the raft toward the middle of the river, and almost immediately feels how the raft is gaining speed on the water. The mountains are so close now they can see the waterfalls that found their way out of the mountains. They are now following their fan-shaped course on the mountain walls until they vanish into the mighty river below. The Donnar River has cut a narrow pass through the rocky mountain, and they now can see strong circular currents of water swirling on the surface of the undisturbed river. The defile walls are so high and steep trees can find no place to take root. They cannot see the sun, even if the time was close to noon.

"No one could attack us here from the shores. The mountains are too steep here."

"You are wrong," argues Maedyv, looking up. "This place is perfect for an ambush, if someone manages to climb on these mountain walls. I wonder if the entire river is like this."

"The village chief said it flows into the sea. I don't think these mountains are endless."

"Look there," says Dytes. "I think the river is splitting in two." "You are right. What side should we take?"

"I cannot tell you, perhaps we should take the left one."

"Left it will be," says Cythun, pulling the oar and turning the raft. "I hope we don't get lost in these treacherous lands."

Slowly they sail to the left side of the river, and as soon as they reach the river fork, Cythun agitates his arms to everyone on the raft, pointing to the left. A gigantic, bearded face was carved into the mountain's white rock, looking their way.

"Now we are certain, beyond that are the Getaes lands," says Maedyv. "This is the face of their old king, Khalfar, the forefather of Armizeg. They will stop us as soon as we pass the carved rock. Do not show any hostilities and hide your weapons."

"And if they will attack us?" asks Dytes.

"Then we will be all dead before we can even draw our swords. Forget about the bow, you will never see them in these thick woods."

The river flows smoothly as they pass in front of the carved figure. a few hundred feet ahead, on the left bank, they see a man waving his hands at them and shouting words in a unknown language.

"Let me speak," says Maedyv.

"You are the only one who can understand what they are saying," says Cythun, steering the raft toward the left bank.

Maedyv waves his hand, too; a sign he understands, and soon the man disappears into the forest.

"Where did he go?" asks Dytes.

"We should dock our raft in place," says Maedyv. "Do not look up into those trees, Dytes. They are watching us. Let's act normal and see what happens."

As soon as Cythun ties the raft to a tree, a few dozen of them, dressed the same as the one on the riverbank, pour down from the trees and cliffs, armed with bows and curved swords. They were at least seven feet tall, and strong. Their long hair and beards made them look frightening. Now Dytes understood why Maedyv told him their sword would have no use in a fight with these people. Only one of the Wolf Warriors would be enough to fight the five of them.

"We come from the Western lands, across the Great Sea, and we wish to see your king. I am Maedyv, wizard of the Western lands, and your king knows me," he says in their tongue.

"What business do you have with him?" asked one in a weathered cape made of sheepskin, with a wolf fur collar.

"I am afraid I cannot say. Your king is my ally, and I ask you to take us to see him at once."

"We have no king. He has left us."

"Then the one who has replaced him; let us speak with him."

"That is his cousin. You may speak with him, but I don't think he will want to see you."

"Tell him I am a friend of Wolbah; perhaps then he will let us pass." At the hearing of Wolbah's name, they turned their eyes to Dolong. "What did he say about Wolbah? How does he know this name?"

"He is a friend of your wizard, Wolbah. His name is Dolong, and he is a wizard too."

The man with a cape looks at them, and after a few moments makes a sign with his hand. The warriors disappear into the woods.

"Do you know how to get into our city?" he asks Maedyv.

"Not from this place. Last time I visited your king I took the Southern road, not the river."

"The river is safer; it's a border for us, and downstream we have warships to protect our lands."

"We will take the ships?" asks Maedyv.

"No, the one you want to speak to is in the City of the Kings, and the city is deep in the mountains. Three days from here. I will send some of my men to escort you, and to be sure you're going where you say you're going. We don't know if you say the truth. You could be spies."

"My men will help you to get the horses on the bank, and then you have to follow them. Do as they say until you reach the king's city. From there you will be under guard to talk to Kothar, the regent. If you live or die depends if he wishes to spare you."

At a signal, three warriors appear from the bushes, and help them take the horses onto firm land. As soon as Maedyv and the other mount them, one was already in front, and the other two behind. Their horses look like a specially breed. They were all black, and much taller than the horses Maedyv and his men have, and well muscled with arched necks, high withers, and sloped shoulders. Long hair covers their lower legs, and their lifted hooves show power and energy. Cythun knew they were bred for war.

"I hope you will convince Kothar what you say is true. If you want to take a break somewhere, just tell the one who leads."

"We will stop for the night," says Maedyv.

"Not if you don't tell them to stop," says the man, turning around and disappearing like the others.

Without a word, the one who leads them spurs his horse and rides, followed by Maedyv and the others. They ride on the steep side of the mountain, and as soon as they reach the top, they see the river that brought them. A few leagues downstream they see the Getaes warships, docked on the Eastern side. The Getaes warrior that led them took a narrow and steep path a horse can barely walk on. They enter a forest with tall firs and beech trees, riding on what once was a riverbed. Suddenly, the lead lifts his right hand, and they all stopped in silence. The other two Getaes come close to him, whispering in their tongue.

"What is it?" asks Maedyv.

"Be quiet and listen," whispers the one who lead them, "there's someone in the forest that has been following us since we started our descent into the valley."

Maedyv listens. Indeed, there was someone in the forest. But what or who could it be? One of the Getaes makes a sign, and slowly descends from his horse.

"We should continue," said the warrior.

The one who descended stays behind, and his horse rode alone.

"Why did we leave him behind?" whispers Maedyv.

"You will soon see."

More than an hour passes since they left him behind, when they hear a scream and a roar, deep in the forest. The rocky walls surrounding amplified the sound of horror.

"What was that?" asks Dytes, frightened.

"I think it's a bear," replies Cythun, looking after his falcon.

They all stop, and the other two warriors dismount. They draw their swords, and wait in tension; ready for anything. The sound of a breaking tree is heard. Approaching them, closer and closer, sounds of a gigantic beast runs toward them. The mother looks to Maedyv with frightened eyes. A few dozen feet in front of them, they see a black beast, falling from a cliff with someone holding onto it. The beast fell on the rocks. It is still moving.

"A black bear," says one of the warriors. "I have never seen one this big. This is a monster! What beautiful monster."

A human was seen getting up from atop the dying bear and walks toward them. As he approaches, they clearly see it is a man wearing a bearskin on his shoulders. His long, dirty hair was falling on his shoulders and in one of his hands he holds a battle dagger, meticulously crafted, with a golden pommel.

"Your friend is dead," he says with a thundering voice. "This bear was after you since you left the river."

"Who are you?" shouts one of the warriors.

"I am the one who killed this bear before he would have killed all of you in that narrow passing," he boldly replies, pointing his dagger in that direction.

"Do you have a name?" inquires one of Getaes warriors. "My name has no importance to you."

They could see this man is even taller than the warrior he stands next to. He must be least eight or nine feet tall. From the darkness of the forest they hear wolves howl, and they turned their head in that direction.

"If you want to take your friend's body, you better hurry, a pack of wolves is on its way. The night is close, and you better hurry to get out from this trap."

"I see you know these mountains," says one of the warriors. "You know we have no time to get out of here."

He looked at the mother with inquisitive eyes, and then at Maedyv, without a word.

"I know a faster way to get you out of the woods. You don't have time to look after your dead friend." He looks into the sky where Cythun's falcon circles.

He took a horse and rode fast through the narrow canyon, followed by all the others. They got out of the canyon and rode into the forest without a path or a trail to guide them. Soon they were in front of a river the horses easily crossed. Upon the safety of the other shore, they look back.

"The carcass of the dead bear will stop them from hunting us. Now you have to follow this river downstream until you get to a village. From there you will know where to go," he says, dismounting the horse.

"I have a question for you if you don't mind," requests Maedyv. The unknown man looks at him, and nods his head in agreement.

"Are you from these lands? I can see you have come a long way. Do you know how we can find the king, Armizeg? I have heard he lives in these mountains, somewhere."

"Why do you want to find him? He is no longer king. Who you seek is his cousin, the new king.

"I am afraid you are mistaken. They said they have no king." pointing at the two Getaes warriors. "They say Kothar is only a regent."

"Yes, he is right," agrees one of the Getaes. "Armizeg abandoned his people and now he is hiding in the mountains."

"What do you know about him abandoning his own people? You know nothing about him!"

"You are right," says Maedyv. "We know nothing about him, well, only a few things."

"What do you mean by that?" he asks, peering at Maedyv.

"Well I know you have his dagger, and you are his friend."

"And how do you know this?"

"I gave the dagger to Armizeg, myself, when he was only five. That blade was once mine, but the little child admired it. I gave it to him when I was visiting his father.

"What is your name?" asks the man, looking at Maedyv in the dawn light.

"Maedyv, but you always called me the Eastern Wizard."

A deep silence took place between them. No one dared make a sound. Even the horses were completely still, as if they understood.

"You are right," he said in his native tongue, so the others cannot understand. "I am Armizeg, and I remember you, but I am not their king anymore," he says, turning his back to Maedyv.

"As long as you'll live, you will always be their king," says Maedyv. "For centuries, they will wait for you to come back. Your people need you."

"How can I help them when I have no will to live myself? I lost everything. My children, my wife... I have nothing to fight for."

"Yes you do, my Lord," says the mother. "There are still children to protect. Not only those of your people, but of the whole world. We need your help. This is why we come all this way to find you."

"And who are you? From the first time I saw you, I knew you were a woman."

"I am Maryia, and Karken stole my son too."

"And how do you think I can help you? No one could bring your child back."

"He is not in Karken's realm. The Great Wizard and Maedyv saved him."

"What? This is unheard of! No one escapes Karken's witchcraft. No one!"

"This one did," says Maedyv. "We saved this child but we still need your help, and that of your people."

"I cannot see how I can help you. I'm just a man who lives in the mountains, waiting for his time to come."

"We need your people to forge ancient weapons. A war is coming in our lands, and if we cannot stop it there, it will cross the sea to these lands too."

"How do you know this? Karken was defeated thousands of years ago. And they are well protected underground."

"Defeated, but not destroyed. He still lies in his fortress, deep in the cave. He rebuilt his armies and now he is ready to march against us. Her child saw it before we had undone the spells that lied upon him. And how long do you think it will take for him to find a way in? He hired spies and assassins among common folk. Sooner or later he will find a traitor to show him the entrance to the city below."

He was looking at the mother and asks, "You are not concerned by this war, if there will even be one, as Maedyv says. Why did you come all this way?"

"I hope to convince you to come with us. My son is ill and he needs your blood. You are his only hope to survive."

"Why my blood?"

"Karken's poison has damaged his lungs and his heart. His blood is poisoned. We need yours in order to cleanse his. As long as poisoned blood runs through his veins the child has no chance to survive," says Maedyv.

"And how do you know that this will work?"

"We don't have any other options. You lost your children, and you know if you had a chance to save them, you would. His mother crossed mountains for days in order to reach the Master Wizard. It was winter then."

"If all you say is true, you will need more than my blood; you will need the knowledge of my people. I know you came here for those weapons. I will ride with you to the king's city. Let's see if my cousin will join our forces."

How do you think they will let you inside?" asks Maedyv.

"Do not worry; I know every tunnel that leads in that underground fortress. My ancestors built them. If it were not for these two I could take you there in no time. There is an entrance not far from this place. We will use the tunnels to travel faster and safer under the mountains. I think the wolves are still after us. If you want I can take you out of here so you can reach your fortress safely.

The wolves howling began again.

"Yes! Thank you!"

Armizeg mounted the warhorse, which buckled beneath his weight. In these lands the woods are so thick it is better to ride on the riverbeds and streams in order to cross. They all now understood why Getaes people use the underground tunnels in order to move from one place to another. Ferocious beasts live in these thick woods. It's close to midnight and a thick fog begins to settle in the valleys.

The Woodsman

"Good, now try to strike from over your head," Wirgos says, looking at Elidoc's hands. "Keep it tight; do not let it turn in your hands. Do not look at me, child. Look at your 'enemy' the stake. Left! ... Good, now right! And.. Stab!

Good, now take a break, and we'll continue with the bow."

Elidoc sheaths his sword and runs into the kitchen. Since his mother left, Wirgos taught him to fight with wooden swords and shoot wooden arrows. For one week now, he has trained with real swords Wirgos specially made for him, forged for his size, and he has exchanged his bow for a faster one. Two hours a day, one before lunch, and another in the afternoon just before dawn, Wirgos trains Elidoc in the art of sword fighting and bow shooting. The child wants more and more training, but Wirgos knows his body is still weak.

"Well, are you hungry?" asks Kolnet. "I have something for you, if you wish."

"No, just water is fine," says Elidoc, taking the cup; emptied in seconds. "I have to go, Wirgos is waiting for me."

"Oh, well, perhaps after. Now, go and be a warrior."

"I will!" Elidoc says, smiling, leaving the kitchen the same way he entered. "I'm back!" he yells to Wirgos.

"Well, that was quick! Come! Take a seat at the straw bale. Do you remember what I told you last time?"

"Of course I remember! It was yesterday." "Then show me what you remember."

Elidoc takes his bow and advances in front of his target made of bales, straw, and wood. He took his bow in one hand, nocking his arrow. A leather quiver holding his arrows attached to his waste. He takes an arrow and places the nock on the string, lifting the bow until the arrow reaches eye level, drawing it in at the same time. In just a few seconds, he releases it and his arrow flies straight to his target with astonishing speed.

"Not bad. Move a foot more towards the left from center. You're taking too much time. The more you take your time, the faster your arms get tired. Just aim and release the arrow. Come on; once again, you're doing great."

Elidoc takes another arrow, and does exactly as Wirgos says.

"See? You are getting closer. You have to breathe, too. Imagine your sight goes with the arrow. Do not close your eyes."

After another arrow, Elidoc hits the red circle, and jumps with joy. "I did it! I did it!"

"Well done! Now try to put all your arrows in that circle so I won't think that it was just luck. He is so proud of Elidoc, learning so fast. He hopes Armizeg will come to save this child they've all grown to adore.

"How are things going here?" asks the Master Wizard, as he enters their training field.

"Well, you can see for yourself. He managed to touch the circle for the first time."

"There is always a first time for everything," says the Master Wizard smiling proudly at Elidoc.

"Focus on your target, child," shouts Wirgos. "Are you listening to us?"

"Do you have news from Maedyv?" he asks.

"No, not yet. But maybe its better this way," says the Master Wizard. I hope they find what they are after."

"There are things beyond us, but I have a feeling he will be alright. Life has given him another chance. Let's hope for the best."

"I hope all this won't be in vain."

"Tomorrow you'll do better," shouted Wirgos, when he saw all the arrows around the circle, and only one inside.

"Let's prepare for lunch; all this fighting has made me hungry." "You are always hungry," laughs the Master Wizard.

"You had enough training for today," said the Master Wizard. "After your afternoon nap you should train your brain."

"He will," says Wirgos. "Anyway, I have to go to see the falconer." "May I come with you?" asks Elidoc, excitedly.

"The master Wizard said you have to train your brain too, and we both should listen to what he says. Next time you may come with me; I promise." Wirgos puts his big, right hand on Elidoc's shoulder. They enter the dining room were food was already on the table.

"All right! Fish and ... what is that?" he asks Larsa.

"Spinach pie," she replies, smiling widely.

"Right, spinach pie. You know it would taste better if you put some meat in it," says Wirgos, looking sadly at Elidoc. "At least we have wine."

"You have wine," says the Master Wizard. "The child is not allowed to drink wine."

"How long do you have until you're done with that book, Elidoc?" asks the Master Wizard.

"I think it will be done by the end of this week," says Elidoc, mouth filled with spinach pie.

"I see you like it, child," notices Wirgos. "It tastes good!"

"Yeah, like boiled spinach," says Wirgos, pouring more wine into his cup. "I will pay a visit to Folmart this afternoon. Do you have any message that has to be sent?"

"No, I don't have any, but what is your business with him? Do you think he has better food?" says the Master Wizard, laughing.

"I just want to ask him about some unfinished business."

"I see. Well, as far as I know, he should be there with his birds."

"May I go with him to see those falcons?" asks Elidoc, looking at the Master Wizard for approval

"Tomorrow," says Wirgos. "I promise. And if Folmart is there, I will have a surprise for you, tomorrow morning."

"What surprise?"

"You know I can't tell you; that would just spoil things. Be patient; tomorrow is only a day away, and it will come quickly."

They finish eating, and each one of them returns to their tasks. Elidoc returns to the library and begins copying the old book into the new one, while Wirgos takes a walk to the fortress city falconer. For Elidoc, this night will be a long one, as he has no idea about what surprise Wirgos has in stock for him. Slowly he stops thinking about it, and he continues to work on the book. The evening came upon the realm slowly. Larsa informs him to prepare for dinner. It was a quiet one, with only Elidoc and the Master Wizard. Wirgos was missing.

"Well, I think Folmart had better food," he says to Elidoc, laughing. "He missed our afternoon training, too," remarks the child, sadly.

"Do not worry; you have time to train. Meanwhile, eat well because you will need it for tomorrow."

"Why is that?"

"You will see. After you finish, you must go and rest because tomorrow you will have a hard and long day."

"Yes, I have bow training in the morning. I hope he will not miss that one too."

"Oh, he won't miss it, that's why you have to go to bed early. He has a surprise for you."

Elidoc finished his dinner, and retreats slowly to his bedroom. He lies on his bed, and closes his eyes. He thinks about his mother, and suddenly felt so alone he started to cry until falling asleep.

"Wake up, child," whispers Wirgos to Elidoc. "What is it? It's not even morning."

"For some it's never morning. Come on, we have work to do. Did you forget about the surprise?"

"No, what is it? Can tell me now?"

"Today we are both going into the mountains, to find you your bird."

"We are going to find my falcon?"

"Indeed, today is the day! Come on, hurry up! Get dressed and be downstairs as soon as you can. We will have breakfast on the road," he says, leaving the room. The child was dressed so fast he almost forgot to wear his socks.

"I am coming!" he shouted from upstairs, as he ran through the door, almost falling down the stairs.

"Where are you going in such a hurry?" inquired the Master Wizard, as he spoke to Wirgos in the living rom.

"We will go to find my falcon, Wirgos and I."

"So that was the surprise? Very well then, you have to hurry, there's a long journey ahead and you have to get back before dawn."

"Come on, my child; let's not waste any more time. The sun will rise soon, and we are still here talking. Take this cloak, the mornings are colder now."

Elidoc wears the cloak Wirgos gave him, and sprints out the door.

"Be careful with him," urges the Master Wizard. "The mountains are harsh even for the strongest of men. Consider the child's age and current health condition."

"Do not worry; he will be with me, on my horse. I will protect him as if he were my very own."

They leave the fortress, headed North toward the mountain range. Elidoc does not say a word, and can barely breathe at the thought he will have his own falcon, just as the ancient warriors once had. He read about them in the books. A pine forest lies ahead of them and soon they take left turn, trying not to cross it. Wirgos steers his horse without using the reins. Soon after they were on a mountain path, climbing toward the mountain peak. Wirgos stops his horse, dismounts, and walks alongside with Elidoc on the saddle.

The path was steep with plenty of rocks that would make it impossible for the horse to carry them both. Arriving near a high rock that almost cut the path like a closed gate, Wirgos takes Elidoc from the saddle, leaving his horse loose.

"You don't have to tie him to something?" asks the child.

"Do not worry; he won't go anywhere if I don't tell him to. We have to walk from here. Their nests are on those cliffs," says Wirgos, pointing toward them.

"Do you think the baby falcons will choose me?"

"You mean eyasses? That's what a baby falcon is called."

"Oh yes, now I remember. Do you think I will find my eyas?"

"Well, let's go and see. Stay behind and watch and me where I put my feet. You have to do the same if you don't want to fall off these cliffs."

Elidoc climbs behind him, watching attentively, every move Wirgos makes. "Look, the falcons are surrounding us!"

"They know we are coming to get one of their offspring. Do not look at them." "Do you think they will be mad?"

"Yes they will, like any parent would. Only they know that with us, their eyasses have more chance to survive than here in the mountains."

"They die here in their nests?"

"Yes, they die sometimes as they do not have food, or because they fall from their nest, but that's part of life. Sometimes one has to die in order for the others to survive. See, they also don't all hatch at the same time. The one who hatches first has more of a chance to live, as they are to be the older ones."

"I thought that they had an easy life and they were safe here, in the mountains."

"Life is not what you think, and as you get older you will see that best part of life is childhood."

"But my childhood hasn't been so great. I almost died, and yet I'm fortunate that I found you and the others to save me from Karken's spell."

"The first of them that learn to fly have more of a chance to make it because they can hunt by themselves and not depend on their parents. Just like humans. You will understand this well, as you get a little older. Now let's see which one will choose you? The one who chooses you will come to you.

As they advance onto the cliff and sit on a short and narrow rock where a falcon's nest was, there were three eyasses with downy feathers. On one side of the nest lay an unhatched egg.

"It seems they will not all make it," says Wirgos, pointing at the egg. "Come on, quick! Move toward them. Let's see if your future bird is among them."

Elidoc moved into the nest but the eyasses ran toward the rocky side, afraid of him. "Well, I guess my bird is not here. Let's go before their parents come."

Sad Elidoc quickly out of the nest followed Wirgos. They were heading to the other side of the rocky cliff where they saw falcons leaving their nest. Just as in the first nest, Elidoc moves toward the eyasses. There were four of them with light brown down. As soon as they see Elidoc descending to their nest, they jump around and hop toward the other side of the nest.

"I guess my bird isn't in this one either," he said, looking up to Wirgos, disappointed.

But just as he gets out of the nest, one of the eyasses lunges toward him, making a high-pitched sound. Elidoc turns to see him.

"He likes me?"

"No, he doesn't like you yet, but he is not afraid of you," says Wirgos." He is the one that you have to take. Be careful with his talons, they can hurt you. Remember what I've told you when this moment comes? Use your cloak."

Slowly, Elidoc approaches the eyas, throwing his cloak over it, completely covering him.

"Lets get out of here before this little thing starts screaming," says Wirgos, helping Elidoc to climb the steep cliff.

"Let's see what this bird is made of," says Wirgos, looking at the eyas' wings and analyzing his talons.

"Do you have a falcon, too?"

"I have them in my fortress. Not only one, but thirty." "Wow! And they are all yours?"

"Only one is mine, and he chose me the same way this one did with you. Now we have to go to and see Folmart so he can teach you how to train him."

"I can see him every day?"

"Who? Folmart?"

"No, my falcon."

"Child, now he is yours, and you will take care of him every day of his life. You have to feed him, train him and watch over him."

"I can't wait for my mother to come." "You must give him a name."

"I will call him... wait! Is it a boy or a girl?" asks Elidoc, turning the bird upside down. "How we can know?"

"He is a boy," Wirgos assures. "I will call him Snowball! "Said Elidoc

"Snowball? Asks Wirgos. "I never heard of such a name for a bird. Why Snowball?"

"Because he has plenty of white down on him, that makes him look like a ball of snow."

"There's a lot you will learn about him. Now let's go back home before the night catches up to us."

They rode fast towards the fortress city as the sun set behind the mountains.

"Well, well, well, now that's a bird," says Folmart, looking at Elidoc's falcon.

"His name is Snowball," he said with pride.

"You know in a few weeks these will be replaced with brown feathers," says Folmart.

"What should I call him then? Nutmeg?"

"I like this one better."

"Then Nutmeg it is," says Elidoc, smiling towards Wirgos.

"Now you have to come here three times a day," demands Folmart.

"Your falcon has to get used to your presence, and as we train him, he will know you are as his master."

"Can we start to train him tomorrow?"

"First he has to learn to fly. After that we can teach him how to hunt. It will take three years until he is a useful bird."

"Oh, no, that much? The Master Wizard told me I would return to my village as soon as I get better. I don't have three years."

"Why do you say that?" questioned Wirgos. "You may take your falcon with you." "Can I do that?"

"Of course you can. You cannot leave it here. Now he is yours, and you are his master."

"I can't wait to see the faces of the children in my village, when they will see Nutmeg!"

"They will be astonished by him," says Wirgos. "Alright now, it's time to go home; the Master Wizard doesn't know we are back yet. If we stay any longer we will miss dinner."

"I shall see you in the morning, child. He will be really hungry then. When they are eyasses they eat six times more than when they are adults, so for a few weeks he is going to need a lot of food."

"May I feed him now?" asks Elidoc, leaving the bird on a perch.

"I will feed him. Go with Wirgos and eat something. I see that you are becoming pale."

"Fine. See you tomorrow, Nutmeg," he lovingly says as he caresses the bird's downy feathers.

Elide and Wirgos leave the falconry court and head toward the Master Wizard's house. Another long night will have to pass until he sees Nutmeg again. Now he is thinking to himself that he was just like the ancient warriors from the old books. He was just missing some strength and a few more years until he will be old enough to fight Karken. But the Master Wizard said that he couldn't. Well, maybe he will change his mind when he knows about the bird?

"How many days until my mother will be back, Wirgos? I have so many things to show her."

Forging a Warrior and Keeping a Promise

"Why are we taking the route?" asks one of the Getaes warriors.

"I need to take something that is mine, from my home," replies Armizeg.

"In which village do you live?" asks another. "I cannot remember any village on our way."

"Who told you I live in a village? A home could be any place," said Armizeg.

They cross a narrow river and ride downstream on the bank until Armizeg stops his horse. In front of them, a huge rock blocks their path.

"What is this place?" asks one of the warriors. "I've never been in these parts before."

"This is the place were my home is," says Armizeg. "You may wait for me here if you would like, or come with me."

They took a detour around a gigantic rock, stopping on the other side. Armizeg walks towards the forest.

"Where are you going?" asks one of the warriors. "I can't see a house in here.." "Because you don't know where to look."

"I'm coming with you," says Maedyv, dismounting his horse clumsily.

"I'll come too," adds Cythun.

Armizeg climbs the steep terrain. In front of them, they noticed a wooden ladder that leads to an opening in that almost rounded rock. They took the ladder and enter Armizeg's home. A cavern carved in the rock with a bed and table, all made of stone. At the table was one wooden chair.

"I never had guests here," he says to Maedyv. "We are not staying long. Help me move this stone, Cythun."

He goes to the other side of the cavern and pushes on a thick, heavy stone that serves as a bench. Cythun helps. Both struggling, the stone finally falls to the floor. Beneath it was carved a cache. Maedyv smiles when he sees it. Armizeg takes out a long sword wrapped in bear fur.

"This is the sword of your father," says Maedyv. "I thought it was lost."

"It was not," says Armizeg. "This sword belonged to my ancestor; Dorbald, and he passed it to his heirs, until it became mine."

"Why didn't it go to your cousin, Kothar?" asks Maedyv, looking at the unusual blade made from metaur.

"He's not of the king's bloodline. You will know when you will meet him."

"I think he will recognize you, if you show him this sword. I remember that it was your people who wrote it in stone and it became a legend among them."

"Indeed, they all know this sword, this is my pass to enter in the fortress."

"So, are you deciding to take back what's yours? You will be their king, once more?"

"Take back what is mine? And what is that? The throne? The city? All the riches beneath these gigantic mountains? No one owns them. They belong to the people and to their children's children.

Besides, you cannot take any riches with you when you're gone, but what you do while you're here will echo for eternity. It's time to leave; the night will soon be upon us," as he wraps the sword in the fur.

"As you say, my Lord," says Maedyv, following Armizeg on the wooden ladder. "I'm not your king, I'm not anyone's king, at least not yet."

"Do you think they will let you in?"

"They will not, but do not worry; I will meet you in the Throne's Hall."

They descend the steep mountain slope and continue to ride toward the City of the Kings fortress. The night was soon upon them. They do not stop until they are at the border of the forest.

"From here, you ride toward that mountain, and the fortress will be in font of you," he directs the warriors, pointing in the right direction.

"Okay, now we know the way. We are grateful, and we thank you."

They follow the two warriors toward the mountain and are soon mounting a beaten road that encircled the mountain. In front of them stood high-fortified walls made of massive, square stones. It disappears into the forest. There seemed to be no end to it.

"Who are you?" shouts a guard from the wall holding a torch in his hand.

"We are the watchers from the river," shouts a warrior. "We have five intruders who wish to speak to your regent."

"What did he say?" asks Cythun.

"He just called us intruders," replies Maedyv.

"That's doesn't sound too good for us. I have a feeling we are in trouble."

"Now, it's too late for us to go back, so let's see what the regent thinks about us," says Maedyv, following the two warriors passing through the massive oak gate of the fortress.

They ride on a wide road paved with rectangular stone that passes through the middle of the fortress. There were no stone buildings, but only some small houses made of clay and straw bale with a shingle roof. The road stopped in front of a round building made in the same fashion as the others around it.

"It's not so impressive from the inside," says Cythun, looking around.

"Don't be deceived," says Maedyv, "the entire city is beneath our feet, deep underground."

"Follow me," instructs one of the warriors, "the regent is waiting for you."

They enter the round building made from the inside around concentrically circles that ends inside a smaller one in the center of it. In the middle of the round room sat a man resembling the Getaes warriors.

"They all look the same," remarks Cythun, "how do they know who is who?"

"I was told you have trespassed our lands," he says, sternly, looking at them attentively. "Are you lost?"

"We are not lost, we have been forced to do so," said Maedyv.

"And why's that? I was also told you want to speak to the king. I have to tell you he left us tens of years ago and now I have replaced him. So, you can speak with me. What is it that you wish?"

Maedyv tells him the story; the reason why they are here, without saying anything of Armizeg.

"I see," says, Kothar, after a long silence. "I heard stories about Karken and the old wars. Our ancestors wrote them in stone. Now you want us to forge weapons for you? But what if we will need them too?"

"You must understand, my Lord, you cannot fight this war alone. We need to regroup and rebound our old alliances."

"Your war is across the great sea," says Kothar, "how will this affect us?"

"If we lose the war then it will be only a matter of time before the enemy's armies will cross the sea. He will not stop until the whole world is under his spell."

"My people don't need a war. Our city is well protected here, and the waters are well guarded, as you could see for yourself. You seek for old forgotten alliances that our long gone kings have made. But now we have no king." "You are wrong, Kothar," booms a voice coming from the dark.

"Who are you to call me by my name?" shouts Kothar, getting up from his chair, heading towards the place where the voice comes from.

Armizeg steps into the light and Kothar stops like he was struck by lightning, looking up at the giant warrior.

"You... you are not dead?"

"No, as you can very well see. You have to listen to these people. Our ancestors fought beside them for hundreds of years and we will do the same."

"But... but... you are not the king anymore."

"Let our people decide if I am the king or not. Let's gather them all in the Great Courtyard."

"Do you think they will recognize you as their king?" "Well, there's only one way to find out. Follow me."

Armizeg pushes a stone, and beneath them a staircase carved in stone ascends from underground. They followed, and soon the underground opens before them. It was a whole city with streets and tall buildings carved in stone and even bridges over underground rivers. In some places they had built barns and stalls for their animals and grains. In the ceiling of that gigantic cave was made openings to let fresh air enter and take out the moisture. As they look through them they see it is nighttime already. As they cross the underground city into the Getaes, people stare with curiosity. They head toward the Great Court in the middle of the city, just in front of the Throne Hall. Tall, carved steps lead them to the entrance. Armizeg, followed by Maedyv, climb the carved steps and soon see Kothar arranged for all warriors to be present. Everyone is asking why they have been gathered in the night.

"I can't imagine myself living here," says Cythun to Dytes. "To be forced to live in the darkness of this cave. Awful."

"They are not forced," says Armizeg. "They live above, in the houses you saw when we crossed the fortress. They come down here only when the night comes so they are protected. They work their fields during the day and watch over there sheep, cows, and goats."

Kothar appeared on top of the stairs, followed by some elders.

"They must be his counsel," said Maedyv, looking at the old ones. Kothar raises his arms, and in a moment the underground city was covered by a strange silence.

"People of this city, I gave an order to gather each one of you here, because after more than fifty years of waiting, our king has returned."

The Getaes people begin talking to one another in rapid succession. They didn't know what was happening.

"I know many of you were not even born, and those who were, are now older," he says, looking for approval from the elders of the council.

"Our king, Armizeg, is back! And he is right here in front of you!" he shouts, pointing his hands at Armizeg.

"How do we know he is the one you say?" shouts one of the elders. "He's right; we need proof that he is the right one!" shouts another.

Armizeg advances toward Kothar, who stands in front of him, and raises his hand. The silence returns among the people. They listen intently to what Armizeg has to say.

"My people, I know I left you for many years, but I could not carry my burden anymore. I had lost what I cherished most in this world, and I couldn't trouble my people with my pain and sorrow. I know our enemies attacked you from across the Dark Sea. I was watching you all this time fighting and building, preparing your beast and your crops for the winter. I was watching your children grow and become warriors like their fathers and their fathers before them; you have become fearless warriors our ancestors would be proud of. You want me to prove my identity? Here's your proof!" Armizeg draws his long sword and lifts it above his head with both hands.

"It's the sword of the kings!" shouts one of the elders. "We thought it was lost since the days of Khalfar. Centuries ago."

"It is not!" yells Armizeg. "It was passed through my family for generations and it was my task to take it further to the next, but my line was broken by Karken's wrath. He took my children, and the king's bloodline was broken."

"It is not!" shouts an elder. "You are still alive, and you will be our king as long as you live!" he says, bending in front of Armizeg. The other elders follow, bowing their heads. All the Getaes people shout his name with joy, welcoming his return. Now they had their king again!

"My people," shouts Armizeg, with his booming voice, "I also come this day, to warn you a war is upon us, once again. These people had come from across the sea to warn me that our old enemy, Karken the Dragon Sorcerer is preparing to move his armies into the world of living. The old alliances must be restored if we all want to defeat him, but to fight with his shadow soldiers they will need our weapons made of metaur! And they will need us to forge them! I am asking you, the wolf warriors! I am asking you, the blacksmiths, and you, who work the land tirelessly toiling in the field! Are you with me? Are WE with them?"

They all shout as one, raising their fists into the air, acclaiming Armizeg king.

"Then let's start building our weapons, and preparing for the war! Now time is our enemy!"

The Getaes were leaving the Great Court all shouting with joy, in unison. "What's your next command, my Lord," asks Kothar, with a low voice.

"Do not feel guilty, cousin, you were here when I was not, and you have nothing to be ashamed of. I will ask you to keep my place once more."

"Are you going somewhere?" asks Kothar.

"I must leave for a while to look after Karken, and to better prepare our people. There's a child who survived his wrath, and I need to see him as well. You have to look over those weapons to be done in time. As soon as they're ready you must send them with our ships."

"And the warriors?"

"How many of them are there?"

"We have eighty thousand ready to leave."

"And those who are not ready?"

"Thirty thousand more. They are posted to guard our borders. Should we take them, too?"

"No, we cannot leave our people unprotected. They should stay where they are. Do we have enough ships?"

Not enough, but they could be built in short time. The only thing is we will require more time to make the weapons. That metal is very hard to work with.

"Then let's not waste any more time! Prepare a ship for the six of us. We leave in the morning," he says to Maedyv.

"My Lord, we cannot leave with your ship," he says, looking at Armizeg. "Why not? Do you think our ships cannot take us across the sea?"

"We made a deal with the pirates, and we must honor it. I gave them my word. Their captain that will be back in four weeks to get us."

"I see. Well, if you gave him your word then, you'll have to honor it. We will sail with the pirates. Now, you rest and quench your hunger. My people will take care of your horses, and prepare them for tomorrow. We'll be there in two days," he says, leaving the Throne's Hall.

"Two days?" asks Cythun, "that's impossible. It took us more than two weeks to get here."

"Well, that's because you didn't use the tunnels," says Armizeg. "Then I can't wait to see them," says Cythun, looking at Maedyv.

"We thank you, my Lord, for everything you're doing for us," says Maedyv to Armizeg.

"No, I thank you for opening my eyes. All this times I thought only about my own sorrow and forgot about my people that I've left behind. I should thank you, my friends, for giving me back my will to live."

A guard came and took them into their quarters after they dined with Armizeg and Kothar. The king wanted to know everything about Elidoc, and his mother was more than happy to tell him the whole story, knowing he agreed to come with them to save the child. They wake up early in the morning, to the request of one the city's servants. Armizeg was already on his horse, waiting for them at the entrance of their underground house. Four more warriors were by his side.

"I thought we didn't need an escort in the tunnels," says Maedyv.

"We don't, but it has been a long time since I've traveled through, from the mountains to the sea. Now they will not allow me to go by myself, as I am their king."

"I have to get outside," said Cythun to Maedyv. "My falcon must know we are going back to the village near fjord."

"What's wrong?" asks Armizeg.

"He must go outside, he has a falcon and he must send him back to the fjord's village," replies Maedyv.

"Oh, I was wondering why we were always followed by that bird. I didn't know it was yours. Very well then, one of them will take you outside and then you will catch up to us in the tunnels. Two men can ride faster than the eight of us. There will be places when the tunnel will be so narrow we have to dismount our horses in order to pass."

He made a sign with his head to one of the warriors and disappears into the darkness of the underground city, followed by Cythun. They ride into the deep and dark tunnels lit only by their torches and lanterns. Droplets of waterfall from the ceiling and a cold air came from the top. After many turns they stop to give their horses water from an underground river. Dytes was moving his torch, looking insistently at the tunnel's walls. He touches them with his hand and looks at his finger.

"Look!" he says to Dolong. "These walls have veins of gold in them. Look!" he says, moving his hand on the wet rock.

"I know! These mountains are made of gold and silver."

"If Vingoth knew this, I am sure that he would want to come here."

In the darkness they hear an echo coming from the tunnels. A small light can be seen in their direction. As it approaches they see it is two torches.

Cythun and the other warrior join them to continue the journey.

In the middle of the mountains they cannot tell what time it was or if it was night or day.

"We must rest," says Armizeg, looking at his horse. "If my horse is tired, yours must be exhausted. We'll make our camp here," he says, pointing to a high flat rock. "If we stay by the river and it rains outside it will be unpleasant to wake up in the middle of the night, covered with cold water."

They follow, and soon they make a fire. Getaes people prepared food for their journey. They sit and enjoy some sheep's meat with cheese, and raw honeycomb.

"Wirgos would be pleased to live here," he says to Dolong.

"Oh, I am sure. I wonder if he is thinner now after all these days at the Master Wizard's house," laughs Dolong.

"Who is Wirgos?" asks Armizeg, interested in the name.

"He's the wizard of the Western lands," says Maedyv. "You will meet him once we reach the White Fortress. Speaking of wizards, you didn't meet your friend, Wolbah."

"Do you know Wolbah?" asks Armizeg.

"I met him once when he came to our lands," says Dolong. "He told me about you."

One by one, they fall asleep. Outside it was already morning. Only the whisper of the river broke the silence of the darkness.

When they finally came out of the mountain, it was evening the following day.

"Finally! I almost missed the sight of the sky," says Cythun, looking up. "Bad news I have, it will rain soon."

"Then we should wait here until the rain will pass," says Armizeg.

"I think it is better for us to go forward," offers, Maedyv looking at the sky. "If it will rain today, it won't be anytime soon. How far are we from the fjord?"

Half a day if we don't stop too often."

"Then we better continue our trip. Maybe tomorrow by this time we will be sailing west, toward our lands."

"I agree," adds Armizeg. "Let's not waste time. Follow me," as he rides in front of them.

"Maryia," says Maedyv, "you should disguise yourself once again. They will not take us on board of their ship if they see that you're a women."

"Yes, my Lord."

One by one, they all follow him with the four warriors ending their column. They pass through a forest that none of them saw before on their way to the river. After a while they exit the forest and head North on rocky meadows. Far in the horizon they distinguish the mountain range lying at the fjord's shores. They were close now, but still don't know where they are. Armizeg takes a sharp left turn, and is now riding on a beaten path. As they approach the mountains, the landscape becomes familiar. They can see the path they took on their way to the Getaes lands. Armizeg takes a narrow path made by beasts that leads them across the mountains by passing through a deep valley. In no time they are on the shore of the fjord. It is almost midnight when they reach the fishermen's village.

"Look! They are still here," says Cythun, pointing at Vingoth's ship.

"Of course they are", says Dolong. "They want the other half of the gold."

"Well, at least they keep their word," says Maedyv, heading towards the pirate ship.

"Who is there? Say your name!" he shouts with a booming voice. "And what are you searching for, near this ship?"

"I am Maedyv. Tell your captain we are back."

"Sooner than we were expecting you back," says Vingoth, appearing on the ship's bow. "And who are the others? As far as I remember you were only five," pointing at Armizeg and his warriors.

"I am Armizeg, king of the Getaes people, and these are my warriors!"

"I didn't believe you would come," he says, still gazing at Armizeg.

"You have to prepare the ship; we have to leave as soon as we can."

Vingoth does not respond, as he is mesmerized by the sheer size of Arming.

"Vingoth! Say something! We must leave as soon as we can!"

"Oh yes! I will tell my men to board your horses and we can leave. The ship is ready to sail, and we have food and water."

"Very well then. I want to speak with the village chief. Would you come to translate for us?"

"There's no need to translate," interrupts Armizeg. "I speak their tongue."

"I promised the village chief before we left towards your land, that if I convince you to come with us I will bring you to meet with him."

"How does he know me?"

Slowly he opens the door and yells with joy when he sees Maedyv in front of his house. He stops laughing, lifting his eyes up at Armizeg.

"You convince the king to come with you?" he says with a trembling voice.

At the light of the candles they spoke of their voyage. The chief insisted on giving them something to eat. The chief told Armizeg how he knows about him, and suddenly, Armizeg's face lit up by the pleasant surprise.

"I came at the right time, and I'm so honored to meet you, we need your help. My people will need your skills to help them build dozens of ships. Would you consider?"

The chief nods his head. He was proud to help the Getaes.

"Our odds are good," says Armizeg. If they would build the ships then the blacksmiths will have more men to help them forge the weapons."

There was a knock at the door. The chief opened, and they saw Vingoth, waiting at the front door.

"The ship is ready."

"Does he speak our tongue?" he asks Maedyv.

"Yes, I speak your tongue," replies Armizeg, smiling at him. "I speak many tongues."

"We are leaving when you are ready," he says to Maedyv, and disappears into the night.

"I think he is afraid of me," smiles Armizeg. "I wonder why?"

"When we got here the chief told us about you, and from that day Vingoth was... scared of you."

"I see. Well, we better leave now."

After exchanging a few more words with the chief they leave the house to head toward the ship. The horses are all in, below the deck, and Dolong, Dytes, and the mother are already in their quarters. As soon as Vingoth sees them, he jumps on the dock, approaching Maedyv.

"I will do my best for your men, but they have to share the space with my crew,. He could have my cabin, if that's all right. I thought, perhaps, judging by his size, it will be too tiny for him to share one with you."

"Thank you," says Armizeg to Vingoth. "It will be more then enough."

Vingoth looks at Maedyv, quickly turning around and jumping on the deck of his ship to give orders to his first mate.

Armizeg shrugs, smiling at Maedyv, as they both board the ship. The pirates stare at Armizeg in amazement. On deck, Armizeg and Maedyv watch the shore disappear, while the others sleep. None of the pirates spoke a word on deck. They were moving slowly. At the rudder, Vingoth is steering the ship, and in the distance they now see the Great Sea.

"I hope we will not catch such a storm as the one we caught on our way," says Maedyv, looking at the clear sky.

"We cannot know what the sea has prepared for us," remarks Armizeg, as he takes a deep breath of the salty air.

Maedyv and Armizeg leave the deck to enter their cabins. Even in her sleep, the mother is fully aware this would be a long voyage. She dreams of what Elidoc has done all this time, and of the Master Wizard taking good care of him. She dreams her precious son is getting well, and Armizeg's blood will finally put an end to the child illness and pain. Her dreams take her back to their life in the village.

Awakening the Warriors

"He's flying! Nutmeg is flying!" shouts Elidoc, running toward the Master Wizard's house.

"Who is flying?" asks Borysth, stopping him. "And why are you running?"

"Nutmeg!" says Elidoc. "He's flying! My falcon is flying!"

"Oh, I heard about your bird but didn't know Nutmeg was his name."

"Yes, and I'm looking for Wirgos, to tell him. Did you see him?"

"He's in the Great Hall with the Master Wizard. I will take you there, but no running please."

"Alright, no running! Now, let's go, come on!" pulling Borysth by his hand.

"Easy child, you look pale. You have to rest and regain your breath. If your falcon is flying now, that's good, but don't worry, he will be flying later, too."

Elidoc remembers what the Master Wizard had said about his health. "You are right; let's walk to the Great Hall."

They enter through the side door that leads into the Healing Room, but no one was there. They pass through the Great Hall, but still, no sign of Wirgos or Master Wizard.

"They are not here," says Elidoc, disappointed.

"If they are not here, they should be outside. Come on, let's find them."

They pass through the Great Hall, and Elidoc gazes at the statues of the old warriors.

"You look amazed. You've been here so many times, yet you look at them as if it's your first time."

"Every time I come here, I feel like it is my first time. One day, I want to be like them."

"What do you mean by that?"

"I want to be brave and strong, just as they were. Look, this one, Ludorn," he points his finger to one of the statues. "He was standing alone against tens of enemies giving time for his soldiers to retreat and make a better defense position to stop the attack. He killed them all and joined them after. Look at his sword! I bet it weights tens of pounds!"

"How do you know about this?"

"I read it in a book. I read about all of them!"

"I see you are not wasting your time here. Let's go now if you want to find them before lunch."

Elidoc still looks closely at each one of the statues as they pass in front of them. Outside, Wirgos and the Master Wizard were near the high wall surrounding the Great Hall's building, peering at the sky. Elidoc approaches them with fast pace, almost shouting to Wirgos.

"Nutmeg is flying! Folmart taught him to fly!"

"Well, it was time. He's been here for so many weeks. Is it that one?" he asks, pointing to the horizon.

Elidoc looks, but sees nothing.

"I don't know, let me call to him."

He takes a little whistle Folmart made him, special for his falcon, and whistles three times. A few moments later his falcon is in sight and comes down toward them, landing on Elidoc's left hand. He quickly put his hood on, and caresses his feathers.

"He has no more white down," proudly displaying his falcon.

"I see he's listening you," says the Master Wizard. "You know you can speak with him?"

"I talk to him every time he's with me, but I'm sure he doesn't understand what I am saying yet."

"Do not be so sure. If you spend more time with him, maybe you will start to understand what he says, too."

"I didn't know that," Elidoc says, with a wondering look.

"Well, ask Folmart, he will teach you how to understand your bird better, now that he understands you."

"If that one is not his, then whose falcon is there?" says Wirgos, looking at the horizon.

"He's not hunting, that's for sure, and it's none of ours," says the Master Wizard." If it was not, then those who guard the borders would have already attacked."

"Let's wait until he comes closer," says Wirgos, whistling one time with his whistle. The falcon seems not to care about this signal.

"It's not one of mine, that's for sure."

Soon the falcon was above them, flying in circles around the Great Hall's building.

"If my eyes are still good, this is Cythun's falcon," says Borysth. "And that also means he is near. These two are inseparable."

"Cythun?" says the Master Wizard. "They are here!"

"What? Who is here?" asks Elidoc, still caressing his falcon.

"Your mother, child. She's back!"

"My mother is back?" shouts Elidoc, as he jumps up and down.

"But where? I cannot see any riders coming this way."

"They could be in the forest, let's wait patiently."

"If it's them, then how did they pass our borders and we not know?" asks the Master Wizard. "They should be six if Armizeg is with them."

"You forgot they have Maedyv with them? I thought after all this time you should get used to the fact he's invisible, or almost invisible, even to you."

"You're right, Maedyv knew better than I, how to disguise himself and his men. If he manages to send his spies into Karken's fortress and they get back from there in one piece. And yes, I have to get used to the idea we may always have surprises from him."

The four of them gaze to the road that goes out from Strebo's village.

"There!" points Borysth, "I see dust rising near those trees."

"I see it now, too, there are definitely riders heading this way but I can't tell if it's them."

"I will go to the gate," says Borysth, leaving quickly.

"So we stay here, or do we go to the gate too?" asks Wirgos.

"I know you want to go there," the Master Wizard looks at him. "Alright, take the boy with you. I will meet you there."

Elidoc releases his falcon and follows Wirgos, who has taken a shortcut through the fortress garden.

Once they reach the walls, Elidoc stands impatiently near Borysth on a wooden box, so he can see beyond them. Wirgos is on the watching tower, looking at the riders.

"I count six!"

"It seems they convinced the warrior to come with them!" says Borysth, smiling at Elidoc.

"I cannot see my mother; they are all men."

"Be patient, if they are six, your mother is among them," encourages Borysth, his hands on Elidoc's shoulders.

The riders disappear from view on the narrow road. "Open the gate! Let them pass!"

"They will be here any moment, Elidoc. Let's descend from the walls and wait for them in the court."

With a loud noise, the riders passed through the gate and stop in the forecourt. "Where is my mother? Mother!"

"Elidoc! My son!"

"Mother?" says Elidoc, looking at the soldier, confused. "My son!" she says, removing her cape's hood. "Mother!" running toward her.

They run into each other's arms with tears of joy in their eyes.

"Mother, I didn't recognized you, and I thought something bad happened."

"I had to ride disguised so no one knew that I am a woman, and because the pirates would not a take a woman on their ship. I am home now, my child. Let me look at you."

"So, this is the child," says Armizeg, with a booming voice.

Elidoc looks at him with wonder. To him it seemed as if he was one of the stone warriors from the Great Hall that has come to life and now he was standing in front of him.

"This is Armizeg, my son.. He is the king of the Getaes people, those you have read about in the books."

"He is so tall," whispers Elidoc into his mother's ear.

"In his kingdom they are all tall, but he is the tallest, Elidoc." "We thank you for coming here," says the Master Wizard.

Armizeg was looking at him as if he just saw a familiar face. "You are looking at me like we have met before."

"I know you," says Armizeg. "I saw a drawing of you on one of my ancestor's books. You are King Derron, the ruler of the Northern Lands from across the Great Sea."

"Well, you are not wrong about my old name and title, my Lord, but now I am just a wizard, not a king. Now they all call me the Master Wizard."

"I am just wondering how all these centuries have passed, you are still alive, and look the same. I thought you were long dead and passed into a legend."

"Many things that are not dead have become legends. Please come to my house; all of you. You must be tired and hungry."

"We must return to our quarters," says Cythun. "Our mission is done here."

"Done indeed, but I insist. I don't think Borysth will need your service today."

Borysth agrees, and gives orders to close the fortress's gate. The soldiers were look in wonder, at Armizeg and his giant horse.

"Let's take our horses, there's just a short ride to my house. From there my guards will take care of them."

They mount their horses and ride toward the Master Wizard's house. Elidoc rides with his mother on her horse, followed by Cythun and Dytes. Only Maedyv and Wirgos are left behind.

"I almost forgot," says Wirgos to the Master Wizard, with a mouth full of chicken. "Your buddies, what were their names?"

"Kelrem, Tykas..."

"And Nysgar," says Maedyv as he stops eating. "What about them, and how do you know those names?"

"They were here, looking for you," adds the Master Wizard. "What did they say?"

"First of all, I want you to know they were not willing to tell me anything. I told them you will be gone for more than two months, and they had to know we are now fighting the same enemy, and if they had a message for you that would have to be sent without delay. Only then were they willing to speak with me."

"I see. So did they make it? Or they just have reached the borders and come back?"

"Not only did they make it, they have been inside Karken's fortress."

"What?" as Maedyv chokes on his food.

"Someone has been in Karken's fortress? Who are they? They must be some very brave warriors!"

"No. My Lord, they are not real warriors, just spies."

"Even so, they are still warriors," says Armizeg. "Without them, real warriors, or we kings as you say, would have no chance to really prepare to fight this kind of enemy."

"He is right," agrees the Master Wizard.

"They said Karken is ready to attack us at any time. His armies are training relentlessly deep below his dark fortress dungeons."

"...and he has hired spies and assassins among common folk," adds Wirgos.

"I saw that for myself," says Maedyv, "when we were attacked in the forest."

"This news is old. We are two months late! Wirgos, what did you do regarding our allies?"

"Well, we have Partogos and Hydal who are ready and waiting for the Master Wizard's order to come."

"They are useless without the metaur weapons!"

"In three weeks from now, my men will bring you the weapons you need. Eighty thousand warriors on horses will ride to this fortress."

"Three weeks will be too long. There's no time to waste! I have to go back to my fortress and send those three to the borders to watch over this army of shadow soldiers."

"Guards! Bring my horse, and fast!"

"If you take your horse, you will not make it. Take mine he is ready and rested. You can use the Eastern passages. They are not guarded anymore."

"How can you be so sure? I cannot risk anything; I have no guards with me." "We will come with you," offers Cythun, getting up from the table. "Dytes and I will escort you. My falcon will see if there's something at the exit. I will send him now so we will know before we enter the passage."

"Aright then, my Lord, please excuse us that we must leave so soon but there's no time to waste," he says to Armizeg.

"You have no reason to excuse yourself. Go. See if you find a way to buy us some time."

Maedyv, followed by Cythun and Dytes, leave the Master Wizard's house, heading towards the forecourt. They take rested horses and ride East toward the secret passage, following Maedyv.

"His falcon talks to him?" Elidoc whispers to Wirgos.

"Yes, and yours will do that too; you just need to learn how to listen."

"Mother, I have a falcon!"

"A falcon? How did you get a falcon?"

"Well, Wirgos and I, we went on, on, on...Elidoc was a bit scared to let his mother know he was up high in the mountains. He hesitated.

"Folmart gave it to him," says Wirgos, interrupting Elidoc's story. "He was a baby bird and Folmart thought the child would be happy to have a baby falcon. Since you were gone he trained him and now he is the bird's master," winking at Elidoc.

"Mother, I wrote a book too," he says with pride. "Well, I copy an old one into a new one."

"You know how to write?" asks Armizeg, with a surprised tone in his strong voice.

"Yes, my Lord, he knows how to write and he's already speaking three languages," says the Master Wizard. "You can speak with him in your tongue. Tell him, Elidoc, what is your wish when you are older?"

"I wish to sail across the Great Sea, visit all the lands, and see all beasts who are in the books. I want to know the truth about your people."

"What do you mean by that? What truth?"

"The truth about how they really are, because some of the books describe them as being uncivilized and ruthless, barbarians; when other books say they were very skillful craftsmen and fearless warriors, who like honey and have a taste for wine. So I don't know which one to believe, and I want to know the truth."

"Well what you just said, there's some truth in those books. I can tell you, my people are very good craftsmen. I can understand why you want to find the truth out for yourself. You should live among us for some time if you want to know better. A warrior's life isn't as the one you see the people in your village. They are very complex people."

"Do you think they will let me to live among them? I've heard they keep all their knowledge in secret and allow no strangers in their cities."

"That is true, but you will be no stranger to them because now you know me, and you speak our tongue, too."

"So, I can came and visit you?"

"Whenever you wish, child."

"You have children, too?"

"I had children...once, two boys of your age..."

"Elidoc, did you tell your mother about how well you are shooting a bow?" interrupts Wirgos.

"Oh yes! Mother, Wirgos taught me and I have my own bow! I can show it to you, tomorrow!"

"Tomorrow we have something else to do," reminds the Master Wizard. "You will take a brake for few weeks. No more training and no more books. You have to rest for a while. Armizeg will give you his blood to replace that which is poisoned. It will require most of the day."

"It will hurt?"

"Elidoc, do you want to be a warrior?" asks Wirgos, looking straight in the child's eyes, sternly.

"Yes. Yes, I do. He turns and asks his mother, "Will my hair grow back after the king gives me his blood?" putting his head down.

His mother orders him to look at her and as she lifted his eyes up filled with tears he cries, "I want to be a warrior, and I want to be strong."

RETURN OF THE SIX

"Stay still and don't move your body," commands the Master Wizard, holding Elidoc's right arm. "It will be much easier if you don't look. Turn your head the other way, and try to relax. Think of Nutmeg and how you will impress the children of your village."

"But I want to see."

"Are you not afraid to see blood?" asks Armizeg.

"I don't know, I have never seen blood."

"Elidoc, listen to what the Master Wizard says, and look at me; don't be difficult," says the mother, holding his left arm.

With a small and narrow blade, the Master Wizard makes a precise slit on Elidoc's arm. Blood flows from his veins into a bowl.

"We have to let the blood drain for a little while," he tells Wirgos and Dlong. Prepare the king for the next step."

Armizeg lies next to Elidoc, but he is so tall, he barely fits on the table. "I will just sit."

"I have to warn you that you may pass out. He needs a lot of your blood."

"Do not worry about me, I have more than enough blood through these veins for all of you."

"He is right," says the Master Wizard.

Wirgos took a long tube made of sheep intestines and attaches a funnel shaped bowl made of silver at one end. At the other end, he pulls over a thin tube with a hollow needle at the end. He made a small slit in Armizeg's arm, and collects the blood in the silver bowl. Dolong hands the other end to the Master Wizard who pushes the long needle in the place where he made the slit. Armizeg's blood flows slowly into Elidoc's veins. They repeat this four times until Elidoc's blood changes color.

"It's working!" shouts Wirgos, looking at the flowing of blood from Elidoc's arm. Elidoc is very lethargic, and unable to stay awake for most of the procedure.

"To be sure, we will have to wait until tomorrow," says the Master Wizard, putting his hand on Elidoc's forehead.

"How do you feel, my child?" slowly waking Elidoc.

"My arms are burning."

"That's good, the king's blood is fighting with what's left of the poisoned blood. By tomorrow your veins should be clean and we will do this one more time."

"You are a brave child," says the mother, with tears in her eyes.

"I feel so... sleepy."

"Let me take him to the house," offers Armizeg. "I'm not feeling weak at all. In my time, I lost a lot more blood than you had taken out of me today."

He takes Elidoc into his gigantic arms. He heads toward the small door that leads them outside the Great Hall, followed by Dolong, Wirgos and the mother. Only the master Wizard stays behind, preparing what is needed for tomorrow.

A guard opens the door at the Master Wizard's house and Armizeg passes through, bending his entire body to fir through the door. He lies the child on the bed and leaves the room without saying another word. In the dining room only Dolong and Wirgos have dinner. The mother stays with Elidoc in their room, and Armizeg rests in the fortress garden.

"What dark thought is upon you, my Lord?" asks, the Master Wizard, approaching him.

"I wonder if my people have left the shores, and are sailing here. Elidoc reminds me of my children. They were very much alike, you know? Now they belong to the past. We cannot bring them back, but we can prevent this horrible thing from happening again."

"Indeed we can."

"Tell me, what if we fail? What if Karken cannot be defeated? And if let's say, we defeat him, once again as our ancestors did? He will still be here, and I'm sure once again he will try to build an army as he has done every single time. We have to find a way to kill him and finish this once and for all."

"My Lord, I don't think Karken can be killed."

"There's has to be a way!"

"Anything it possible, Maybe one day we will find out how to do it but for now we need to stop him. All we can right now is fight his armies and stop them from take over this world."

"I don't think you will find this in your books. Maybe you should look somewhere else."

"We would do everything and anything to find it. Maybe it's not something but someone."

"What do you mean?"

"Maybe someone will know how to kill him; a person, man or woman; I do not know. Maybe this person will come to us one day. Maybe this person can be someone that is now defeating his poison."

The Master Wizard quickly caught on to what Armizeg was hinting. "Or maybe this person is already here?"

"Are you thinking about Elidoc?" as Armizeg nods. "I do not know. He is a strong and smart child but..."

"Time will tell. I have a feeling there is something special with this boy. Thousands of years have passed and no child could be saved, and now? Look at him. You took him right back from Karken's claws! Maedyv had found a way to send his spies into his realm and they came back unharmed. Karken has a weakness; I can feel it!"

"Indeed, since the day Dolong brought him here, we have come a long way. But for now, we have to fight him with what we have."

You are right, the child is still very young; there is no way he can do this now. I hope Maedyv will find a way to deceive him. You have to tell Partogos and Hydal to bring their armies in your realm. We must deceive Karken and make him think we are capable. "We cut the trees on his mountain, where your fortress is, and we put shields and armor on them. His spies will see them from far and will not dare to approach us. At night we light more campfires than usual, that way they will be sure that we have a big army. This will buy some time until my people come."

"This may work. I will give orders by tomorrow."

"No, we have to wait until Partogos and Hydal's armies are here and we'll cut the trees at night so no one can see what we are doing. How long it will take them to come here?"

"A week, from the time they received my message. I will send it this night."

"As soon as they are here, send one to Maedyv, too, and tell him to spread word among common folk that our armies are counting hundred of thousands of soldiers."

"Brilliant! Thank you!"

"I thank you; I'm more than glad that you have sent your people to come and rescue me! All these years I was thinking I have nothing left to fight for. You gave me hope for my soul and for my people. I should be thanking you."

"Now you have to rest. Another long day awaits us. I hope after tomorrow he will not need any more of your cleansing blood, and soon his hair will grow back."

"I will be here as long as you need me. My time here will not be in vain if this child will be saved."

"Tomorrow I will know more." Armizeg nods, and enters the house.

The Master Wizard heads to the library to write the message for the two kings. The time for deception has come.

It is morning, and Elidoc is awake and alert.

"Well, that's looking good," says Wirgos, looking at Elidoc's blood. "Do you think I will be able to train again after this?"

"Of course, and even better than before. Now your body will be strong like it was once, or even stronger. You have the blood of a warrior king coursing through your veins, child."

"He is right," says the Master Wizard.

"Do you mean that he will have my equal strength?" asks Armizeg, inquisitively.

"Of course," says the Master Wizard. "Your ancestor's blood now is flowing through his veins."

"As it once flowed through my son's," as the king looks lovingly at Elidoc.

"His hair should start growing in a few days, and if I am right, in few weeks you may return to your village."

"What about Karken? Is he still looking for him?" the mother asks. "That, I do not know, but do not be afraid."

"Now, you two have to rest," looking to Elidoc and Armizeg. "My Lord, you have lost enough blood and your body must be tired. Please listen to my advice and do not get up for a few hours and please, eat some greens."

"Yes, I will rest."

Elidoc asks the king, "Do you have mountains, rivers to fish in, or falcons in your land?"

"Yes we do. All of those, but we use eagles. Golden eagles. We hunt with them." "Golden Eagles? I've never seen one."

"That's because the live only in my lands. My people hunt wolves with them." "They're hunting wolves with eagles? How big they are? This is amazing!"

"They are very large birds. Their wings are much larger than a falcon's and their talons are stronger and more powerful. They look like bear claws."

"Bear claws? I have never seen those either!" says Elidoc, who is now up on his elbows, interested.

"They are this big," shows Armizeg with is arms spread wide. "Do you think they hunt falcons, too?"

"Falcons? Oh no, they are both birds of prey. They are like... cousins. And besides, a falcon is faster than an eagle."

"Then why are you not using falcons?"

"A falcon cannot hunt a wolf."

"I've heard they called you the wolf people? Why is that?"

"Because in those forests are so many wolves, and the old is our emblem; a wolf head, that makes a howling sound when the wind passes through it."

"I've never seen a wolf either."

"Well, this is what they look like," showing him a wolf head made of gold, attached to the chain around his neck.

"It's look like a dog!"

"Every dog once was a wolf. Did you know that?"

"Really? Then my dog was once a wolf too? Oh, I miss him so much."

"Don't be sad; I've heard that soon you and your mother will return to your village."

"Really? I can't wait to go home."

"Do you think he will recognize me after all this time?"

"Oh, you can be sure about that. A dog never forgets his master; no matter how long he doesn't see him. And a dog can have only one master. Remember that. Don't be sad, child, you will have so much to tell your friends. How many of them now how to read and write?"

"None that I know. We have no books there. People said books are forbidden."

"I see. Do not worry; I have a feeling you won't stay long in your village; you will get bored soon, and although that place may always be home, your feet will take you where your soul wants to go."

"Why do you say that? I miss my friends."

"I am sure you will miss Wirgos and all the friends you have made here. I know that, because now the same blood flows through both of our veins."

"Maybe you are right. I will miss Wirgos... and Borysth, and Folmart... and even Larsa with her food. I don't even mind the veggies now. I grew to like them, and the fish, too. The Master Wizard told me once I can stay here, if I want to, but in my village... I have my grandparents, my dog... and my old friends..."

"I thought you want to sail across the sea, not to stay in your village. You can make all your dreams come true, Elidoc. This world is big and beautiful and it's all here for you to experience."

"But now I'm just a child."

'Time will pass so fast, you will be a man in no time. Look how far you've come, and now remember the day you came here. Time passes quickly."

"Yes, it feels that way." "How old are you now?" "Almost ten winters."

"Another seven or eight more, and you can leave your village to see the world, my child. Do not worry, you will get older for sure, but you will never be ten again. So you must enjoy this time. Elidoc took a deep breath and lies down on the table, staring at the ceiling. Wirgos told him once all great things begin with patience. Even if Armizeg didn't tell him, he knew he had to be patient, and he had to wait. Whatever he was waiting for, he knew it was filled with adventure.

WHO DARES WINS

"What news do you bring?" groans Karken, from his dark throne.

"Strange things have happened these past days," replies Troko, looking up at his master, sheepishly.

"What things? Speak!" shouts Karken.

"Partogos and Hydal are moving their armies to..."

Karken rises from his throne, wings reaching the ceiling, unfolding in a furious rage, "To where? WHERE?"

"They are moving North, to the Fortress City."

"WHAT?" Karken's evil voice carried so far, his flying beasts fled the Throne Hall in fear. "How many are they? Did you see their weapons?"

"I cannot be sure. My spies tell me they are more than eighty thousand all together."

"When did they leave their fortress?" "Four days ago."

"And it took four days to get this news to me?! I should kill you now! Generals! Prepare our armies!"

"My Lord, if we leave now, we will be there in two weeks. And that is if we move by night."

"Ahhhh!!! Tell me, Troko; what do they know of OUR plan?"

"I don't believe they know anything."

"So, you are unsure?"

"My Lord, it is impossible to cross those borders; I don't even understand how this could happen. They are well guarded; even our assassins cannot pass them."

"Do not tell me it's impossible! They have done it!" bellows Karken, enveloping Troko with his wings of shadow.

Turning to he's General, "General, when are you ready to march North?" asks Karken.

"As soon as the night comes, my Lord."

"That is more than half the sun cycle!" Karken yells even louder.

"We cannot move our armies in the daylight, my Lord. The soldiers cannot walk into daylight, and we will be seen. The enemy has their spies too, right on our borders."

"Troko! You disappoint me again! You will march with them! As a soldier you are useless!"

"Yes, my Lord."

"Now leave!"

"We march as soon as we can. If they regroup at the Fortress City, we have to fight them there," says Karken. "Eighty thousand are not so many if they don't have weapons."

"Lord, if they know they cannot fight us, why are they gathering?"

"Maybe Troko is right, and they don't know about your plan, my Lord. How could they know? No one can cross our borders without being seen by our guards."

"Can you guarantee that with your soul?"

"No, my Lord."

"Now leave! Leave, I said! Do not come back until you are ready to leave the fortress."

In obedience, the general silently exits the Throne Hall heading toward the dungeons where his soldiers train relentlessly. He gives orders to his officers who continue to shout orders to the troops.

Karken's war machine is moving forward to the cave's exit, waiting for dusk, and orders to march.

"We are ready, Master."

"Are you sure?" As Karken rises from his throne, dissipating toward the exit.

He flies above and between the soldiers, checking them one by one. He wants to be sure they are prepared for anything. Outside the sun is setting over his kingdom. He gives the order to march. Tens of thousand of soldiers pour through the cave's exit, heading North with a fast pace. No sound, not even a small could of dust from this enormous army of shadows. Only the forest beasts and birds from the Man's Lands run, frightened from this army of evil shadows. What they are unaware of, is the falcon sending messages to the Master Wizard's realm, making him fully aware the enemy's army is headed their way. Tykas, Kelrem, and Nysgar follow them closely, carrying the crystals with the poison from the Elidoc's body, so Karken cannot sense them. Before dawn, Karken's army finds shelter in a dark cave, where they waiting for dusk to come once again.

"There's no need for us to stay here," says Tykas. "We must return to our fortress."

"You're right, said Kelrem, "but it is not our fortress we should return to. We will go to the Master Wizard's fortress. It is there we must be. This is where the battle will take place. I sense this."

"We must move now, then. We have no horses, and those evil shadows move faster than we possibly can."

"We need a horse. Maybe we can smuggle from the next village," suggests Tykas. Kelrem agrees. There is just no other option.

"He is right; it's the only way to get there before they do," agrees Nysgar. "We have no choice."

They run through the forest when they suddenly hear dogs barking wildly in the distance. They change their course, and head toward the sound of the dogs.

"There!" says Nysgar. "I see smoke," he points to show them.

"We need to get rid of these clothes," says Nysgar, throwing his cloak t the ground. Tykas and Kelrem then follow. They enter the village calmly, smiling at everyone they see along the way, searching for a horse or two. They continue to walk on the dusty street, when someone stops them.

"Good day to you," greets the man. "Where are you heading?"

"We are from the village of Loend," says Kelrem, "and... we have lost our way."

"Loend? I never heard of that village."

"It's in the Eastern lands, across the Black Mountains," says Nysgar, smiling at the stranger.

"You are far from home. The mountains you seek are over there," says the man, pointing his hand East. "You can take this road, then turn left toward the forest. Just stay East and you will find your way back to your lands."

The man turns to leave, and continue his walk.

"He had no idea what he was talking about," whispers Tykas. "He has never heard of the Black Mountains."

"Shhh...listen," whispers Kelrem. "I think I hear horses."

"I hear them too!" says Nysgar, excitedly. "This way!"

They approach an old barn used as a stable and see two brown horses grazing in the small court.

"There are two. We should find one more."

"We don't have time," whispers Kelrem. "You will ride together on one."

Kelrem and Nysgar slowly unleash the horses, and whistle for Tykas to join them. They ride at a slow pace until they reach the forest. Karken was behind them. They gallop among the trees, not looking back.

"If Maedyv was here we could use one of those passages," says Tykas. "But he's not here. It looks as if we have to take the long road."

"Which way do you think Karken's army will take?" asks Nysgar.

"Not the easy one," says Kelrem. "They will not risk being seen, even if they are going to war. He still hopes they don't know about his plan."

"By this time, the Master Wizard should have received our message," says Nysgar.

"Maedyv is with him, so don't worry, they will find a way."

They continue without stopping until they reach the Master Wizard's realm.

"Wake up!" shouts Kelrem to Tykas, asleep behind him on the horse.

"What! What is it?" taken by surprise.

"We are not alone."

On the plains between the fortress and the village of Strebo were tens of thousand of soldiers in camp. White tents, arranged in a circle, with soldiers building fortified walls made of turf brick and sharp poles buried in trenches.

"I have never seen such an army! Who brought them all here?" asks Tykas in utter amazement.

"By their flags, I can say there are two armies, or more," Nysgar says.

"We have to find Maedyv. He must be in there somewhere," says Kelrem, already riding toward the soldier's camp.

"Wait! Come back! He would still be in the fortress," yells Nysgar. "He has no business there."

Kelrem ignores him, and continues to ride toward the fortress.

"Let them pass!" shouts Borysth, when he sees them coming near the gate. "I never thought I would be so happy to see you again," says Tykas.

"Me either!" Borysth smiles.

"What ARE all those things? We thought they were soldiers until we get closer."

"That's our decoy," says Borysth, with a crooked grin. "It was Armizeg's idea. If it works the same for the enemy, as it did for you, perhaps it will buy us some time."

"Who?"

"Armizeg, the king of Getaes people."

"He is here?"

"Buy us time for what?" interrupts Nysgar. "The enemy will be here in three days."

"For the Getaes warriors to reach our realm," says Borysth.

"Is Maedyv here?"

"He's with the others in the Great Hall. Go now, I will join you later."

They dismount their stolen horses, and allow the guards to water them, and take them to a grassy paddock.

"We are here for our master, Maedyv," says Kelrem, to the guard standing in front of the door.

The guard allows them pass into the Great Hall. "Maedyv, I think your spies are here," says Wirgos.

"You look exhausted," says the Master Wizard, as he heads towards them. "We received your message just in time to make arrangements for this war."

"They will be here in two or three days at most," says Kelrem, taken aback by the size of Armizeg.

"We need three more days," says Armizeg. "I hope our plan will work." "He is Armizeg, king of Getaes people," says the Master Wizard. "Forgive me, my Lord," Kelrem bows. "I was unaware. It is an honor."

"Who I am does not matter. What matters right now is how I can help win this battle."

"We saw your decoy," says Nysgar. "It will work to delay them."

"If this can stop Karken advancing for one more day, until my people arrive, it will be more than enough."

"Tell me," says Maedyv, "what else can you tell us about his army? Does he have any war machines with them? Cavalry? What kind of weapons do they have?"

"My Lord," replies Kelrem, "they came on foot. No horses or war machines. They move faster, but only by night. During the day they hide in caves. Swords and bows are their only weapons; they have to move fast so they carry no heavy weapons."

"He still believes you don't know anything about his plan," says Nysgar.

"We could use this to our advantage. I hope he will send his spies before he decides to attack," adds Wyrgos.

"We cannot fight without those weapons! That is for certain!"

"Partogos and Hydal, do not forget to tell your men to light as many fires as possible, and if they have spare tents, put them up; we must appear as if we are many, even if we are few."

"We'll give orders to our generals," replies Partogos. "How far are they from us?" asks Armizeg.

"Two or three days, at most," Nysgar tells him.

Armizeg nods, says something to one of the guards who left the Great Hall in a hurry.

"Did you see Troko?" asks Maedyv.

"We did. He is among the soldiers for some reason."

"Wirgos, we need you here!" yells the Master Wizard, interrupting him. "We have few weapons left, and Maedyv has some metaur arrowheads. Send someone to give them to those on our first line of defense. If they could kill even one, perhaps Karken will be deceived and believe we have the weapons to kill him."

"Leave now, but return before dark," orders the Master Wizard, taking Maedyv aside.

"So we will have to fight at night then," Maedyv tells Armizeg. "If we can hold until dusk, maybe we can follow them when they seek darkness."

"I don't think he will risk it. I think there will be only one wave, and I can't tell you how it will end. Without my people, there's no sense to fight them."

"Do you think they will cross the borders?" Dolong asks, holding his hands on Elidoc's shoulders.

"I'm afraid they will. Karken cannot cross them, but his soldiers can. You have to take the child and his mother across the mountains before it's too late."

"And go where? If the battle is lost we will have no place to hide."

"You're right, but you will at least have a chance to live longer than the rest of us." "What do you think he will do with you and the other two?"

"The only thing that he can do is to make us prisoners. Let's not think about it. Our help is on the way. Take the child to my house and let's prepare for the night.

Likely, this is the last quiet night we'll have for a long time."

Dolong and Elidoc leave the Great Hall, headed toward the Master Wizard's house. "Wait!" Elidoc yells. "I have to see Nutmeg!"

"You will see him tomorrow," assures Dolong. "Do not worry, he will be there waiting for you."

"Then let's move faster, I have to prepare my bow and arrows for tomorrow," pulling Dolong's hand.

"You are too young for this battle, child, and you cannot kill them with your arrows. Let's see your mother, maybe she's worried because she didn't see you the entire day."

"She will understand; we are preparing for war, Dolong."

"Oh, dear child, I hope you will never know what a war brings."

"They are fifteen leagues from our borders," says Cythun, entering the Master Wizard's house. "My falcon saw them hiding in a cave before dusk."

"So it will be this night," says the Master Wizard, rising from his chair.

"I will wait for them," says Armizeg, as he gets up from the table. "My sword can stop some of them."

"Mine too," adds Wirgos, also rising.

"My Lord," says the Master Wizard, "it is not wise for you to go to the front line. It is there we will have the most casualties. It will be there the enemy will strike hardest."

"And that's why I must be there. These people will need all the help we can give them. The success of all depends upon our first line of defense."

"I agree with him," says Wirgos.

"Very well then, Maedyv and I will be on the second line with the cavalry."

"We must go and check all the fortifications we have; work until dawn to fix what remains," Armizeg tells Wirgos.

Wirgos agrees, and both leave the Master Wizard's house, headed toward the Southern border.

"Do not worry, my Lady," says the Master Wizard, looking into the mother's frightened eyes. "If our defense fails, Dolong will take you across the mountains. It will pass some time until Karken can reach those far lands too. Not many people live there, so he has no interest in those lands."

"I wonder how long we will have to run from his wrath. He reached us even here, where I thought we were safe."

"He's not coming for you, my Lady."

"No, he's coming for all mankind," interrupts Maedyv. "And we will stop him!" he shouts, hitting the table hard with his fist.

"Dolong knows what he has to do," says the Master Wizard, leaving the dining room. "Trust him."

The mother nods in obedience, and heads to her room. She packs the few things they have.

"Do we leave now?" asks Elidoc, sadly.

"Not now," says Dolong, "but we have to be prepared."

"May I stay on the watchtower, Dolong?"

"It's not safe, child. I'm sorry. Your safety is our greatest concern."

The mother enters, and Elidoc asks, "Do you think the Master Wizard will save all those books from the library?"

"There are too many books, my child. In times like these, people's lives are more valuable than books. Besides, what use they will have if there's no one left to read them?"

"I understand, but... I hate Karken!" shouted Elidoc.

"Tell your soldiers to light up every one of those lights," Armizeg commands the general. "Make them prepared for battle!"

The general disappears into the forest, headed toward the fortified camp.

"Here," Wirgos says to Cythun, "I took these from Maedyv. Use them wisely. I only have these twelve arrows to give you."

"How I will know who to aim for first? Nysgar says they all look the same." "Look for those who give orders", says Armizeg.

"Hard to know that by night," says Cythun, arranging his arrow in a handy way. "Do not worry; all this meadow in front of us will be on fire as they approach." "And how do you know they will come from that direction?" inquires Cythun.

"It's the only way to move with that large an army. They have no other option. We will know in less than one hour," Wirgos says, looking at the setting sun. "It will be a cloudy night."

"Karken is near," Maedyv tells them. "His spells are now fighting with the Master Wizard's spells."

Cythun's falcon was descending toward them and lands near his master.

"They are moving at a rapid pace!" he whispers to Armizeg.

Armizeg signals, preparing the archers behind them, They wait in silence, for Karken's soldiers to come out of the woods, but no one comes.

"Where are they?" whispers Wirgos. "You said they are moving." "Maybe our decoy worked," says Cythun, counting his arrows.

"The more we wait, the closer we are to light," says Armizeg. "If they will not attack soon, the battle will not be for this night."

For hours they wait, hidden by fortified turf walls. Cythun's falcon suddenly takes off, flying East.

"Look there, Eastward, on that wooded hill; I see lights coming our way. Unfortunately, I believe war may begin tonight."

"No, they are too far to be Karken's soldiers, and they are not using torches!" "Then who could this be?"

Thousands of torches approach in rapid succession. The tension is palpable. "They are on horses!" says Wirgos, drawing his sword.

"Silence!" whispers Armizeg. "Listen!"

"It's my warriors! They are here!" yells Armizeg. "The Wolf Warriors! They are here! Light up the fire so they will not fall into our trap!"

Thousand of arrows with their tips ablaze fly into the night's dark sky, lighting it up like a meteor shower. The meadow lit, and burned with gigantic flames, transforming night into day.

Tens of thousands of bearded, longhaired Wolf Warrior horsemen poured down from the Eastern hills, thundering across burning meadows.

"They are not afraid of fire?" asks Cythun, amazed, watching their horses jump effortlessly over burning trenches.

"No. We invented this defense. They know where to ride, do not worry." As they approached they split into two flanks. One flank continues in there direction, while the others head to the forest, where Karken's soldiers await the fight.

Armizeg descends from the walls, mounting his warhorse, and rides toward his warriors.

"Look, the wolves' heads," Cythun shouts to Wirgos. "That's where the howling came from!"

Wolf heads made of silver with mouths agape, snake-like bodies in the form of a windsock atop a wooden pole, trailed majestically behind their standard bearers.

"I never expected for you to arrive so quickly," Armizeg tells one of the generals. "Who here is in command?"

"I am," replies the general, "but Wolbah, our King, showed us the way."

"Where is he?"

"He is with the others who are chasing the enemy."

"Let's go! We will head toward the forest were the second flank is."

Armed with their curved swords made of metaeur, the wolf warriors bring destruction over Karken's soldiers who are now were fleeing into the forest, heading South while Karken flew unleashed above the Wolf Warriors. The gold embellishing their armor protected them form his witchcraft. Armizeg's warriors hunt them down relentlessly. They only have until dawn. Daylight weakens them even more as they try to reach the darkness of a cave that they passed the night before. Opposing resistance, Karken's soldiers fall on the ground like sheaths of wheat under the heavy strike of a scythe, transforming their bodies into ash.

"Where is Karken?" shouts Armizeg to Wolbah.

"He should be hidden somewhere," says the wizard. "There's no sense in going after him."

"General, go South until the sunset. Do not leave any of them standing," bellows Armizeg.

The general nods, and with a sign of his hand, a few thousand warriors head South. Armizeg and the others now head toward the fortress where Master Wizard is waiting for them. From the high of the Great Hall's plateau, he watches all the battle. The wolf warriors join the camp of the two armies of king Partogos and Hydal, while Armizeg and Wolbah enter the Fortress City.

"You won the battle!" shouts Elidoc from the watchtower, as he sees Armizeg entering the forecourt.

"Not me! The Wolf Warriors won the battle! What are you doing up there? You should be sleeping."

"He insisted in watching the battle from up here, my Lord," answered Borysth, looking at Elidoc and his mother.

"This is not a place for a child, he said. Come on, I'll take you home; both of you."

"I thought Karken's allies had encircled you," says the Master Wizard, looking at Armizeg and Wolbah.

"I thought so, too, until I heard the sound of our standard, the wolf head," says Armizeg.

"When I saw that meadow all on fire, I thought the battle started," says the Master Wizard. "Then I saw the torches heading toward Karken's position and I knew something else was waging."

"There's not much left of his army," alerts Armizeg, "and those who managed to escape our first strike are now hiding until night comes. He will not be able to rebuild his army for a long time to come."

"He will turn to the people for now," says Maedyv. "He will pay them and then deceive them. In their desire for more power and riches, the new kings will join him."

"But they are not our allies?" asks Elidoc. "You said once we are all fighting the same evil."

"For now we have only two allies," replies the Master Wizard

"Three," added Armizeg, looking to Elidoc.

"You cannot protect us all the time," says the Master Wizard. "Your troops should go back home. You have your own people to protect."

"I may leave half of them here until you think there's no need for them. Thirty thousand will be more than enough. They are all warriors and nothing else. Use them for this."

"If you think you will not need them, I am more than thankful. Partogos and Hydal will have their own realms to protect, and Karken will not stop here. We won this battle but we are far from winning the war."

"At least now we have more time to enforce our defenses, and our borders too," says Maedyv.

"We need to build war machines," says Wirgos. "I know your men are good at that. Yes, we will keep them for a while."

"We could help with that," offers King Partogos. "With your warriors here, Karken will not dare to go into a battle for a long time."

"But one day he will," says Dolong, entering the room. "I could not find his writings anywhere; he took them with him when he left from here."

"Dolong!" shouts Wolbah. "I'm so glad to see you again!"

"I didn't recognize you in this armor," says the wizard, smiling and walking toward him. "I thought you were one of the generals."

"I'm far from that. I've heard about your visit and the reason behind it. I didn't miss the chance to come back here."

"And I'm glad you did. Without your troops we would have never been here in time."

Wolbah nods, smiling to Armizeg.

"Without you, my King, they never would have left our realm. They just follow their king."

"All this will be in vain if we don't find a way to destroy Karken," says Armizeg to the wizards. "You know that better than me. Now we have time to search, and this should be our priority."

"We did it for thousand of years," says Maedyv. "There's no spell or weapon that could kill a shadow. All we can do is to make him stay in his damned stronghold."

"That's not enough," says Armizeg. "It's just a matter of time until he will try to attack again."

Wirgos adds, "Maybe we have to fight fire with fire." "What do you mean by that?" asks Maedyv.

"We didn't try to fight with his own weapons. That poison, that you took from Elidoc's body... what if we made a weapon out of it?"

"If we do this and if we would succeed from the first try, we would not a second chance."

"Do you have any prisoners?" says Wirgos to Armizeg. "Yes we have a dozen."

"Well, maybe we could test it on them a see what it does."

"We tried asking them questions, but they never talk. As soon as Karken commands, they die without saying anything. Their souls belong to him," says the Master Wizard.

Elidoc and his mother look at them with fear in their eyes.

"It means he will come back after me?" asks the child.

"No Elidoc. Thanks to you, Karken will not be able to take any child for a long time. Not for hundreds of years or possibly thousands," says the Master Wizard, putting his hand on the boy's shoulder.

"So we can go back home now?"

"Yes you can. Now that we are all safe for some time, you can go back to your village and take your lives back; it will be a new normal, nothing is like you knew it. You are stronger because of this experience."

"The village people will ask you where have you have been all this time," Maedyv tells the mother. "You should know what to tell them."

"What should we tell them? A lie?"

"Mariya, in war times, the truth should be protected by lies," says Elidoc, smiling to Wirgos.

"He is right," says Maedyv. "You should stick to the story you told in the villages here. You have been visiting your brother, Borysth. Tell them about Loend; not many people have ever even heard of it."

"I cannot wait until we get there. I have so many stories to tell to my friends," says Elidoc, excited. "Or should I lie to them, too?"

"Just tell them the truth; they will not believe you," he says, laughing. "Dinner is ready," shouts Larsa.

On the table was a smorgasbord of geese, chicken, roasted beef and pork, smocked eels, trout with cheese and butter, oysters steamed in almond milk with spicy mulled wines, stewed cabbage, tarts and custards.

"Oh my," Wirgos' mouth watered intensely. Almost dropping his cup, he says, "It's like a wedding party."

They all took their places at the table, thoroughly enjoying their feast. Only, Elidoc seemed to be bothered.

"What is it, son? You don't like your chicken?"

"No it's not that," whispers Elidoc. "I don't know if I will be happy in the village... I already miss our life we have here."

"But we are still here."

"I know, but still... and I don't like chicken anymore," he says, with tears in his eyes.

"You don't miss your grandma and your grandpa, and your dog?"

"I do but... I don't know...can we bring them all here?"

"Elidoc, your grandma is too old for such a long and perilous journey. The Master Wizard told you to could come back whenever you want, and we can stay here and never return to Sargem if that is what we choose."

Elidoc stops crying. "We return to the village, stay for a season, then we come back here."

"Alright, anything for you, my son."

Elidoc begins to eat, amused by Wirgos' endless hunger. The first to leave the dining room was Armizeg, who rejoins his warriors, checks on casualties. He gives direct orders for the next day, and returns to the fortress. The entire fortress is asleep, except Maedyv and the Master Wizard, who are talking outside.

"It will be a quiet night," says Maedyv as Armizeg approaches. "I hope you will stay with us for a while."

"I will stay until the child and his mother leave," he replies.

"I see that you like him very much," says the Master Wizard, smiling at Armizeg. He peers into the cloudless sky, thinking of his own children.

"I have a feeling there's something special about this child. Maybe he is the one who will find a way to kill Karken."

"After all he has learned here, he will be a great and wise warrior. If he's the one that will put an end to all this...only the time will tell."

"Indeed," says Maedyv, "After all that training Wirgos gave him; all those books he has read, and all the suffering he endured from the poison and medicine; now he has the mind of a wise man."

"His childhood was stolen from him," says Armizeg. "He saw things no child should see, he felt pain no child should feel."

"Maybe that's the way it should be," says the Master Wizard. "If all this had it not happened, Karken's evil would never end."

"Yes, I think that's the way it was meant to be. I wonder if he will find peace there, in his village."

"I think he will be obsessed with fighting Karken for the rest of his life," says the Master Wizard. "It is in his blood now."

"Unfortunately, this may be true," says Armizeg.

"You saved him, my King," says Maedyv, looking deep into hiseyes. "But I also given him all my sorrows."

Maryia is ready to leave, and does not want to delay. "Elidoc, are you ready?"

"I will be down in a moment, Mother." "They are waiting for you! Hurry up!"

"Who is waiting for me," says Elidoc, from the top of the stairs. "Your friends," she says, heading to the front door.

With his hand full of books, Elidoc walks slowly on the Master Wizard's Entrance Hall.

"Here he is!" shouted Wirgos, as Elidoc opens the door.

The court was full of soldiers, and all who knew him gathered in front of the door.

"We are all here to wish you well on your journey," says the Master Wizard, helping him carry the books. I see you chose the good books."

You told me to take whatever book I like, but it was too hard to choose; I wish to take them all."

"Well you chose wisely."

"Elidoc," says Armizeg, bending toward him, "take this as a gift from my people."

"But... but it's your wolf..."

"I want it to be yours, so when you are old enough to sail over the Great Sea, and come to my realm, you will be welcomed by those who keep watch of those borders. They will know who you are and will escort you to my fortress."

Armizeg took the heavy, golden chain from his neck, and put it around Elidoc's.

"You are a very brave and wise child. Do not forget whose blood courses through your veins. You are a warrior."

"Thank you, my Lord," touched by his generosity.

"I will escort you until the borders; we will meet at the gate," Armizeg says to Dolong.

"Wait, not so fast," says Maedyv. "Here, take this crystal, so every time you feel lost just point it at the sky and look through it. You will always find the right way back."

Elidoc took the shiny crystal and started turning it on all its faces.

"Like this," shows Maedyv. "You hold this side toward the sky, and you look here... see?"

"Oh yes, I can see lines of light."

Elidoc jumped to Maedyv, embracing him with his small arms.

"Elidoc," says king Partogos, "in the name of my people, I am honored to give you this."

From under his long cape, King Partogos takes his sword, and hands it to Elidoc. "A real sword? Is it for me?"

"Yes, Elidoc. It was forged by my ancestors in the time of the old wars, and passed through my family's line. Now it is yours; to remind you there are people you will have to defend and protect. One day it will serve you well," says the king, embracing him.

"Someone else is waiting for you," says Borysth. "He is asking if you are leaving without him."

"Who?" Elidoc wonders.

Borysth points his finger to the sky.

"Nutmeg!" shouts the child.

His falcon flew above the fortress, waiting for his command. Elidoc blows in his whistle, and the falcon descends like as lightning strike, landing on his arm.

"We are going home, Nutmeg," caressing his brown feathers. "There you will have plenty of rabbits."

Elidoc hides his face, as he begins to weep.

"Oh, child," comforts Wirgos, "you will not start to cry now? Warriors do not cry, my child."

"I will miss you all," he says, looking to the Master Wizard.

"Well, you may stay here," the Master Wizard says, looking to Elidoc's mother.

"We cannot leave grandma without letting her know we are alive and safe; and my dog. I want to have my dog. Mother told me we will stay just a season, and then we will return."

"Then you have no reason to be sad. We will see you again soon."

Helped by Wirgos, Elidoc mounts his small horse the Master Wizard gave him.

"I will miss you, child," whispers Wirgos, at Elidoc's ear, his eyes filled with tears.

"Why are you crying? I shall return. Don't let Maedyv see you cry," he says grinning, through his own tears.

"Larsa, I hope you will still give him fish and salad," shouts Elidoc, loud enough for all to hear. "He said he loves it! Thank you Larsa, for everything you've done for me!"

"As always. I will wait for you to come back to prepare another feast."

"See you soon, my child," the Master Wizard takes his hand. "Don't forget what you've learned here."

"I will remember everything."

"It's time to leave," says Dolong, already on his horse. "We have a long road ahead, and we don't want to spend the night in some forgotten place."

Elidoc and his mother ride behind Dolong, following him on the fortress streets until they join Armizeg, who waits at the gate. They travel the mountain, passing under the waterfalls, and crossing the narrow bridge heading toward the village.

"Do you think he will come back in a season?" Wirgos asks the Master Wizard.

"Do not worry, the child will return in his time; he left part of his soul here, within each of us."

www.ingramcontent.com/pod-product-compliance
Lightning Source LLC
Chambersburg PA
CBHW030529030726
47495CB00004B/919